CARAPACE

by

Davyne DeSye

ISBN: 978-0-9988747-1-5

First Edition.

Cover art by Gordon Whitesides.

OTHER BOOKS
BY
DAVYNE DESYE

HISTORICAL ROMANCE

The Phantom Rising Series:
For Love of the Phantom
Skeletons in the Closet
Phantom Rising (forthcoming)

SCIENCE FICTION

Soap Bubble Dreams and Other Distortions

CONTENTS

ACKNOWLEDGEMENTS

First, I'd like to thank Pat LoBrutto, a New York editorial consultant who told me early into things that my writing was great and that I should finish this book. Knowing he had spent decades in the publishing houses in New York City, this was a tremendous encouragement! I'm sure he doesn't remember me, but I will remember him always for his kind words.

Next, I'd like to thank the most wonderful readers in the world, Bob Simon, Evie Phallon, Dana McAuley, Thomas O'Meara and Stephen Reid. They read this novel chapter by chapter, told me where I'd screwed up and helped me fix where I'd gone wrong. They helped make this book better and they get credit for a lot of improvements. Any errors still existing are mine.

Finally, I want to thank my family – my parents and my kids – for all the support they give me (not just in my writing, but in life) and for all their tolerance when I am babbling on and on about the latest "life" I'm living in my head. Most of all, my thanks go to my amazing husband who reads every word I write on a day by day basis, and is my first and best reader. And that's only the smallest of the things that make him wonderful.

Thank you all!

To Ed and Anita
For who you are, and all you've meant to me.

Carapace (ˈkarəˌpās), *Noun*:

1. A hard shell on the back of an animal.

2. An attitude that someone has developed as a protection against other people.

Merriam-Webster

CHAPTER 1
KHARA

It's a ninety-five degree afternoon as stifling as sex under a rhino. Got to be a hundred percent humidity, maybe a hundred and ten. I can barely breathe the thick air. I'm just finished with my latest session, clothes stuck to my skin, waiting for my dismissal. My back presses against the rough-brushed chrome doorway of Dominique's Bar. I suck in a full breath in preparation for the final kiss.

I guess calling it a kiss is a pretty gross misnomer – I did my fair share of kissing when there were just humans around, and I remember the difference. When I think about it all. Which I don't.

Deep throat kiss from an alien named Ilnok – my master, my provider, he gives me hits of the drug I need to get through my horrible, endless days. He kisses me and sucks the last of the sugary sweetness from my stomach, sweetmead that I drink because he loves to suck it out. My head arches back as he towers two feet above me. His four jointed limbs wrap around me; his hard black shell presses against my breasts. I close my eyes to the sight of his mandibles open and against me. I close my eyes rather than look into the lidless, oil-slick facetted eyes. My squeezed-shut lids don't keep me from feeling his cat-tongue-textured palpus against my tongue, the end of his palpus slithering down my throat. I've long since learned to stifle my gag reflex. The drug I took at the beginning of this session has worn off, and I'm near the end of my ability to cope with this crap – not that I have a choice. He finally breaks loose and goes back in. I'm dismissed.

I throw myself into the passing stream of bodies. I want to race away, but the crowd has its own pace. I push my way down a street packed with humans and the taller, silent aliens. More aliens these days than ever. The rhythm as we press against each other in passing is the daytime song of the city. I pray for night.

After my latest session, I can't handle the touch of so many. Even after two years, the sight of aliens on our streets, their touch, hasn't settled into the familiar. Earth of my memory belonged to us – humans – and I can't let go. I wish I could. Lord knows I'm trying.

I rake fingers through my mussed hair, try to ignore the way the rough fibers of my loose shirt chafe my tender breasts. Suddenly, I'm face to face with a human in the crowd. Once upon a time, I might have thought he was a good looking guy. He holds me at arm's length and stares me down with I-want-you eyes. Then he pulls me in and presses against me, thigh-to-thigh, shoulder-to-shoulder.

"Let's go," he says in my ear.

The words register, but I don't get his meaning. My brain's blank. He signals me to follow. I'm almost beyond noticing because all I can think is that I need a drink. I press past him without a word, like he's not even there. He grabs my breast and it's enough to gain my focused attention. I notice his rank and insignia, and recognize his high status in the alien corps. He has the power to claim humans, although not me.

Screw you, Traitor-man, I've already got a master. I swallow the bile his kind brings to the back of my throat, wondering how many of his fellow humans he's used or killed in the service of his masters. It's disgusting that he thinks he can reward himself with me. I jerk away, squeeze my way down the street past other humans, other aliens, trying to get away from the hot press of alien-and-humanity.

"Hey. Get back here." His outraged voice yells from behind me. Then louder, "Hey!" The crowd comes between us and he's gone from my mind in the same instant.

The street stinks of sewer and garbage and puke and piss. The city was never meant to support this many. I push away from the middle of the street, toward the buildings, hoping to avoid the sun and the thickest part of the crowd. I trip over the legs of a woman sitting on a doorstep of what used to be a hotel. She's holding a baby who cries as I fall to the filthy pavement. I pull myself upright before I get stepped on. I look back at the empty expression on the woman's face – has she noticed the child is crying? – horrified for mother and child and the hell we live in. I press on, supported by my need for a drink.

Refugio's. My favorite bar. If I can just get past the chittering doorman. I squeeze in behind, lost in the press while the doorman concentrates all four upper limbs on keeping some creep out. Got to have credit or rank to get in, but I'm not a stranger here. Doorman knows me, knows who I belong to. I'm almost in before Traitor-man grabs my wrist – I can't believe he wanted me enough to follow me! There are plenty of others he could have claimed, prettier and more willing. It must be a power thing. Well, tough luck for him.

I pull free again leaving skin from my wrist under his nails, and wish I could leave the burning pain with him, too. I'm in.

I find a seat at the bar. Never as crowded in as out. A whiskey appears – the tender knows me. I hold up my thumb and he swipes my credit ring for payment.

Nearby, three young boys, long greasy hair, slop down cold beer, slop in rice mash. They shake their heads violently through blue-lighted swirls of dust motes and bang their fists on the bar in time to a screeching guitar up on stage.

"Training sucks, man," screams one, "glad you got us out." He smashes his beer mug into his friend's, sending sickly looking globs of beer into the air.

"No shit," yells his friend.

Wait until you're done with training and they decide how they want you.

I slump lower over my drink, savoring the sour smell. It's not like before the invasion. . . I throw my drink back, finishing it in a great burning gulp, somehow controlling the urge to smash the heavy glass on my head or theirs.

I'm going to need another hit soon; I'm thinking too much. Another whiskey appears to replace my empty. I order a beer to drink with it. Have a slug of each. Feels good to get the sweet and sour taste of Ilnok out of my mouth. I concentrate on that, trying to keep my mind numb, trying to hold on one more day, trying not to think about the patches in my pocket.

I lose the battle and am slapping a patch on my jugular when I notice the man. Scruffy. Big. Just short of ugly, with a potato nose that overshadows his thick upper lip. Same one I've seen maybe twenty, thirty times this month, not just here. I'd guess he was tracking me, but I'm not sure it can be done in the dense humanity streetside.

The drug-induced swirl behind my eyes runs awhile, emptying me, scraping out my self-disgust, my anger, before I order another set of beer and whiskey and slide toward the man.

"Whaddya want with me?" I ask, not looking at him, knowing I can't focus anyway. He scours me with hungry eyes for a long while before peering down into his drink.

"You're a fighter," he says. He looks up and around as though afraid someone will overhear us. With the screeching guitar, I almost don't hear him.

He watches me with his dissecting eyes as I snort and pick up my drinks. I pause, dizzied by my sudden movement. "Leave me the fuck alone." I move back to my abandoned seat, still warm, ready to heat the back of my throat with rotgut for the third time in ten minutes.

Without warning, Traitor-man is there pinning my arm behind my back, and crushing my throat with the other. He's squeezing my throat so high he doesn't notice my collar-monitor under the high neck of my shirt that tells everybody I'm claimed. Through my self-inflicted haze, I blink at his image in the mirror behind the bar. He grins his triumph at me over my shoulder.

I try to pull away, wanting to kill him for touching me again. Sorry for the moment my shirt collar is so high or that I'm not wearing my own insignia which would show I'm taken, protected, but I hate wearing that shit. His hand tightens on my throat. He pulls my arm higher behind me. My wrist burns where the nail marks he left in me still bleed under his grip. My peripheral vision darkens as I start to pass out.

Then he lets me go. Gasping for air, I turn to see a shocked expression on his face. His eyes are open, rolled up toward the low ceiling. He falls like a board to the damp darkness at my feet. The ugly human I approached earlier at the bar pulls me over the large lump.

To my besotted senses we seem to melt through the wall at the back of the toilet and into a tunnel. The man's hand is clasped over my torn wrist. With a curse, he pulls my now-ripped shirt

6

collar closed over the bright splash of red from my collar-monitor when it goes off, and pulls me faster.

With a mix of nausea and relief, I realize Ilnok wants me again. Better the evil I know than the confusion this man has caused in me with his rescue.

Through another wall and I'm standing in a dim restaurant kitchen. Humans scurry around us preparing food. No one is surprised at our appearance. No one misses a beat.

"I have to go, I need to . . . ," I begin.

"I know. I know all about you and what you do," he answers. He makes his way to a cabinet, and brings me a bowl of the cloying sweetmead Ilnok loves to take from me. It's a large serving bowl, and he fills it, somehow knowing how empty I am. Well, except for the booze. I hold out my credit ring on my upraised thumb but he ignores it.

I stare into the mead at the ruby reflection of the monitor at my throat before I gulp it down. It is even more sickeningly sweet as a whiskey chaser.

"You're a fighter," the man says again, this time at normal speaking volume, then pushes me across the kitchen floor and through a door into the teeming street. I know what he wants. He's part of the rebellion – one of the hopeful who believe we can win against these alien invaders. I'm not. I've given up all hope.

"I am Samuel," he adds before letting go of my shirt.

Turning back, I fight the stream long enough to say, "Fuck off, Samuel."

CARAPACE

The slamming of heat and sunlight against a mind ready for cool darkness is nauseating. I want to puke. The taste of beer, whiskey and sweetmead combines with the streetside stench of human sweat and almost pushes me over the edge. I can't puke. It will mean I need to drink more sweetmead for Ilnok. To Ilnok, I am larger and more amusing than a beer mug, but as a drinking vessel, I have to start full or be useless.

Pulling at my choker in the fetid humidity, I press toward Dominique's – Ilnok's favorite lair.

Ilnok is in the red semi-darkness with his siblings (team? crew? – I've intuited a connection but not its clear form). He leaves my monitor lit until he's undressed me, which he does with slow, distracted movements. I'm almost happy to have the scratchy pants away from my not-so-private parts again. In the dim red light, I lean toward him as his mandibles open, ready for a long kiss, but he barely moves his palpus into my mouth. I lay backward over his lap with my arms and head hanging toward the floor, my legs and body open to him. He moves his antennae over me, my smallness, my softness that is my – our – vulnerability. Beneath the relaxed occasional click and wave of antennae that passes for conversation among these aliens begins a low ticking that's almost a purr. I'm glad for the patch at my neck, and the drinks I've had. I'm content for the moment I'm safe.

CHAPTER 2
NESTRA

I lie on the high dais, my jointed limbs and antennae interlocked with those of my queen. Our mandibles are open and against each other; our palpi writhe together. Behind and below the trance that allows me to accept the chemical download from the queen, my mind wanders in languid circles.

Shame always comes with despondence. With stooped shoulders and diarrhea. In their logicky way, the engineers explain the interlocking chemical affiliations of the two, but I like to think of the one following the other. Like extreme drunkenness and hangover. If I think of despondence as hangover, I always know when to stop guzzling Shame, when to retire to my quarters, perhaps to regurgitate my meal in subservience to the nausea that comes with Shame. But I *know* when to quit. And so despondence has not led to death.

Now, I cannot accept any more of the chemicals. And with an uncontrollable/anticipatory shiver that runs up my armored body like an earth tremor, *Do not try to push any more Shame in.*

CARAPACE

The queen, feeling my need through our intimacy, disentangles our limbs, our antennae, and then further opens her mandibles and pulls her palpus from mine. Queen Tal is far from empty, and I will be recalled soon to continue the chemical off-loading, but I need the respite, however brief. I shudder with gratitude at the disconnect, registering the slight gurgling sound that accompanies my shudder. I am too spent to be embarrassed at the sound. I lie on the dais, long triple-jointed limbs akimbo, gathering what strength I have to remove myself from the throne room, from the decidedly-not-looking courtiers, and others of my people from other continents – visitors waiting for recognition and audience.

Sooner than I think I can, I pull myself upright, and with a dearth of protocol which I hope will be forgiven, slump from the room, all four arms wrapped around my hard blue-black shell. My squeezing arms are the external manifestation of my internal struggle to maintain control. I do not cling to myself in fear someone will touch me – to touch me would mean that brother's death at the hands of the queen: instantaneous, bloody, public execution. With my body so loaded with the queen's Shame, I am safe now except from the queen herself – the one from whom I most need to be free. And so, with no one who will touch me, no one to support me, no one who can pull me along, I jerk myself from the queen's presence with all the haste I can muster.

I lock my quarters to intrusion, resentful as ever of the distant escort. The tinkling of bells as the lemon breeze moves the branches of the blossom-heavy homeworld tree behind me does not soothe me. I lean over the shoulder-high vomitorium. I methodically bring up the meal I ingested before my session with the queen, noting how little of it has benefited my body through digestion. My slim fingers prattle at the control keys on my lower arm above my pincer ordering a heavier scent: something that will *smell* like the limbs of a Consoler wrapped around me, since no Consoler will risk what they would taste on me.

I lower my body to the cushioned floor amidst an orchestra of pops and cracks from all six of my limbs, and begin the private mantra that will rid me of the Shame. I hope for the several hours it will take to tread the mantra at least once. The chemical concentration within me will take time to dissipate.

I am not quite through the first recitation when I am summoned again. I sigh and try to visualize the sigh as an exhalation from all my pores, as a mediocre cleansing where the real thing cannot be had. I know my duty as the queen's Shame Receptor and understand the resentment is a residual chemical side effect of the Shame. I am annoyed at being unable to shake the feeling of resentment by understanding its cause.

I rise and look to my terminal for some random words of benediction, pressing my high right pincer against the touch pad to renew the phrase of well-wishing. My screen changes to read,

Gather your strength from those whom you serve.

Chrenu VII, Book 6, Gru

CARAPACE

I know the reference. It is a quote from the Gru parable wherein my people are taught the satisfaction of serving the whole and the compensation of seeing those around you swell and grow on your efforts. But in my frame of mind, the quote feeds my feeling of resentment, of being exploited, rather than diminishing it.

I clear the screen with a swipe, and leave my quarters, unable to stop imagining the words counsel me to *gather my strength from the queen.* With a guilt that gnaws at my innards like hunger, I follow my escorts back to the queen. It will be late when I recall my noon meal from the vomitorium and eat it. I hope it will satisfy.

The escort leaves me standing in the low archway to the queen's private bedchamber. Like everything else that surrounds the queen, the chamber strikes me a blow. Where I seek out tranquility, serenity, sights-sounds-colors which sing a gracious gentle symphony to the slow rhythm of my soul, the queen seeks disharmony bordering on painful.

The immense cushioned bed-pit is strewn with food and bright, colorful cushions. The soft pale limbs of at least two humans protrude from crumpled linens. The bed cushions themselves are stained or otherwise splashed with discordant colors. Since my last visit to the chamber, long rapier-like metal stakes have been added to the ceiling above the bed-pit giving me the impression the pit rests in the open maw of some multi-fanged monster.

The queen is not visible and I do not catch her scent. Without an order to enter, I cannot bring myself to cross the threshold. Knowing I should turn away from the visual cacophony and take advantage of every additional moment to meditate and purge myself before receiving a fresh off-loading, I still cannot stop myself from watching the two brothers moving to and fro in the far corner of the chamber. With a voyeuristic ache, I watch as – between bending to clean some mess and turning to shove debris into the chute – they find an excuse to touch each other. Just a brush, mandible to mandible, as one passes the other. A tender tap of antenna against the throat of the other. Wrist locking for a moment with wrist.

Sharing. Sharing as I have never done with another. Yes, I take the queen's Shame. I "share" more intensely – and with the queen! – than these two share. But it is not true sharing. It is duty: I receive the damaging chemical concoction from within the queen that might cause her precious mind or body to weaken. I perform the job for which I was bred. And in so doing, I am forbidden by the queen to share.

Ah, to share, as part of an unspoken discourse, small brushes of feeling and sight with someone I can call friend… I ache with the sight of it, and yet cannot turn away.

I weaken myself, coveting what can never be mine. And now, do I also mix my own shame with that of my queen.

I turn from the brothers to discover the queen behind me, mandibles pinched into a cruel smile. Only now does her color/scent register. The distraction provided by the brothers was almost absolute.

CARAPACE

"Majesty…" I bend my head backward, antennae curling in subservience back and downward, hoping to cover the effulgence of fear that runs through me and knowing the queen smells it, regardless.

The queen brushes past me and addresses the brothers. "Clear the room. Quickly, curse you," and turning to me, "Almost altogether worthless, wouldn't you say?" Again the cruel smile.

One brother begins moving a drugged human from the bed, and ushering it through the door at the back of the chamber. The other brother continues cleaning the shapeless debris from the back of the room. The queen sweeps the near side of the bed cushions free of food and beckons to me.

"Would you like them?" the queen asks, black cruelty sharpening her words. "These brothers?"

My ache intensifies as the queen toys with me. The queen has sensed my interest, and without knowing why I might be interested, she pokes and prods, hoping to find a wound. I cannot imagine how to answer.

"Of course, you don't. You have no need of worthless brothers, no more than I. I'll do them a kindness and have them destroyed when they've finished here."

I look again to the brother cleaning the back of the room. With a sickening jolt, I recognize the messy debris being thrown into the chute as numerous small human body parts. The stain on the far side of the bed cushions is human blood.

14

You overestimate me. You cannot keep raising the threshold without destroying me, as well.

I turn to the queen, who watches me with her large glittering eyes.

"Majesty," I say with a slow deep breath, "shall we begin?" I am pleased the words are spoken without the waver of emotion.

The queen studies me a moment longer before breaking into a rich thrumming laugh. Then sweetly: "Come dear, strong Nestra. Come lay beside me."

The incongruity of her kind tone almost breaks me.

"Sweet, sweet, calm, good Nestra." The queen pats the bed cushions. Her voice is silken, her features wicked and amused. "Don't worry about the mess. My workers will have this cleared long before you rise again to consciousness, I promise you. Come dearest." She pats the bed cushions again. "I need you." The queen's mandibles pinch again into a cold, cruel smile.

Shivering in an attempt to maintain my control, I sit beside the queen.

"There, there." The queen brushes my mandible. She speaks with a tenderness that slices like a razor on human flesh: it cuts deeply and, at first, it seems there is no pain. "There, there. Open to me dearest."

I fall with gratitude into the comfort of routine and open myself to the kiss that will begin the off-loading. I begin the mental exercises that will help separate my mind from the damaging influx of chemicals. One last thought bubbles to the surface as I sink into the dark trance that comes with the chemical transfer – a thought I refuse to claim as my own.

Save me.

CHAPTER 3
SAMUEL

The meeting with my ant contact is on for tonight and I'm meeting my man at Refugio's to learn the time and place. I go early hoping to see Khara. I search the semi-darkness of the bar – darkness pierced by flashes of blue light – but Khara is not there. Still, I must wait. I order a drink and settle myself.

Sitting at a round, roughly varnished table, I rub my finger into the deepest of the gouges – until I become conscious of the tic and control myself. I sip chilled vodka. More often, I pour vodka down the drain in the floor under my table. After making a show of drinking down the last bit in my glass, I rise and purchase my fourth drink, slurring my request.

I return to my table by a circuitous shuffling route. Without even a sip of my drink, I drop my head on the table with a loud *thunk* and perform my snore and drool. I attempt looking relaxed out cold while tensing and releasing the major muscle groups. Nowadays, I take every opportunity to maintain my stamina and strength; it's too easy in these times for us to physically wither away in hopelessness. I refuse to do that. I'll fight until I have no fight left in me, until I die.

It's not bravery that's propelled me to lead this rebellion – it's my faith in humankind. I believe we can overcome our current overlords. It's sad, but despite this faith in my species and how few of us are left, I trust few individuals. Too many – out of fear or self-interest – would betray us. And so I act as I am tonight to keep suspicious eyes away.

While I wait, I listen to the conversations around me for anything useful to the cause. I have often, under the cover of supposed incoherency, heard of a planned ant raid on one of our cells or discovered that a certain person had joined the ant corps. I hear nothing of use tonight.

Spittle tickles my cheek. After a time, I jerk my head off the table, wipe my slobber on the back of one hand, and sip my drink, now warm as spit.

Two skinny women at a nearby table laugh at me, gray faces smeared upward into wry smiles. We all try to find small reasons to laugh, to keep going. But, if the rumors are true, ours is the last continent on which humans survive. I've even heard of human purges in cities not far from here. Maybe it's just my own brand of pessimism but I think before long we humans will be gone, exterminated for the crime of no longer being useful. I believe when enough larvae ripen, the only living sound in our cities will be the rasping and clicking of ants. I want to laugh with the women, just to remember what it feels like. I can't.

My chin is almost touching my chest, head bent over my newest drink when Khara slouches in and collapses onto a barstool. Over the weeks I've been observing her, Khara's routine has become predictable. I watch her without raising my head, sneaking sidelong glances which I hope will go unnoticed. Certainly unnoticed by her, but one can never tell who else is watching. Rodriguez, another of my men, is here, but he doesn't watch her in particular, as I'm drawn to. Unobtrusive in his guise of sleeping – chair leaned back against a wall, mouth open, arms folded across his barrel chest – he watches everyone through dark eyelashes, learning patterns, watching for alliances or betrayals.

Khara runs long fingers through her curly, dirty blonde hair, and pulls herself upright on the stool. Her eyes are closed. She is whipcord thin, but not small boned. She looks young – maybe twenty – except in her face, which has lost any mark of soft youth. Her cheeks are hollows below pronounced cheekbones, her lips thin. Without being summoned, the ant/tender brings her a drink – whiskey, no ice. Not a small glass either.

The tender grabs her thumb and swipes her credit ring. She doesn't respond. It's as though she doesn't even know the ant has touched her. She makes no effort to confirm the amount he charges. Her hand falls to the bar where the tender drops it, palm up, fingers curled. Her other hand closes around the drink. After a moment, her head rocks back, off balance, before she catches it and jerks it forward to hang over the drink. Stoned again.

CARAPACE

My impression of Khara is of someone bleeding internally. Whole on the outside, yet broken inside, dying unobserved.

My lieutenant, Michael Bellamy, enters the bar. A tall rubber band of a man, he glides with his customary elegance to the bar near Khara. Blue neon shines on his taut ebony arms and shoulders as he lifts two beers and heads for my table.

"I don't want a beer," I say as he reaches the table.

"Just my effort to be hospitable, Mate, but I take no offense at your rejection." He checks his original motion and puts both beers down on his side of the table. "I shall simply have to finish them myself." He laughs with his usual good nature and holds his palm to my back for a moment of comradeship.

Leaning toward me and making a close examination of my face, he says, "The whites of your eyes have achieved a rather remarkable crimson. How many of those bloody things have you had?" Bloody. It is the closest thing to a curse word Bell ever uses – and never in front of "the ladies" – perhaps making this one exception in deference to its British origin. He always utters it with relish, prolonging the "l" sound. I can't help but smile. I'm sure my eyes aren't red. He's supporting my act.

"A couple," I say, answering his question. I smile, blink with a slow dip of my lids, keep my eyes at half-mast. The beauty of my caricature is that it's easy. My play-acting extends to the physical, which is a realm I'm comfortable with. I don't have to be witty, or charming, of which I am neither. I'm not like Bell.

He smells of beer already. And cigarettes. I can't help wondering what new connections he's made to come up with the cigarettes. The ants don't like them – the smoke irritates their eyes or their pores – so they've become next to impossible to come by. But, Bell has connections everywhere.

He's the rebellion's number one answer man. If we need information, he gets it. Everyone likes him. Everyone trusts him. He doesn't have to play the careful charade I play because no one would dream of suspecting or distrusting this man. Me included. In my case, not because I'm seduced by his likeability but because he's proven himself time and again.

"You're not going to have any luck with the ladies in your state, Mate." His chiseled features are painted with sincere concern, one eyebrow raised in emphasis.

"Damn," I say.

"Look around, lovelies all around us." He motions with both arms, a ringmaster, tantalizing. The gray-faced women watch him, drooping faces around eyes gone coy, wishful, inviting. Bell is an attractive man. His dark skin stretches over tight muscle, and leaves his teeth and eyes almost glowing. Fine-boned features show his Somali lineage. His British accent charms old and young.

Bell smiles at the gray-faced women. In this, he's not acting. His appreciation of women is genuine and, perhaps for this reason, his ability to woo, legendary. One of the women arches her back, and her body is like her face. Gray, tired, dried out. Bell pushes himself back from the table and glides over to her. He talks to her around his broad, glittering smile. Then, after a chivalrous bow, he excuses himself, goes to the bar and returns with three glasses of vodka. The women move their chairs closer to his and one reaches under the table to put a hand on his thigh. He raises his drink and the clinking sound of their three glasses mixes with their laughter.

I suppress my annoyance at having to wait for the information I need. Bell's a good man. He won't make me late.

Khara hasn't moved from her place at the bar. I rise from the table, drink in hand, and stumble across the floor. I trip over the back leg of her barstool, elbowing her in the kidney as I fall to the floor. She grunts as I bump her, but the noise is more exhalation than indication of pain. My fall is choreographed well enough to look spastic and unplanned, but to leave me with no bruises. I can't have bruises. I have my own ant master to which I must account.

I pull myself to my feet, retrieve my glass from the floor, and drag myself three seats down on the bar, glancing sidelong at Khara. I don't understand my attraction to her. She's an addict, barely surviving. Perhaps it is her powerful tenacity I need, that the rebellion needs.

I first noticed Khara because of her complete and almost corporeal aloneness, because of the space she clutched around herself, even in the constant crowd. I took her solitude to be a façade at first, or a cover, or a mood, but the darkness of the hole she had dug for herself seemed too rich not to be genuine. I followed her and waited for her alliances to surface.

This is what I've discovered: She is a bodyslave, used by the ants as they choose, the perfect submissive. Yet, she hasn't sworn allegiance to the ants. She has no human acquaintances. She sleeps in the downtown dorms – not even returning to the same space or the same dorm night after night – rather than with the other slaves in their pet hotels. She is either completely inside herself, or completely empty. She needs no one. The perfection of her solitude intrigues me.

One of Bell's women laughs – it's a shrill titter – gaining my attention. Bell has his arm around both, and they are headed toward the back of the bar. Bell smiles at me and holds up two fingers.

Two minutes? Both women? Either meaning would fit.

Khara finishes her second – maybe third? – whiskey and drops her head to the bar.

Yes, she is hemorrhaging. Is this strength, or the weakness of someone unable to fulfill her own death wish, someone who's chiseling away at a life she's too impotent to just crush?

Soon, I think, not sure whether this means I'll approach her again soon, or that soon her body will just give up and die.

Bile rises to my throat as she slaps another drug patch to her jugular. I watch her, trying to learn her, as tears drip down her face. She scratches her cheek with long thin fingers, as though the tears make it itch, but without any apparent knowledge she is crying.

I rest my head on the bar. Eyes open, I watch the dull blue flash-flash on the counter top and listen to the space around me. I wait for Bell. I wish I could sleep but I can't afford to be less than vigilant.

Bell soon scoops his beers from the round table and joins me at the bar. His women are gone.

"Made some new friends, I see," I say.

"I have had the good fortune to persuade them to join me for a meal a bit later, Mate." He doesn't gloat. He seems surprised at his "good fortune," though I'm not.

"What about Charlotte?" Charlotte is the code word. "Aren't you meeting her later?" I lift my head, glance past Bell to Khara. She is looking at me. The intense focus of her green eyes strikes a jolt, and I find it difficult not to react.

"Oh, my word." Bell opens his eyes wide, as if caught in a real-life dilemma. Khara struggles to maintain focus but can't. She's looking through me, and then away.

"You are correct. How could I have forgotten?" he says.

"Maybe I can help?" I ask.

"Would you? I was supposed to meet her at 2100, but it seems I have now double engaged myself."

2100.

"Where?"

"She wanted to meet me on Decatur, but I told her the back alley of the Comfort Inn was more convenient."

In the Comfort Inn back alley. Too open for comfort, but also non-negotiable. I check my watch. Almost time to go.

"I'll go and make some excuse for you. Do you suppose Charlotte will believe me?" I'm just finishing the conversation.

"Of course, Mate. She trusts me." A smile pulls at the corners of his mouth. He stands, suddenly solemn, takes my hand and shakes it. With that gesture, I feel he has wished me luck and safety in my coming rendezvous.

I glance at Khara as I shuffle from Refugio's. What makes us trust the people we do?

I want Khara to trust me.

CHAPTER 4
KHARA

Emptiness and fullness at the same time.

Emptiness. My stomach is empty of sweetmead, or anything. Hunger gnaws at me with dull teeth, coring me. My throat aches from repeated brushes with palpi, but there is no palpus in my throat now.

Yet I'm full. My left leg twitches every few seconds – maybe my body's unconscious effort to fight where I've given all conscious effort away – and with each twitch I feel myself still anchored to the table, feel something still within me, between my legs.

No.

The thought drifts behind my eyes, red, angry, neon wrapped in cotton.

No.

I don't know what the hell it means.

My hand floats along the warm surface of the wooden table I'm on. Up and down, up and down, looking for something. My fingers close on a patch, and the realization I have an avenue of escape burns in me, outshines the empty hunger and the heavy fullness. My hand brings the patch to my jugular. I don't feel my way – my body is dislocated – but my arm moves with a muscular memory of the movement that will bring the patch to the correct spot.

The drug-induced swirl begins anew. I follow the disconnected relentless thought – *No* – down the swirling drain to the black hole at the bottom, and disappear.

CHAPTER 5
FATCHK

In the warmth and darkness of the private den, I approach my bond-brother. Red light glints off the shell of his body and limbs; red hues reflect off the dark wood paneling of this small lounge. I have secured the heavy, ornate door to this room to ensure privacy from others who may try to enter from the club through which I have just passed. I did not scent-identify any of the brothers in the club and hope none recognized me.

"Sorm'ba," I whisper, naming my brother, in the human fashion of greeting. I have adopted this human convention as yet another way of supporting their fight for survival. I am careful to do this only with trusted comrades.

"Fatchk," rasps my brother.

It is unnecessary, this human-style greeting, because we clasp each other, graze each other with mandible and antenna, and taste each other's identities. Knowing each other by signature smell and taste, we relax to large cushions. As I lower my body, I wonder how this room was furnished when it was a human space. Then, it might have had tables, chairs, couches – as humans prefer. Now, it

28

is equipped in the manner we favor, with large pillows into which our bodies can recline for more comfortable sharing. Our bodies close together, we intertwine our limbs for our brief and risky meeting.

"There is danger," says Sorm'ba. I taste the undertones of his statement and understand the danger is that which is inherent in our rebellious activities, and not any particular or new danger.

"Yes," I answer, and reflect the flavor and scent of understanding.

"If the humans are to have a chance, they need many more things," says Sorm'ba. The space surrounding us thickens with the desperate scent of the need.

I wait, exuding patience and calm, undertoned with the need for haste due to our personal danger.

"Five cartons," Sorm'ba says, and follows the statement with the flavor of the antibiotic medicines the humans use. At the end of this transmission of information, Sorm'ba adds the punctuation that will let me know he is moving to the next item in the list of required items.

"Much," he says, and follows with the flavor of machine grease, made overwhelming to indicate the huge quantity indicated by the vague communication of amount.

"Pistons, ten," Sorm'ba continues, leaving the barest taste of the metal, since the flavor of the metal matches many machine-made components.

I trill a sound of questioning, and lick out with the mild sour green-yellow flavor of a question regarding the size of the pistons needed.

Sorm'ba answers, and then continues with the list of needed supplies and components. I listen and remember, the catalog a concoction of scent and flavor and sound that weaves together into a work of art and that will stay with me easily.

I compliment my companion, my bond-brother, my friend: "Thank you for the excellent organization of the list, whose flavor is distinctive and memorable."

"Yes," says Sorm'ba. He is aware of the sublime structure he has prepared, but is warmed by the compassion behind my unnecessary praise.

Our brief meeting ends with a strong combined flavor of the need for secrecy, the smell of trust, and of well-wishes tasted palpus to palpus. I move from the small darkness of the private room and into the crowded club. Even as I focus on each of the brothers and search for signs of recognition, of flavor-scents of suspicion, I ignore the uses to which humans are being put by the infected of my kind. I leave the club and am away.

CHAPTER 6
SAMUEL

I stumble from Refugio's into the thick night and I catch myself against the dark wood panel outside the bar, pretending to regain my balance. In a wobbling, drunken fashion, I turn this way and that, surveying my surroundings. In the flickering death-dance of the neon sign above the bar, I can't see anyone watching me, but spy at least one human member of the ant corps moving back and forth, back and forth, across the street. And there's always the possibility of someone hidden in the shadows.

I have to find a way past the ant corps member's relentless path. If I can enter the alley just beyond him, it'll be difficult for anyone to follow me to my rendezvous point without my detection. The path from the alley to the Comfort Inn is circuitous and only deliberately made.

I trip off the sidewalk and fall to my knees in the street. I've gained the ant corps member's attention. Teetering, I stand and turn back toward Refugio's. Tripping back up the sidewalk, I stumble north ten yards to the service alley that feeds Refugio's. I bend forward in the mouth of the alley, careful to remain visible to the ant corps member, and wretch.

Drunks vomit. Vomit-covered drunks are amusing, but only at a distance. In close, they stink.

I stand and make a show of wiping my mouth on my bare arm, wiping my hands on the front of my shirt. I spit into the street and wipe my mouth again on my arm. Then I lurch across the street toward the ant corps member and the alley beyond him. He shortens his insistent path which would bring him close to me, turns from me, and paces several steps away.

"Hey." I slur the word and gesture to him with my arm. He glances at me over his shoulder, contempt clear on his face in the streetlight, but he doesn't answer. He takes another couple of steps.

"Hey, buddy," I say again. I stumble into the alley and out of his sight. I fall against one wall and am lifting myself to my feet again when I hear him pass the alley mouth behind me. He mumbles something down the alley toward me, but he is too much the coward to say it so I can hear him. I continue down the alley. I hear him off and on at the mouth of the alley as he paces by but I no longer have his attention. This is good. It means he was not there to watch for me specifically.

I can feel the vodka's effect on me when I am free to walk, to stop my act. I despise the slight feeling of impairment. I stop at a street vendor and purchase a serving of greasy noodles and meat, served in a paper cone, and continue toward my meeting. Two of my people pass me on the crowded stretch near the Comfort Inn, but we don't acknowledge one another.

I slide into the wide alley behind the Comfort Inn. There is a light above the service door near the over-flowing trash bins, a streetlight at the entrance to the alley, and an orange-yellow crime light at the back of the alley. There is a brick column, attached to and jutting from one wall, and there are the huge trash bins to stand behind, but the light in the alley will cast shadows. Nowhere to hide.

I stand with my back to one wall, head down, peripheral vision keeping me aware of my surroundings. My ant contact hasn't yet arrived.

Within minutes, a small ant – an ant barely taller than I am – glides into the alley. My contact, Fatchk. There are no introductory pleasantries.

"Timing gears," he says, and tells me the sizes. "Piston rods. Gaskets." The words are formed with difficulty. The list goes on. Weapons, medications. It's a wish list I have to try to fill by stealing, trading, buying with pain. The price is high, but necessary. I hate that I live in this world, and so do as needed. We all die, but not under this yoke if I can help it.

Most of the parts are for the fleet of vehicles we're attempting to restore. I don't know if the ants destroyed and disabled so many to keep humans foot-bound on our streets or because the fumes bother them. I don't care. They have their flying vehicles but they're not often in the city and we wouldn't know how to use them anyway. We need instant mobility if we're to carry out the planned attack and, therefore, we need parts. And gasoline. We're having a hard time finding much gas at all.

I repeat the list. No notes, no written records – I have to remember what's needed, in which sizes and quantities. I assume once I've repeated the list, our meeting is over.

"Come," he commands, and steps out from the alley into the street. This movement into the public eye is unusual, but then we've never repeated a rendezvous point or time. Perhaps we're now also changing the rules regarding method. I once asked Fatchk, in my own attempt to analyze, predict, and understand, how the time or place for our meetings is chosen, and by whom. His answer was surprisingly un-antlike:

"Habit kills."

I knew at the time it was all the answer I'd get. I also understood that within the ant side of the rebellion, patterns were being broken and extraordinary actions taken. I can't pretend to understand the ant involvement, but won't deny their assistance in our fight.

I step onto the sidewalk behind and to the left of Fatchk. He chatters at me in his language which I can't comprehend. He turns toward me, and I'm braced for additional angry chatter, am prepared to look complacent and submissive in response. It's the game we're playing tonight for anyone who might be watching.

"When?" he asks, then turns away from me and continues moving down the sidewalk. He's asking when I might have the parts available. I wait until we've moved far enough that no one who may have heard his question will hear my answer.

"Unknown." I shuffle after Fatchk as he increases his speed and moves across the street. He turns toward me as we step up the far sidewalk.

"Seven days," he says, and then chatters angrily at me again. I act my part. I open my arms and bare my neck. He moves away from me again. I follow. I have the pain of panic in my chest as I wonder how to respond to this latest request. I can't imagine how I'll fulfill the parts order in just seven days. For every part the ants notice is missing, one of us dies. For every disturbance of factory operations, one of us is beaten. My factory doesn't even produce all the supplies requested.

"Impossible," I answer. I keep my voice toneless, devoid of the panic rushing through me.

"Imperative," Fatchk answers. He snaps his head over his shoulder, mandibles first, in the odd, mechanical fashion of the ants.

I can't answer. I don't have an answer. My mind races through the deceptions necessary to fulfill the order. I want to explain to Fatchk that speed may translate to sloppiness, to the deaths of my team members. I want to ask the necessity for the quick turnaround time. I can't. Fatchk escorts me into a dark alley. He backs me against the wall and places a pincer, open, at my throat above my monitor. I am not afraid of Fatchk. He has proven himself time and again.

"Dangerous times," Fatchk says, sibilant. "Must move faster. Larval production is up. The queen's madness is rampant."

Madness?

I don't have an answer. Fatchk wouldn't be pushing me without cause. Fear slices through me, and I don't care for its taste. Like blood in the mouth.

"Do you wish to die?" Fatchk isn't asking me if I want to die, but the grander question of whether I want the human race to die. I want to shake my head from side to side – NO – letting his pincer cut into my neck to show the vehemence of my answer; however, the slices are marks I couldn't explain to my own master.

"No."

"We make aggressive move in queen's court. We risk much. You must risk much." Then Fatchk releases me and slides from the alley.

I move deeper into the darkness. I'll wait before I leave this alley for my home. Unless someone is watching us, no one will notice Fatchk and I were in this alley together. And if someone is watching us, we'll both be dead soon. I use the time to solidify the parts list in my memory, and to think through what has to be done. Who must be contacted.

On my way to my home – my master's home – I stop at the Camelback and set a meeting for tomorrow with a warehouse manager for medical supplies. This stop requires more vodka, and more excruciating, slow, diffuse communication. I can't move fast enough. My impotence fills me with anger. I show the world emotionless stoicism. It's what is required of me.

CHAPTER 7
NESTRA

Waking in the warmth of my own bed-pit, clothed in the delicious comfort of darkness, I relax for a long moment. I revel in the peacefulness I find within myself, exploring its depths. I slept after treading the mantra many times.

A heavy, serene sigh escapes me.

"Bless you my dear queen." I leave the rest unspoken, knowing the likelihood of eavesdroppers. *Bless you for controlling your gluttony long enough for me to recover. But then, with what evil have you engorged yourself while I slept? Are you needy of me yet again?*

I chastise myself for my uncharitable thoughts and chuckle as I realize my spirit is too light to do a proper job. A small mental pinch is all I can manage.

I wonder if it is day or night. I am hungry.

"System." It is the default name for the computer. Most others have chosen nicknames for their terminals, but I use the default "System." Everyone else has brothers, friends. By the tens, or the hundreds, or the thousands. Everyone except those specially bred – females of the species, like me, like the queen. I have no bond-friends, nobody to share with, and I confirm my enforced isolation by refusing to name the computer as if it is a bond-friend.

My bedside terminal wakes at my summons and the screen shines red in the darkness. I intend to ask the time, but decide I do not want to know.

"Minimal lights, System." Dull red light oozes from the far end of the room, barely bringing the room out of blackness.

I light smokeless candles, cut the system lights and eat a light meal, tranquil in the fragrant, velvet dark. After a time, my need for interaction, for sharing – although I do not consciously form the word – draws my mind from its quiescence. I equate the need with a desire to emerge from my quarters.

Please let it be day so I might enjoy the garden. "System, time of day?"

"Early afternoon. You could consider the meal you just consumed your noon meal."

"Music, please." Satisfied, happy, I scrape myself clean within the comfort of the candlelight to the lulling classical tones I so enjoy. I gather my painting supplies and, as usual before leaving my quarters, touch the terminal for a random quotation. The terminal lights up:

Gather your strength from those whom you serve.
Chrenu VII, Book 6, Gru

The shock of the words hits me as a pincer to the gullet.

"System?!" Never since awakening from larva to consciousness on this planet have I seen a quotation repeated. Never. I take several panicked breaths.

Random doesn't mean without repetition, I remind myself. In a random system – even one with thousands or millions of variables, one quote might be followed by the identical quote. *Mightn't it?* I touch my terminal again.

Civility is borne of belief in the society and love of the individual.
Semlach, Epoch II-9.32.00007

I touch the screen again, and obtain a third quotation. Another sigh. For two years, I have wondered if perhaps the system anticipates my various needs, my moods, and finds an appropriate quote. Now I console myself with the idea the system produces quotes in a random manner.

My guilt speaks volumes. I have attached a meaning to a phrase that gnaws at me. I move into the hall, hoping to escape the dread that envelops me. Instead, it settles on my back, cloak-like, as my escorts move in to flank me. I force myself to slow my pace as I head for the gardens, knowing I can shed my escorts there, and hoping to cast off the foreboding that now shadows my short-lived tranquility.

I step into the warmth of the sunlight – a warmth different from the blanketing warmth of the darkness I have enjoyed all afternoon, but soothing nonetheless. I give an involuntary twitch of my shoulders as I shake off my escort at the entry of the garden. No other of my people is allowed within this, the queen's private garden, which makes it the sole space I have discovered – outside my own quarters – where I have any measure of freedom. I'm thankful that she does not come here often, of late.

Moving across the trimmed lawn, I enter the shade of my favorite tree – the shape of the leaves resembles the hands of my people beneath our lower pincers. Encased in the protection of the gardens walls, I am content, embraced by the spaced shade trees and the artistically arranged flower beds.

I am happy to notice the human gardeners work quite a distance from me. The soft-bodied, larval vulnerability of humans makes me uneasy. I stay away from humans, much as a hatchling would keep away from an old relative's collection of breakables – with both a fear of breaking the collection, and a complete lack of understanding as to why one would collect such mad, useless items. With a hatchling's high rasping voice the thought comes, unbidden, *Someday, when I'm old, I'll have a collection of such things.*

I shudder. *Never. Never shall I have such a collection of delicate rag dolls.* I glance at the humans as they clip and shape the low shrubbery. *I've seen enough of how the queen uses her fragile collection.* I force my eyes from the humans, repulsed, yet thankful only these creatures work the garden. Should I ever touch one of the humans, they will not taste the queen's Shame on me. And so my escort stands down when I enter the garden, undoubtedly bored, blessedly uninterested.

CARAPACE

Before I sit on the stool I keep under the large tree, I make a final effort to shake off the black shroud of guilt that has engulfed me upon the reappearance of the enigmatic quote.

I take nothing from the queen but her Shame.

I drop my painting supplies to the loamy ground, plant my feet, and shake myself in a tremulous wave that moves up my body. I twitch my legs, from jointed ankles up my body, out my four arms, up my neck and head and to the tips of my antennae. As I shake my head, the files and scrapers under my mandibles jam against each other and let loose an uncontrolled garbled sound that would be a screech if I put any air behind it. I know the guard, my escort, watches my twitching and ululation as a sign of madness. I do not care.

I cannot change that they treat me as someone diseased. And so I am. I carry the queen's sickness within me.

The wave of twitches, smaller this time, washes over me again. My antennae again sweep through the open scents of the garden. Mellowed, I pull my supplies from their sack and move through the small ritual of arranging the canvas, the colors, the scents, before relaxing, head thrown back, eyes not-quite-focused on the sun-sparkles that dance through the leaves above me.

I wait for the moment when inspiration will lay a color-scent-flavor picture in my mind which my fingers and pincers can only crudely recreate. It is this odd process of translation from the uncapturable illumination to its two-dimensional depiction that fascinates me and draws me over and over to the canvas.

I allow my mind to enter the state of free association which I find akin to the madness of dreams. I am always happy to discover something new and surprising within myself in the process. My turbulent thoughts mix with my transcendent relaxation until flashes of image coalesce into a dark pattern of patches with thin shimmering web-like strands waving, diaphanous, in a fragrant darkness.

Ah, a perfect representation of my mood.

In the center floats a warm bead – a golden dewdrop – shining like the web strands, and somehow floating in their grasp.

This I cannot name, this golden beckoning bead. I recognize the darkness of my guilt, of the queen's Shame, and the shining lines of my own peacefulness that make the background. The image settles upon me with a surety that allows me to begin the translation to canvas.

When I can name the tempting dewdrop, I will have named this work. And with the tingle of pleasure that accompanies painting, I dash my lower pincers into the paints and began mixing shades and flavors on the palette into the bruised color of my inner self.

As I paint, I enjoy the garden: the colors, the scents, the textures, the mere knowledge I can walk amongst the trees and bushes and flowers without trailing an escort. I caress the canvas for a time with paint-laden pincers, then find myself staring, foggy-eyed, into a colorful patch of dancing flowers, petals bunched together so closely that the blossom resembles a ball.

I return to another dab of paint and the press against the canvas. My pleasure is tainted by the unhappy coincidence that the human gardeners move into my field of vision so often today. As I sit, I am entranced by the slight movement of large white flowers upon a bush of deep green, waxy leaves. I am relishing their heavy fragrance as it moves over me on the breeze when the humans move again into view.

With a rasping sigh, I lift my arm and ready myself to continue my painting – I am adding the delicate, shining web-lines (with their flavor-scent of serenity) over the dark background with the sharp tip of one pincer – when something about the humans catches my attention. For the first time, I focus on them.

Soft light-colored bodies, naked of any armor, I find them as vulgar and inappropriate as an unsheathed sex organ. I watch the humans as one bends to clip and shape a small bush, and the other, close at hand, digs weeds from around the base of the same shrub. Disgusted, ready to turn back to my painting, I register what the humans do *between* each movement of clipping and digging, register the touching that must have attracted my attention.

The humans are . . . no. No, I'm anthropomorphizing. But now I cannot stop watching. As the one human stands from its digging to move around the other, it brings the back of a dirty hand to the cheek of the other human. As the clipping human moves the sheers from one hand to the other, the hands of the two clasp for a moment. Then, digging, clipping, clipping, clipping. Then again, a brush of a touch, shoulder to shoulder – and now, spectacularly – mouth brushing against cheek. Clipping, clipping, digging, clipping.

Sharing. With an exquisite ache in my abdomen, and a shortness of breath, I stand. *And yet, it is not possible, all our studies say they cannot . . .*

I cannot take my eyes from the gardeners, who do not speak to one another, who do not often look at one another, but find a way, within the confines of their chores, *to share.*

I am standing mere feet from the closer of the two humans, looking into the softness of its liquid eyes, with no recollection of having moved across the lawn. The humans stop mid-motion and look at me, obviously startled. I can smell their sudden fear. The digger stands and the clipper backs to stand with the digger.

"I will not hurt you," I stammer, before remembering the humans will not understand my speech. Lowering my antennae and pincers, I open my arms, and do not otherwise move, hoping my subservient motionlessness will communicate my pacifism to these inferior animals.

One human moves to clasp the other's hand. The contact between them is a shock that leaves me shivering. They bow and back away, move around the low shrubbery until several small bushes stand between us. They stare with their jelly eyes. Their rejection is a weight on my chest.

Even these repulsive creatures have what I cannot have. I wrap my four arms around my torso to quell the ache there and moan. At the sound, the humans drop their tools. They wrap their arms around each other – I almost cannot bear the sight – and continue to back away from me and out the back gate until I am alone in the garden.

Heavy, hurting, I return to my painting. The pain within fires me with energy for outpouring, and before long, I have dashed a bold golden dewdrop into the center of the painting. With yellows and browns, I give it depth, until its visual richness makes me lust for a taste. As I trim the gold with a thin bead of red, I recognize it. *I have seen this in the fugue state I enter for downloading.*

'Tal's Strength.' I name my painting aloud, and shiver with a violent spasm.

I know now why the golden dewdrop is so tantalizing to me. Queen Tal: You have something I need if I am to keep living.

Strength.

CHAPTER 8
SAMUEL

I wake with the knowledge it's four forty-five in the morning, within minutes of the time I awoke yesterday, and the day before that, and again before that. It's impossible to gauge the hour by any daylight, because the room in which Tamerak's bed-pit is located is windowless, and always red-dark.

Tamerak breathes lightly in trance-state. Soon, he'll rise from his semi-seated position against the edge of the bed-pit, and we'll begin our morning ritual of cleansing and eating before heading to the factory. I'm like a beloved dog to Tamerak: well-trained, worthy of affection. I imagine to myself Tamerak has come to rely upon me to some degree, but I never let these imaginings convince me I'm indispensable. As with a dog, if I appear rabid or otherwise unreliable, Tamerak will put me down. I'm careful to remain dependable and affectionate.

This puts me on the same level as the bodyslaves who whore themselves to the ants even though Tamerak does not expect physical intimacy from me. I know – were Tamerak to ask –

47

I'd perform whatever physical acts requested to continue my life in this position of relative safety. And I think he knows it, too.

I help Tamerak scrape himself of the evening's waste excretions. I prepare his predigested and regurgitated pap for a morning meal. Neither of these tasks nauseates me. I've become accustomed to my degradations, and suffer them willingly. In exchange for the price I pay, Tamerak trusts me to some degree, and indulges me with kindness in a world where trust and kindness are rarities. My obedience has purchased me security, ephemeral though it may be.

I'm impatient to get to the factory this morning, as I know how much we have to try to steal in less than a week. I'm sick with the knowledge that in our haste, there'll likely be a price to pay. Thankfully, while this factory is ostensibly producing parts for the machines that are tearing up roads outside the city and getting the land ready for the agriculture of ant-style plants, there are several parts that we can use in restoring our vehicles.

Once there, I get busy with the books, looking over production figures, planning shifts and schedules, and accounting for any changes made necessary by new directives from the queen. It's my job, and Tamerak leaves me to it, trusting me, as always, to get the most from the humans that work for him. Tamerak is the factory's contact with the outside, the liaison to the world of ants, and I'm his inside man. Things run with smooth efficiency in Tamerak's factory.

I force myself to review my assigned parts in my mind before I attempt to discern what I can get from our factory. I have to consider which parts we've stolen in the recent past, and who works on the production of the various parts – factors that will turn mere mistake or coincidence in to a pattern recognizable by our captors.

I always tend toward the side of caution, but can't with our newest parts list. Our position must be precarious, given this latest push – and if our position is so precarious, then I have to take risks. I've long believed our time of extinction was approaching. Better now to risk much and lose a few than to lose it all. Lose the war, our lives, our planet.

At my normal time for checking production, I descend the stairs to the floor. I stop at Jan's workbench, touch her on the shoulder as I comment on her efficiency. I touch the huge, dark-skinned, quiet Eli, at the bench nearest Jan's. Without comment. I stop and touch Steve, Davey, Debbie, and Sturm. With each touch, I am sending a message: *I need one. Today you must, without preplanning, try to take one. Whether it be piston, bolt, washer. I need one.* Each person knows they'll be on their own – no preplanned distraction, no prearranged pass-off. *I need one. Get me one if you can.*

I haven't often used this method of gathering parts because of the risk on the individual thief of being caught with the part. The sentence is death. And I've never called on more than one. Today, I tap eight. I know some won't get an opportunity; I pray

49

none will be discovered. I also know each will make their best effort. We know what we fight for.

I'm careful as I walk amongst my people to also touch those who are not active in the rebellion, like Stella, who is too old, too scared. She's lost everyone important, except a grandson. She hopes to stay alive long enough to make sure he's taken care of and hopes to buy his continued life through her own obedience. She won't join us. Death is forever on her shoulder, and weighs too heavily for her to see that death rides us all. I can't fault her. There are many here like her, young and old, hoping to ride through the storm. They don't buy into our brand of pessimism, our doomsday opinion that humans won't weather this fatal storm. I sometimes touch these. They take the touch as comfort – human flesh to human flesh – a form of communion we all crave. And these touches buy our people a measure of safety as well: if anyone is watching, they won't see it as the signal it represents among the rebels. It's a shame with my rebels, this touch isn't comfort but an assignment that comes with the metallic taste of fear.

There are also those on the floor – humans – who would betray us for some small favor from the ants. It sickens me our own kind would betray us for some ephemeral special treatment. Extra food or credits, or perhaps a more comfortable sleep space. But we've always had these pathetic creatures among us. I try to shake them off. And I refuse to touch them, to give them even that small comfort. I damn them all to hell and hope fervently that *that* hell is worse than the one I now occupy.

Done with rounds, I trudge with heavy heart back up the metal stairs to the catwalk and look back over the floor. My people. Even the wretched traitors are my people. I console myself that the risk and burden I just placed on a few will – I hope – benefit all.

I force myself back to my desk to continue looking through accounts and requisition requests, to work as though nothing were being risked. Force myself not to stand on the catwalk watching. I take my second break of the day as the first, walking amongst the workers on the floor, urging speed where necessary, expressing gratitude at efficiency. Same as any other day.

When the workday is done, I stand with Tamerak and two other ant-guards as the workers file out past us, random workers searched as they leave. I grit my teeth as Sturm is searched, but the search is cursory. Nothing's found. This means either Sturm hasn't managed to steal a part, or that he's gotten lucky. I stand, as always, with my hands clasped behind my back, to all outward appearances, uninterested in the process. Two more workers file past without being searched. Then Davey. He's the youngest of my people in this factory, and one of the most fervent. The ant-guards stop and search him. Pat him down, ask him to remove his shirt and shoes. This isn't unusual. Davey says nothing, which also isn't unusual.

"Open mouth," one ant-guard intones. It's obvious he's not one of the ants who is fluent in our language. Most of the guards aren't. Not that it matters if they are.

Davey doesn't listen. I can see now, from the way he holds his jaw, this is how he has chosen to smuggle his part. To give him credit, though fear is now apparent on his face, he doesn't look at me, to me.

"Open mouth," the ant says again as the other hits Davey in the gut.

Davey grunts around the part in his mouth – a gear too big to swallow. At the second blow to his stomach, he opens his mouth and the gear falls, spit-covered, to the ground.

"What?" the ant asks. I bend to retrieve the part. I don't hesitate to hand the gear to the guard, although I know Davey will now die and his death won't even buy us this gear we need. My heart aches for this young boy even though I know there's nothing I can do. Nothing whatsoever, other than choose to die with him.

The guard takes the part with one pincer, hands me his pistol-shaped laser gun – or whatever the mechanism is – with the other and says to me, "Shoot human."

My breath stops in my chest and my heart beat pulses in my face, my fingers.

This is unusual. This is my own test. I know in that split second that if I don't shoot Davey, the guard will shoot us both. Do I choose to die with Davey in a fruitless, brave gesture?

I don't hesitate, although my mind is filled with a silent scream. I pull Davey out of the line, put the gun to his forehead and push the contact trigger. Davey falls backward, with a neat black hole in his forehead. I hand the pistol back to the guard. I can't act on the anger that courses through me. I can't allow myself to shake, or vomit, or weep. I wish in that moment I'd turned the gun on myself.

No one screams. No one moves. I know none of my people blames me. I blame myself. I put Davey in this danger today.

The guard pulls the next person in line forward, Jan, and searches her with unusual thoroughness. Clothes off, boots off, mouth open. Short hair inspected. I can't breathe.

Nothing is found.

The rest of the line files through, some searched in cursory fashion, some not, as though nothing extraordinary has occurred. No one looks to where Davey lies, even after the pool of blood from his head grows and spreads to where we stand. Blood soaks the soles of my boots. Bloody footprints lead out of the factory.

No one else is caught.

I stop twice on the way back to Tamerak's house to vomit. I can't wipe Davey's eyes from my mind. Davey's surprised eyes, and the third eye I opened in the middle of his forehead. Tamerak rubs me with his pincer after the second time but says nothing. I'm relieved he doesn't question me regarding the incident. Of course, his loyal pet would know nothing of the smuggling.

CHAPTER 9
NESTRA

I cock my head to one side and watch as my high left pincer twitches open and closed. The twitch has worsened since yesterday. Without moving my head, I rotate my focus to watch each of my three remaining pincers. The slim delicate fingers beneath my lower pincers show no sign the tremors have started in any of my other forelimbs. Without looking, I can feel the tremors in my legs.

I have been unable to ignore the symptoms of physical disintegration since falling three days ago in the hall outside my quarters. Of course, the escort made no move to assist me. I had been sure I had stumbled over something. Pulling myself to my feet, I searched for the obstacle, only to find the hallway clear of anything that might have tripped me. I questioned the guards.

"What did I trip on? Did you see it?" Still searching the ground.

"No, M'Nestra," spoken in unison.

I felt foolish when, after another moment of bending and searching, I had sniffed at the guards, tasting their surety of my madness emanating from their pores and evident in their clenched mandibles. I noted their stiff torsos, the rotation of their heads, one eye turned toward me.

I straightened, and led them down the hallway at a brisk pace, only to trip again moments later. This time, I recognized my own dragging leg as the culprit, and recovered my balance before falling. I slowed my pace after that, careful to concentrate on lifting each leg and placing it before me. It was the next day I noticed an odd blind spot in my right eye as if certain facets had died. And now the tremors.

I am dying.

I know my condition is not yet irreversible. With proper nourishment and rest, time enough to rebuild my strength, I can recover from this sudden onset of Shame-induced decrepitude.

But I also know my queen. The queen's appetite for killing and torture is increasing. She easily kills humans and almost as easily kills our people. At the rate with which the queen is disposing of humans, I wonder how long her courtiers will continue supplying her with their own well-trained pets. I have already noticed a decline in the quality being supplied, but my own knowledge of the pets – and their use – is limited. Deliberately. I shudder as I recall the queen's many uses for humans – always involving their blood, and often their deaths. The queen must appreciate the mild suffocation which comes with having her pores covered with their sticky red fluid. Must also appreciate the flavor. It is a flavor I have no interest in discovering.

CARAPACE

I am dying.

Anger rises within me at the thought. Anger directed at the queen. *Is this another symptom?*

I should meditate, make some effort to relieve the negative chemicals which flood my system, but I cannot rouse myself to the task. Despondence.

Yes, dying.

With a sigh, I push aside the texts which describe my condition. The tapes clatter away across my bed cushion. I choose, instead, my favorite philosophical text, which contains not only quotations, but analysis. My favorite passages are marked.

Ancestors, help me. Where logic and education cannot heal me, give me comfort. Give me faith.

Today I seek an unmarked passage. The passage speaks of loyalty, and I need the reminder that my instinct for self-preservation is base and unworthy. That I should focus on loyalty to society, to colony – and in my particular situation – to my queen. My search is rewarded – I am pleased and proud of my familiarity with the ancient writings – and I take comfort in what I read. I breathe easier, peacefulness settling over my trembling limbs, as I follow the annotations to related passages.

Settled, almost ready for the meditation I need, I turn to my favorite passages. I scan in haphazard fashion from one to the other. Until I come to one that undoes me.

Gather your strength from those whom you serve.

I almost yank the tape from the player and throw it across the bedchamber.

Did I mark this? I cannot recall having marked the passage, but I must have. I read it, re-read it. I have marked no annotations. The quote is the only marked passage on the screen. I force myself to read the annotations and analyses in an attempt to relieve myself of the meaning I have assigned the quotation: *Take your strength from the queen.*

No!

"The queen commands your presence." The system announcement – despite its gentle tones – startles me. Panic surges through me with the irrational fear I have been caught with unauthorized contraband, and the sick knowledge I am not physically or emotionally prepared to accept any Shame.

"The queen commands your presence." The system will repeat the announcement until acknowledged.

"Thank you, System."

My escort will be waiting. I clean and feed myself, fearful and unable to focus on anything except the tremors that afflict me.

I lead my escort to the antechamber off the throne room where the queen awaits me.

CHAPTER 10
KHARA

Samuel is following me. He shows up at Refugio's and the streetside feeding bins where the sponsored eat for free. He watches me, a dole expression sewn into the cracks around his eyes and full mouth. I don't care about his apparent need, the need of the rebellion. I'm not a revolutionary. Survival is my goal and I'm well kept by the enemy. My fight is to live another day without giving the aliens anything more than the shell of my body. It's a fight that takes all my effort. I have no energy left for Samuel.

I spend even more time with Ilnok, covered with the juices he loves to lap from me, full of the mead he longs to take from me. I do whatever he demands. I'm a good pet. I sleep at his feet when I can't stay awake any longer. I escape him when I'm allowed.

"You could rise in their ranks, work with them, become a member of the ant corps," Samuel says to me one night at Refugio's. The insult is so huge that for a while, the words circle in my head as I try to figure out what the hell he means.

Then the words come clear — *work with them... ant corps.* Beyond pissed, I swing my mug at him, determined to make him pay for the insult. He stops my arm short, covering himself in the rest of my beer. His hand is immense on my arm, his grip steel. "But you haven't," he says. His hungry eyes move over me, dissecting me. They don't leave me as he mops my beer from his face.

"I don't believe in you," I hiss. I'd spit at him, but the cottony after-effects of my addiction make that impossible. "I could turn you in, bastard. Leave me alone." I jerk my arm from his grip and move away, down the bar. When I look back, he's gone.

I order another shot of whiskey and beer, wondering at my warning. Why haven't I turned him in? Why am I hurt that he's gone from his seat at the bar? I slap another patch on my neck, unwilling to let my train of thought derail me from my willing acquiescence.

Before the drug can take me, Samuel's words ring in my head once more — *you could work with them* — and anger explodes in me again. I slam down the shot and drain the new beer in front of me. Ilnok will be calling me soon and I don't want to be thinking about Samuel's words when I'm with Ilnok. I order another set, desperate to let the crashing music of the two-man band fill my head. I imagine I can feel Samuel watching me.

A strong hand closes around my upper arm and pulls me from my seat, drags me backward off my stool. I pull against the grip, hand clawing at the steel hand, accomplishing nothing. I trip backwards, sideways, unable to get my feet under me as I'm dragged into the bathroom. In the toilet stall, I'm released with a violent push. It's Samuel. His face is tight with anger. I'm too stoned to be scared even though I should be. Vertigo overcomes me and I fall to my knees.

"See that white spot?" he demands as he points to a white chip in the back wall of an open stall. His thick mouth is pulled taut. His body is tensed, menacing, and his fists are clenched. He steps toward me. I flinch, sure he'll hit me, but he doesn't. I want to crawl away.

"Stand up. Do you see that white spot?" His words are controlled bursts of sound, full of command, but not loud.

My head spins as I answer yes and push myself to my feet. He grabs my arm, almost pulling me from my feet again, and I'm in the tunnel again. I stumble as he pulls me along. I want and don't want to make him drag me, as pride and need battle within me. We come out of the tunnel into a small living quarters. A ragged group of young humans – training age – sit and stand, packed into the small room. They're bent over equipment benches or books, industrious. Samuel releases me and I stagger forward. All eyes are on me. Each youth is an internal combustion engine powered by hope.

"For the kids," Samuel says as he steps around me. He takes a deep breath that is a sigh. His anger is gone. "Help us," he says. He turns my face toward his own, gently, almost with a caress. His hand is large and soft against my cheek and chin. A finger lingers against my face. "You believe in the human race," he whispers, "you believe we can survive this. You haven't given up yet. You believe."

I pull away from the softness of his touch and look around at the faces that watch me, feeling my anger build like a belch, threatening to break free. I want to hit Samuel for daring to speak to me with such gentleness, for being so tender in his touch. I'd rather he hit me. The sensation of his hand moving across my cheek burns as though the nerves are on fire. I squeeze and pull at my cheek in an effort to get rid of the sensation. They're still watching me. I hate them.

"How can you say I believe?" I scream at them, shocking my own ears with the sudden volume of my outburst. "You don't know what I do!" I stare at their bare, virgin throats, watch as the ruby glare at my own throat ignites in their eyes. I lift the choker toward them. "My master calls me." I shudder, nauseous with self-disgust. My master. I'm willingly owned.

Samuel squeezes my shoulder, turns me toward him. He is a brick of a man. I jerk away from his grasp.

"You do whatever they want. *Whatever* they want." His voice is warm with understanding, his mouth sensual and soft under his fleshy nose. As I watch, he pulls his high collar down to reveal a monitor of his own.

I'm speechless. I close my eyes to the sight of him.

"Will you help us build? Defend? Defy?" he asks. His voice is caramel strength. Then softer still: "We need you."

I don't want this.

CARAPACE

I wish I could melt into the twisting haze behind my eyes. I want a beer. I want the blindness offered by the patch. I want out of here. Out of this room, out of this world, out of the knowledge that Samuel exists.

"Go to hell," I say. I open my eyes and try to regain my balance. I'm crushed by the weight of their eyes upon me.

Pushing through the group and into the street, I know I have to find a sweetmead vendor on the way to Ilnok. I squeeze my eyes shut to release the tears that have gathered there, push them violently from my face. I suck in a full breath of the rank street determined to shake off the panic Samuel has planted in me. There is comfort in routine, even routine violation.

***

I don't see Samuel as often, and he doesn't look at me anymore. Maybe he's trying to remind me by just being there, to make me feel guilty. I'm beyond guilt. He makes it easier for me to ignore him, to go on living as I must.

I'm now Ilnok's favorite pet. He takes me to the most exclusive of their clubs, rank with hedonistic splendor. He lets others feast on me, enter me, as I lie prone on a table before them. I'm ornament and banquet for them. I gorge myself on sweetmead and let them drain me. They taste of my soft body that so fascinates them until my patch is useless to me, and I lie shivering, shuddering, sore. Even as I hate them, I'm thankful for the proud human favorites that watch and wait their turn. Thankful for the relief they provide my body and mind. But thankful most for the patch and the numbness that allows me to endure another touch of an antenna, another penetrating kiss.

"You may leave," Ilnok says, clicking with the effort of our speech. His companions chitter with laughter as I squeeze my knees together. I push myself up on my elbows. A new, young boy — years younger than me — stares from his seat on the wall, tears littering his hairless cheeks and chest. An ant — I've adopted Samuel's word for the aliens — gestures toward the kid with a long triple-jointed limb. The kid shakes his head, crying. I can see he's terrified, that he was brought here unprepared for this level of submission.

Aw. Poor kid. Didn't want to join this club?

Some unidentifiable, dark, stabbing feeling runs through me as finish the thought and I realize the coldness behind it.

The ant gestures again but the boy doesn't obey. Just sits there, eyes round. The ant rises, chattering angrily, and pulls the kid up by his monitor. The collar snaps open.

The ant clicks in English so we humans can all understand, "For disobedience, this one will be killed."

I'm stunned into motionlessness with a patch halfway to my throat. I've seen bodyslaves die, but never an outright murder. The loud clicking and snapping that surrounds me as the ant grips the boy's neck startles me into movement again. I slap the patch to my neck. I gather from the noise and gesturing that the group doesn't want the mess made in their splendiferous clubroom. I slide across the table toward Ilnok. I'm sitting before him in my own juices.

"Master," I say, raising my voice above the din, "may I –" I almost can't finish the sentence. I throw my head back, spread my arms as if to embrace him, open my legs, press my breasts toward him. I'm the picture of subservience. "May I kill it?"

My words descend on the sudden silence. I feel myself redden, lighten, with the onrush of my drug, the audacity of my request. Ilnok opens his mandibles and I throw my head back to accept his kiss amid the gentle whirring of what I have come to recognize as applause. The boy is mine.

I expect to be escorted as I lead the boy away and I have no fucking plan for what comes next. But I'm not followed. It's just another sign of how little Ilnok and his crew care. I entertained them today, first with my body and then by asking if I can kill the boy. What a good slave I am. Now, with the disobedient boy out of sight, the kid's also out of mind and they can go back to their play. Plenty of fun to go around.

The shivering boy marches in front of me. He hasn't pleaded with me or said a word in anger. I hold his wrists together behind him, pulled toward his head. The skin covering his back is so young and resilient, his back, buttocks, and thighs, beautiful. He reminds of someone, but I can't – don't want to – think who. For reasons I can't understand, I'm angry with the kid.

In the dressing room, I order him into his clothes. He cries but obeys. The exhausted haze I'm moving in doesn't drown my self-disgust as I pull my pants over the sticky residue on my skin. I'm crippled with my need for a drink.

Wrists now tied in front of him, I lead the kid to the street. I tear my shirt collar open and down, leaving no question of my rank and status. I don't want to be stopped or interrogated.

Refugio's. I want to order a whiskey, but first pull the boy to the toilet. Groggy, I search for the white chip and pull the kid into the open stall. He faces me and takes off his shirt. His arms are limp at his sides. He bears his neck in the standard symbol of subservience and then starts to take off his pants. I can hit him, or have him. I want to hit him.

Instead, I reach past him, push the back wall. My arms shake as if my body is pressing beyond its limits. Nothing happens. The boy moves to the side. He watches me with pale eyes trimmed in red. His face reveals nothing, no fear.

"Samuel!" I cry, too tired, too drained for this. I strike the wall, hit over and over at the white chip.

Then we're through. I push the boy. He tightens his pants around his trim waist with a long drawstring. He stares at me, expressionless, waiting.

"Walk." I throw his shirt at him. He doesn't catch it. It crumples at his feet. Hauntingly, his eyes don't leave mine.

"Someone will help you." I turn and step back into the toilet. The wall closes between us.

I've already forgotten him in my need for a drink.

CARAPACE

Whiskey, another patch, and I'm letting the streetside mass take me to a dorm where I can sleep for free. My exhaustion helps bring sleep as I settle to the padded floor of the shelter. I press my body toward the wall, away from the other bodies, too raw for even human touch. I let myself fade away.

***

I'm drinking down sweetmead, all I can stomach. I haven't eaten, but – much to my surprise – my spirits are high. My monitor glows off everyone and everything around me. I slap a new patch to my throat, looking forward to the oblivion it offers and begin the press streetside to Ilnok.

A door opens beside me, and Samuel drags me through. The kid is there, with several others. He shines with the hope his new friends have given him. Samuel smiles at me. The softness of his full lips captures my eyes for a long moment.

"Fuck off, Samuel," I say. His smile grows, and I'm tempted to return the smile. I find I can't. I pull the door open, push into the press of the crowded street. I've had a good night's sleep. I'll be able to face Ilnok today, stronger.

CHAPTER 11
SAMUEL

I can't stay away from the home I share with Tamerak much longer this evening. I've met with two of my contacts tonight – one wiry old black woman who had good news regarding the medical supplies we have to deliver in two days, and one small round gray man who works at a factory much like Tamerak's, but hasn't been able to get many of the vehicle parts we need. I didn't ask how many of his people he's lost in his efforts. It's a bitter, unworthy question. We're all doing what we can.

We've done well at our factory, but we still don't have the needed quantities. Thankfully, Davey's been our only fatality. So far. I am haunted by Davey's face as he fell to the grey floor of the factory, by bloody footprints. I don't flinch from the memory. The pain associated with it is both my penance and how I honor his bravery.

The kitchen is empty, except for Bell, who's come in smelling of cigarettes again. With the satisfaction of the well-fed, he covers his mouth with a fist to mask a slight burp. Following protocol, he didn't join my meeting. Now, he's sitting with his chair rocked back against the yellow, water-stained wall, feet crossed on the table, head leaning back, a faint smile on his face. The low light glints off his carved features.

"Where have you been?" I ask, curious again about the cigarettes.

"Dining and dancing, Mate," he answers, pauses a beat, then, "with an absolutely sublime blonde at the Club Atlanta."

"They don't allow cigarettes inside the Club."

"More's the pity." A wistful sigh that is full of satisfaction. "I found myself a pack. Smoked one on the way here. The flavor's a bit off, but, I miss them all the same." He is smiling at me. He pulls a red and white pack from his shirt pocket and gestures like he's going to toss it to me. "Want one, Mate?"

"Thanks, no," I answer. I wouldn't mind a cigarette, but these aren't the days of old when another pack can be easily come by. Anyone else would be hoarding them instead of offering one. I won't take advantage of Bell's friendship and natural generosity.

"Any new leads on gasoline?" I don't want to pressure Bell – I ask this question every time I see him – but we're short on gas. No matter how many trucks we manage to piece together, if they don't have go-juice, we may as well not have bothered.

"I'm working it, Mate. Trust me. Something will come to the fore."

It's not the answer I want. In my mind, I list other sources I can ask – not that anyone is better connected than Bell, but I've got to try.

"How's the new boy?" he asks. His head is back against the wall again, and his eyes play over the two dusty, dirty fixtures set into the low ceiling.

"Smart," I answer. "He's doggone smart. Knows a bit of their language, worked with their computers. Good contacts." We can't send him back to where he worked with their computers, but he has lots of information that'll be useful. "Thinks Khara walks on water," I pause, then smile as I say, "I'm not sure she doesn't. Gutsy gal."

Not many things to smile about these days, but a young boy saved, a new recruit, and Khara . . . Khara's involvement is something to smile about. I've hoped for some time we could gain Khara, but never thought she'd start with such a spectacular, risky stunt. I hadn't been sure she had enough left inside her to care.

Bell drops his feet from the rickety wooden table one at a time. The sound is loud in the small room. He leans forward to bring all four legs of the chair down. His face is as serious as I have ever seen it.

"You're not trusting..." He doesn't finish the sentence. His head cocks to one side and then straightens. "Are you?" He squints at me and I wonder if I have ever seen him look so solemn.

I'm confused. She saved a life today at great risk to her own. She asked for nothing in return.

"Well, I don't see..."

I suppose Bell can see the confusion written on my face. "It's simple," he says. "She's a drug addict." He stands, paces the tile floor toward a sink orange with rust, and then back. "She can't be trusted. She sells herself for her miracle patches, and she'd sell you, too – believe it, Mate." Bell looks anxious, which is unusual on a face that is always good-natured, smiling, finding the joke in every situation.

I'm slow to answer. Bell has excellent instincts and has been my lieutenant since the beginning. I trust his judgment. But I'm not making sense of the vehemence of his objection.

Is my interest in and instinctive trust of Khara so extraordinary? Wrong?

"She hasn't sold me out." I say the words. "She hasn't sold anything but her body. Certainly not her soul, if I'm any judge of character. She proved it when she saved that boy today."

"Samuel!" Bell's voice is raised. I lift my eyebrows in surprise. He takes two deep breaths and, voice at a normal level again, says, "You really think she risked anything? She's in with them, Mate. You heard the boy. She *asked* for him, and they gave him to her. How bloody likely is that? It's a set-up. She didn't risk anything."

This isn't an interpretation I want to accept, but it adds up as more likely than the one I had assigned to her actions.

When I don't answer, Bell says, a small smile on his face, "Come on, Mate, who you going to trust? Bellamy?" – he places a hand, fingers steepled, on his chest – "or a known drug addict?" He lets me think for a bit. I take the moment, weighing my instincts about Khara against the logic of his statements. Then he says, "Do you find her that attractive?"

I still don't answer because I can't deny Khara has my notice, although not – I don't think – for the reason he's suggested. I lost the woman I loved in the invasion. I won't allow myself the indulgence of that kind of relationship again. Won't.

"I've seen you watching her." He stands, and crossing the room to put a consoling hand on my shoulder, he says, "I know, Mate, I know. And they call them the weaker sex."

I'm unsure whether to trust myself, unwilling to trust Bell's characterization of Khara.

He turns to go, as if this discussion is over, but for some reason I can't let Khara go. She could be an asset, I am sure of it, and I can't make myself believe she's with the ants.

"I still think we could make use of her," I say, just as he reaches the dingy hallway leading out of the kitchen.

Bell turns. He is not smiling, but he doesn't look angry either. He looks worried. "You can't let her in, Samuel." He walks back to me. We look at each other, and in the silence I remember all the times Bell and I have saved each other's lives. I should trust what he's saying, but I keep circling back to Khara.

"She'd sell herself to anybody – you, me, anybody – for another hit, and she's sold herself to *them*, Mate. Use your head. If you are that attracted to her, go to her. But *don't* let her in." He is very serious, very sincere. His voice is intense, but low. He's wrong about my intentions toward Khara, but still...

71

He stands there looking into my eyes, and I know he's right. Khara has already told me she doesn't want any part of the rebellion. She's already threatened to turn me in. I can't risk what we have. Not now when it's heating up and the risks have grown so great.

I sigh, feeling the weight of responsibility in my chest.

"Right," I say, and clap him on the back. "Right."

Images of Khara shift past my inner eye: sitting at a bar stoned, wending down a street unsteady on her feet, slumping senseless onto a mat at one of the downtown dorms, sleeping . . . young and strong and . . . yes, beautiful, in the escape of sleep.

Bell's right. I have attached emotion – attraction – to the idea of Khara. And the events of today make a lot more sense from his angle than mine.

Bell is still looking into my eyes. Searching for something. He asks, still unsure of me, "Right?"

"Right," I say again, tired now. Ready to head home.

We head down the hall and slip outside into a dark alley, then turn in opposite directions. I'm weary and sad. Upset with myself for seeing something in Khara that intrigues me, knowing Bell is correct, but thinking of Khara regardless. I'm weaker than I thought. Emotional attachment of any kind – even if it's simply the feeling of certainty or curiosity – is a luxury I can't afford.

As I move through the shadows of the reeking alley, I scan the alley with all my senses, always on the lookout. As I turn back to see if Bell is still in sight, a lighter flares at the end of another hard-to-come-by cigarette.

CHAPTER 12
KHARA

"Khara."

My name. It arrives with my whiskey and beer. Oddly accented – antly accented – barely heard over the band and the subdued drunken laughter from the party at the end of the bar. There's no ant seated near me who could have spoken. I look to the ant-tender as he swipes my credit ring for the drinks, and then moves away. I must've imagined my name from him. Even Ilnok has never called me by name.

I'm over-tired. I throw back my whiskey and reach for the beer. I'll collapse soon, maybe without needing another patch to level my mind into mere exhaustion. The noise in the bar washes over me, battering me with its rhythms. I raise my beer to my lips. It's warm and flat.

"Khara." Again. Clearly from an ant. From over the top of my beer, I see the tender in front of me, another whiskey in his pincer. He slides the drink toward me across the countertop and reaches for my free hand. My credit ring.

I swallow beer around the sudden lump at my throat.

"Did you say something?" I ask. My first word is a croak. My throat is raw from my time with Ilnok and I haven't used my voice today.

"You did not kill the human." The tender speaks without the force of announcement which Ilnok always uses, yet the words flatten me. Ilnok never asked and I figured nobody ever would. I had done my good deed and forgotten about it. But now...

The thrill of fear rushes through me giving me the same spinning nausea that comes with a patch. I'm clear with the preternatural awareness I imagine comes right before death. I recognize the need to run, yet don't have the energy or volition to move. The tender swipes my credit ring, then holds my hand in his slim fingers a moment longer. I'm trapped.

I look side to side to see if anyone else has heard the ant's accusation. No one. No one to hear the accusation, no one who will understand what transpired between us before the ant acts on the death sentence he'll soon execute.

The tender releases my hand. Disconnected from conscious will, my other arm lowers my beer mug to the wooden bar top. In the clarity of my fear, I hear the slight kissing sound of the mug connecting with the wet ring on the counter.

The tender moves away. Moves away! I don't know what to do with this.

Run. Run. Run. The thought plays over and around the red pit that has opened in my mind, thumps in my brain in time to the music. I can hear my heart beating in my ears and I can't stop watching the tender. I want to believe I've imagined its words.

The tender doesn't look toward me, isn't watching me. My mortality, my imminent death rests on me with such weight I can't breathe without panting.

After long minutes of tortured waiting, the tender returns with a fresh beer and places it next to the full whiskey. My eyes flicker to the half-full beer held in my white-knuckled hand, then back to the tender. His mandibles move as he speaks a single word: "Downtime."

I don't know what he's talking about.

"Downtime. Midnight," he says.

"The bar?" I'm confused. I feel like a fool, making small talk and waiting for death to come across the bar. I expect his pincer to sever my jugular.

"Midnight," he repeats. He takes my free hand and swipes my credit ring for the beer. He stalks away.

My mind dances in circles. I fumble in my pocket for a patch, finger the plastic shield – *tik, tik, tik* – then drop it to the bottom of my pocket, and down the half-full beer in one gulp. I keep looking to the tender but he doesn't approach me or look toward me again. I shake with need for a patch as I stare at the new beer, the whiskey, wanting them but unable to drink. I need clarity of mind more than the patch or more booze. It's amazing how fear can clear your head.

Run. Run. Run. The thought continues to beat within me. I try to focus on the implications of our conversation, on the fact I remain alive. Thoughts tumble and choke in knots.

I'm not dead.

A meeting. Why? Extortion? All an ant could take from me – other than my life – has already been taken.

I'm not dead. The tender could have killed me in my chair with no question, no repercussions. He should have killed me.

I'm not dead . . . and neither is the boy. This second thought is a minor comfort to me now. In my confused terror, I almost wish I'd killed the kid. Almost. It's a revolting thought of self-preservation.

Almost midnight. Do I dare go to Downtime? Do I dare not go?

The tender comes over again and takes both drinks. I'm frozen to my stool, arms stiffened against the bar top, anticipating more words. He wipes the bar top before me as if I'm leaving and moves away.

I drop from my seat to the floor, weak and unsteady on my feet, and leave Refugio's, hand in my pocket, fist full of patches.

The streets are almost empty. The pavement bleeds heat up into my face, hot currents of revolting smells. Whether it's the vile odor or abject terror, my gorge rises and I puke. I wipe my mouth on my shirt and keep moving. Downtime's not far from Refugio's.

The doorman swipes my credit ring on my way through the door. Like Refugio's, Downtime is full of noise, although this noise is harsher – a ruined jukebox bellowing loud, distorted music, and too many people. And ants. Here, I could almost believe we're not mortal enemies, humans and ants, with the gambling and dancing and mingling.

I move to the bar and order a whiskey. A small ant – only about a foot and a half taller than I am – approaches me as the tender moves to fill my order.

"Let me purchase your drink," he says, leaning into me. I brace for the fatal bite of its mandibles, then realize as he leans closer and repeats himself, he's trying to be heard over the din.

One day ago, I'd have moved to another spot on the bar. I'd have shown my monitor to let him know I was already owned and moved away. My world has slipped sideways. I don't know how to react. I stare into his enormous eyes, wishing, as I always do with ants, to read some expression there. Small sparks of light from the disco ball flash in the facets of his eyes.

"Can you hear me?" he asks, louder.

I nod.

"Let me purchase your drink." It's less of a question than a statement. What will happen if I refuse?

I nod again.

My drink arrives, and the ant pays. Although I crave the warm potion at the back of my throat, want to wash the foul taste from my mouth, I don't drink. I hover over the whiskey, allowing the fumes to torment me, waiting for the next step.

"Drink," he says. "Drink."

I can't lift the glass, fearful of what will come after.

"Drink," he says again, with no more force than the first time.

I doubt drinking or failing to drink will change anything – and I want the numbing comfort of it – but with my head already spinning from fear and the booze I've had, I push the whiskey away.

"I don't want it." What a damned lie.

"Let us dance now," the ant says. He holds out his lower pincer toward me, and I'm struck with the oddity of such a human, gentlemanly gesture from this creature.

I turn away from the ant. I've noticed what passes for dancing in this place. The humans are dancing, or having sex, or both. The mixed human-ant groupings are for penetration of one kind or another. No thanks.

I drop into routine. Without looking up, I pull down my shirt collar and display my monitor with the markings that indicate my rank. He can't claim me. I expect him to go away.

"Let us dance now," he says again, and I'm forced to turn toward him, to see if he has somehow missed my monitor.

He's looking at me, can't have missed my meaning.

"Do you see – ?" I start, but he interrupts me, leaning into the space above my shoulder. He speaks so quietly I don't hear all he says. But I hear the last three words:

" . . . kill the human."

Panic shoots through me again. I'm frozen except for my breathing which is hot and fast.

"Let us dance now," he says again.

I take the pincer he offers, shaking, wondering if allowing this ant to use me will buy my life. And for how long. Ilnok will not hesitate to kill me if he learns I didn't kill the boy. Ilnok, despite my being his favorite toy, will use me, then kill me, then use me further, as a lesson to others.

The small ant moves me across the dance floor toward the back of the bar. He stops when my back is pressed against the dark, rough wooden wall. It's strange that in such a crowded bar we are relatively alone.

"Should I get undressed?" I've only been with Ilnok and his crowd; I don't know what passes for play in a bar. In none of the human-ant groupings do the humans appear to be fully undressed. Nor fully dressed. I'm in new territory.

"Take off your shirt."

I do as he says. I find myself switching from fear to the disconnected state I enter when I'm with Ilnok. I pull a patch from my pocket, but the ant pins my wrist to the wall near my shoulder before I can get the patch to my jugular.

"You will not need your drug."

Tears fill my eyes. I blink, registering desperation, fear, and self-loathing all in the same moment.

"You did not kill the human," he says. It strikes me the phrase has not changed since I first heard it from the ant-tender in Refugio's. As though it's a code that requires a response.

My breath coming fast, my skin prickling with instant sweat, I take a long moment before answering. "No," I answer with a sigh. *Will I be killed with this admission?*

"You work with Samuel."

"No!" I answer. I don't understand the vehemence of my response, or why Samuel leaves me so uneasy.

"I work with Samuel," he says.

"What?" I can't believe I heard the words. My wrist is still pinned to the wooden wall and my fingers begin to tingle.

"You work with Samuel. I work with Samuel." He speaks barely loud enough for me to hear him. "Have information for Samuel. Will you remember?"

It all clicks into place. I understand. I'm both relieved and angry. Damn Samuel, damn him.

"My hand." I unclench my fist, and the patch falls to the ground. "I won't use the drug. Please let go of my hand."

The ant releases his grip and I bend to retrieve the fallen patch, shove it into my pocket with the others.

"Nestra, Shame Receptor. You repeat."

"Nestra, Shame Receptor," I say.

He places his two high pincers on the wall next to my head and his two low pincers between my bare arms and my torso. He opens his mandibles and extrudes his palpus a short way. I lean my head back and open my mouth.

"No need. This is deception. I do not use humans." He finishes his statement with something in his own language. Maybe a curse, or a call to some ant deity. It's new information to me: All ants are not like Ilnok.

"Nestra wishes to share. You repeat," he says.

"Nestra wishes to share."

"Nestra will share with humans. This will weaken loyalty to queen." As the ant speaks, he pulls one high pincer and one low pincer away from the wall and tucks them in tight to his torso. To anyone watching, this will look like he's using them on me.

"Humans may learn information from Nestra."

I repeat this last sentence. He makes me repeat the entire message, then again.

"Tell Samuel," he says. "I am Fatchk." He extrudes his palpus a short way again. I lean my head back and move closer, but fight the ingrained urge to open my mouth. I think I understand the show we're putting on, but part of me expects to be disciplined for not opening myself.

"Nestra is good. I . . . ," He pauses, apparently searching for the right word in our language. ". . . admire Nestra." He lifts my shirt to me with one pincer, and says, "I admire you."

He stalks away, leaving me speechless against the wall, shirt in hand.

He admires me? Tears fill my eyes again.

The ant leaves Downtime without pausing at the bar or interacting with anyone else. I pull my shirt over my head and return to the bar, to my abandoned whiskey. I repeat the message in my head. I bring the glass twice to my lips, but I don't drink.

He admires me. Even if he is only an ant, this ant has dared to give me more than I would give myself.

I guess I'd better find Samuel.

CHAPTER 13
SAMUEL

I've seen Khara twice today, but made sure she didn't see me. She is not at all practiced at perceiving the spaces and crowds around her – which follows, given her complete self-absorption.

The first time was this morning, on the way to the factory with Tamerak. Khara stumbled down the middle of the street, being spun and bounced by the shoulders and hips of humans as hopeless and oblivious as she. She looked like she was coming from an all-night session with her master, and I couldn't imagine her coherent enough to do anything but stumble by accident into a spot where she could sleep. Stoned again.

Now, the second time, I see her as I make my way to one of the meeting places where we in the rebellion can gather with safety. This time she seems more coherent and seems to be more aware of her surroundings, looking for something or someone. Probably a bar.

Bell was right. Khara is too weak in her struggle for survival to be trusted. She doesn't seem to have been punished for her "daring rescue" of Rex, which leads me to conclude it was not a rescue at all, but a planned attempt at sabotage or spying. If so, then the ants are as foolish as I am in believing Khara could be counted on, could be strong enough to stay focused on their mission for her.

In retrospect, I find myself surprised at my earlier interest in Khara, at my willingness to trust her. Perhaps I singled out Khara as a symbol of the humanity I am trying to protect and wanted in that symbol to protect her, save her from an untenable circumstance that is killing her.

And yet.

And yet, I still make my way toward her – ready to duck behind something if she turns in my direction – and pass within inches of her, elbow almost jostling elbow. I inhale her scent as I pass, searching for I-don't-know-what. Perhaps the telltale smell of whiskey. She doesn't smell of whiskey, but smells rather pleasant. Like sun-dried laundry.

Stop it, I scold myself, surprised I could become so fixated. Bell was right.

I pass through a shop selling used items of various kinds, abandoned human items that no longer seem as compelling in the waste the ants have left us – a folding TV table, an elaborate candelabrum, a small glass vase complete with a drooping bouquet of silk flowers, lots of other things.

I exit through a back entrance, cross a short strip of alley and enter a door marked "Deliveries Only," which leads to what used to be an illicit gambling hall. It's now a warehouse of detritus, with overturned tables and chairs, and gambling chips and papers and the odd bit of torn cloth strewn like confetti over the surface of the floor. It's difficult to move through this room without creating some noise in the passage, which suits us, as it alerts the sentries of any arrival. I crawl into the dumbwaiter and it moves toward the basement. I've been recognized.

In the basement, I move to the vault that once held meat for the restaurant that fronted for the gambling hall. It's small and cold, but no longer provides refrigeration.

Diane and Tanner are there, and while waiting for me, seem oblivious to my entrance. Diane, straight black hair hanging around her Asian features, gazes at Tanner's somewhat effeminate profile, and in her look it seems she's feasting on his ear, his downturned eyes, the microscopic pores of a chin that almost never needs shaving. Tanner looks at Diane's hand as his long fingers caress her knuckles. He smiles and raises his eyes to her almond-shaped ones, and she smiles back, both smiles seeming to say much, but not to me. They've been inseparable since they found each other. I would almost guess they'd wish the invasion upon us again if this is the only way they could find each other.

Diane and Tanner, as one, turn their youthful faces toward me. I expect a mild look of embarrassment from one or both of them for expressing such intimacy in front of me. Instead, I feel the flush of the discovered voyeur.

"Samuel," Diane says, nodding her head in greeting. She smiles and then clicks at me in the ant language, showing off for me with the air of a child looking for praise.

"What did you say?" I ask.

"Just a greeting. It means something like 'hive-brother.'" Tanner nods in agreement.

"You know I'm no expert, but it sounds great." I squeeze her on the shoulder to reinforce my flimsy praise. "If I wasn't looking, I'd think you were an ant." Tanner laughs out loud, and cups her cheek, his pride glowing in his face.

"You have a report," I say, by way of starting the meeting.

"In the queen's garden," Tanner starts. My eyebrows rise. While Tanner and Diane act as gardeners in the queen's sanctum, they don't often learn any information there, as the queen is always there alone, and thus there is nothing to overhear or learn. It's dangerous work because the queen's penchant for killing humans seems unquenchable. Most of the information Diane and Tanner learn is in the bars where humans and ants intermingle. Their facility with languages has taught them much of what they know of the ant's tongue.

"It was weird, man," Tanner continues. "There we were, just trimming and stuff, and this ant comes into the garden, like usual. The other big one we told you about. We were cool because that one never bothers humans, you know?"

I suppress a smile at Tanner's vernacular. Considering he speaks three languages – and is now learning the ant's – it must be an affectation, and one I find amusing. "Go on."

"So we weren't worried about getting close to it and stuff, and we needed to take care of a couple of plants near it, you know."

Diane takes up the story. "Then all of a sudden, it was standing right there in front of us. It scared me to death. I thought maybe it's just like the queen, and maybe Tanner and I were going to die right there." She takes the time to squeeze Tanner's hand while looking at him for confirmation.

Tanner nods. "Right, man."

Diane looks back at me. "Then it opened itself up to us. You know, head back, arms open. Like they do when they show their submissiveness. Then," Diane pauses and swallows, as if afraid I won't believe her, "then, it said, 'I won't hurt you.' It was really strange."

"Totally weird," Tanner adds.

"We left. But we wanted to know what you think. What should we do? Anything?"

I can't think what this new information reveals. Ants don't approach humans with anything other than demands or pain or death. I should pull them from the garden, but this is the one place where we can have humans inside the walls of the capitol complex and still expect them to retain more than a one- or two-day life expectancy. It's a tactical advantage I don't want to have to abandon.

"Stay away from it. From now on, treat it with the same deference – *and distance* – as you give the queen. Don't jeopardize yourselves, but keep working there. Report anything else with it. As you know, no one else has the freedom to enter and exit the capitol complex. You're needed."

"Can do," answers Tanner, with a smile and a thumbs up. Diane nods, glances at Tanner, and squeezes his hand again.

I leave them there, and start toward Tamerak's home, hoping I haven't just consigned them to death.

***

Khara wanders the street near the place where I showed her Rex was safe. She paces, restless, and searching for someone. She's a traitor after all. She's searching for us. I'm thankful when I pulled her into the back pantry room she was disoriented and drugged and can't now find her way back. I'll pass the word we're not to meet there any longer. I'll pass the word to stay away from Khara. I curse myself for a fool. My interest in Khara has endangered us.

I stay and watch her to satisfy myself she can't remember the doorway. After some time, she leaves, heading toward Refugio's and a drink. I follow, wondering at my motivation. I tell myself it's not attraction or fascination, but to ensure the safety of the rebellion I may have compromised. Once at the bar, she resumes the decomposition she seems determined to accomplish, with whiskey and beer and a patch at her throat. When I leave, her eyes are glazed, as usual.

Disappointment lies heavy in my chest as I make my way to Tamerak's. Disappointment in her, even more in myself.

CHAPTER 14
NESTRA

The queen reclines across the huge gape-jawed throne and its covering of garish cushions, her relaxed posture belying her rage. A drugged human lies tossed at the base of the throne, sprawled in the attitude of complete oblivion, spittle escaping its open mouth. It is small for a human, little more than half the height of the queen, and unharmed, as yet.

As yet. I shudder.

I pull myself straighter in an attempt to look dignified as I wait on the dais at the side of and behind the queen. An echoing pop sounds from the joint between my abdomen and thorax as I straighten, which defies any attempt at dignity. The queen rages at a courtier and does not react.

"I asked for a projection of time needed to complete fertilization and maturation of the final brothers needed!" The rasp and screech of the queen's demand makes many more cringe than the courtier addressed. Although all try to hide their fear, the bright red scent in the large room is unmistakable. I wish I could close my pores, as I need no additional negative chemical reactions within myself. I try to meditate through the queen's storming.

"Majesty, the larval development on those maturing is excellent and should be completed by the end of the week . . .," grates the courtier, but the queen interrupts with a scraping roar.

"Final brothers needed! Time!" The queen twitches forward with her two high, larger pincers and the whole of the audience crests back in the face of her rage. All but Dev'ro, the queen's most trusted advisor, whose mandibles pinch cruelly toward the unfortunate courtier from his spot at the base of the dais.

"Majesty, if you could visit the crèche more often . . . ," mumbles the courtier, and the queen roars again.

"I cannot spend all my time spilling chemicals into eggs! I am not merely a breeding machine!" I hear several sharp rasps of surprise from those in attendance and look up to see the queen re-sheathing her phallus. The shock of the audience at the queen's lewd display colors the already palpable scent of fear in the room toward teal-violet.

I sigh around the edges of my mandibles, and the queen spins on me in obvious fury, multi-faceted eyes gleaming. Appalled at my own unconscious breach of protocol, I throw my head back and open myself, but the queen growls and spins back to the courtier.

The courtier does not answer. There is nothing he can say. The queen is the only one who can awaken the waiting eggs and begin the final maturation process, and yet she suggests she does not have the time, while demanding a projection for the completion of the work force. The unfortunate creature rocks backward, opening himself. I pity him and fear, given the queen's obvious instability, she will kill him on the spot.

Queen Tal needs me. She is overloaded and losing control. And yet, I dread receiving her sickness into me. I pull my attention away from the court, and begin again the cleansing mantra, hoping to concentrate over the clamor. *My duty.* The thought runs under and around my feeble attempt at meditation.

I am not aware of the remainder of the audience, but know, at least, the queen has not killed the courtier. I pull myself free of my semi-trance when the queen rises and strides past me into the antechamber at the back of the throne room. I follow in haste, knowing her rage will not brook any delay.

"Ready yourself!" she roars, and this is all the preparation I am given before she pounces on me and begins off-loading a rancid brew into me. I am barely able to enter the life-sustaining trance before the bitter Shame pours into me like regurgitated poison.

***

Fugue state. The protective mantra floats as colored sound, scented sound, as a singing, roiling coil of crystalline bursts of color – mutable, fluid, flowing. I float, unaware, unattached, all but unconscious, except for the awareness which allows me to separate the toxin from my *Self.* Evil, bitter, black, bruised, omnivorous, acid, poison . . . Shame. A voracious flood of horrors cascades into me.

Indeterminate time.

In the midst of the disordered fusion of mantra and self-sense and near hysteria, I feel the ordered sensation of coiling and unfolding as if breathing. Half-formed visions/sounds/smells/tastes coalesce and separate, change in hue, flavor, scent, tone. I tread the path of the mantra in an effort to keep some slight hold of my own sanity amidst the turmoil and fetid corruption. Tread the mantra and follow its loose winding path.

And there. There in the midst of jumbled images/sounds/scents, there coalesces a beautiful, glowing, golden dewdrop, which hums and vibrates, and gives off the sweet/tart scent of warm fresh fruit. Within the cocoon of protection I have woven about myself, I shudder at the beauty and attraction of the warm throbbing bead.

Indeterminate time.

Floating, wafting, but focused on the golden bead, drawn . . . drawn.

Indeterminate time and hesitation, and then . . .

Reaching, touching – shuddering at near contact, trembling at scent . . . quivering . . . and finally, lapping the smallest taste.

Fugue and pleasure. Fugue and warmth. Fugue and joy. The smallest taste, and yet immense pleasure and warmth and joy.

Indeterminate time.

Floating, treading the mantra, with greater ease.

Then, the spiral march up the web of the mantra toward the call of light and breath and consciousness.

Awake.

***

The queen lies still as I pull myself away, wrap my limbs around my own shell, fingers and pincers tapping on my own back. It's strange, but I feel I have just awakened after a pleasant dream, with only dim recollection of it.

"I go to the breeding room," says the queen. She is quiet, coherent. I wonder why she tells me this much. "But I will need you again later. You may go." She does not look toward me, but instead seems subdued. No cruel pinch of mandibles. No leering thrust at me as mere tool, indispensable yet disposable.

"Majesty," I murmur and move toward the door. From the thickness of the off-loaded chemicals, I know I will have trouble dragging myself to my rooms, but also know how much I need the solitude and solace found there. I pause at the door and turn to open in the ritual bow to the queen. I am astonished to see the queen still sprawled where I left her.

"Majesty?" I ask, surprised.

"Go," she mutters, and then pulls herself to her full regal height and swipes a pincer in my direction. "Go!"

I am even more surprised to discover I do not need the support of the doorframe to turn and leave the room.

***

I move down the corridors toward my rooms, aware of the escort behind me. They keep their distance, knowing I often falter after my sessions with the queen and unwilling to walk too close, to perhaps touch me if I flail or fall.

I do not falter. I move with slow steps, yes, but halfway to my rooms, I realize my careful pace and meticulous attention to my feet on the path of the corridor before me is more habitual than necessary today.

I am stronger after this session than usual.

I stop in the corridor and stretch, and feel a bubble of humor rise in me as the guards stop, each exuding the orange aroma of surprise, followed by the sour green-yellow flavor of questioning. They do not question me with words, however. No doubt, they want no interaction with me at all in my current state.

I move on, called by the thought of my rooms, and rest, and the dissipation of the poisonous concoction within me.

***

I tread the mantra quickly, less ponderously than is usual for my first time through after a session with the queen.

Perhaps the queen has been behaving herself and the Shame was less thick than usual. But even as I try to explain the ease with which the poisons are dissipated, the weight and depth of the poison I absorbed did not seem less.

The lemon breeze and the soft music wafts over me, lifting my mood further. I should walk the mantra again, cleanse myself further, since the queen will, without doubt, call me again soon, but I cannot bring myself to feel the need.

Do I have time to relax in the garden? Perhaps to paint?

The desire recalls to me my last painting: the beautiful golden dewdrop, glowing in its desirability. *Tal's Strength.*

The connection crashes on me as I also recall tasting of the dewdrop during my recent fugue state. *Tal's strength!*

The nausea which I have avoided through my pursuit of the cleansing mantra threatens now. I am washed with my own shame and guilt as I recall what seemed a dream – a beautiful, enticing, entrancing dream.

It was no dream . . . No dream!

And now I have done it! I have taken strength from the queen!

I cringe with the horror of my own wickedness in taking from the queen. The weakness that descends upon me with the whirlpool of my own castigatory shame overwhelms me, and I lower myself into the cushioned floor of my bed-pit and tread the cleansing mantra again, and yet again, before I am summoned to the queen. Even after the cleansing and rest, I still feel weakened by my own shame and only muster a feeling of some normalcy upon swearing to myself I will *never* commit such an unimaginable breach again.

CHAPTER 15
KHARA

Samuel's gone. It's clear that I saw Samuel as frequently as I did because he was looking for me, following me. And now, with a message burning in me, with these fucking withdrawal symptoms as I try to wean myself from the patch, with fear of reprisals for a failure to deliver the message, Samuel's gone.

Damn Samuel.

I'm in a new bar, afraid to go back to Refugio's and face the ant-tender who first spoke to me. I finish my whiskey, throwing it back, burning the opening to my sinuses at the top of my throat. Damn Samuel! Anger fills me, threatening to bring the whiskey back up. Not just anger. Rage.

My existence, such as it is, was bearable. Endurable. With alcohol and the patch, yes, endurable. At least for today. I never thought about tomorrow. Today and tomorrow strung together in my mind, with the knowledge of what I force myself to do each day, would be one day too many to endure.

I realize my rage is directed at myself. I *allowed* Samuel . . . allowed him to what? Awaken me? Samuel with the soft mouth, and the warm eyes.

Samuel has violated me. Damn him! I was surviving. And now, I'm pregnant with a message that means nothing to me, other than fear and a loathing for Samuel that he put me in this position of danger. I cringe each time an ant comes near me with a dread I don't feel even at Ilnok's most cruel moments. Will I be killed for failing to deliver the message?

I finger the patches in my pocket. I want so much to forget Samuel and the message. Instead of the patch, I order another whiskey. The booze doesn't help my nausea, doesn't do a hell of a lot for the shakes. But, it does help me space out a bit, does help me get away from the pain of existence.

As the tender approaches, the ever-present fear washes over me again as a wave of skin-prickling instant sweat. My breath comes fast. Nausea again, and I groan as the tender deposits the whiskey on the bar top and swipes my credit ring. He doesn't look concerned.

Now my least favorite withdrawal symptom. I throw myself back off my stool and stumble toward the bathroom for another bout of diarrhea. Ilnok doesn't care for diarrhea either. It's the one of my bodily fluids that seems to annoy him. In fear for myself, I've managed to control it during my time with him, which makes for worse nausea and cold sweats, but these are better than having Ilnok decide I'm not useful any longer. From the bathroom, I lurch into the street. My fresh drink sits on the bar top, untouched. The world sways around me and my bones ache.

Heat from the street, the close buildings, the bodies everywhere. More ants than humans. Panic-induced sweat coats my body. I imagine panic-sweat tastes different and fear Ilnok calling me now.

I have to find Samuel. I finger the patches in my pocket again, but I won't be coherent enough to search the passing bodies with the drug's seductive swirl blinding me. My teeth chatter through another flash of chills.

Somehow I manage to keep my hands in my pockets, fists clenched around what I so very much desire.

I decide to risk Refugio's. The toilet. I'll find Samuel, regurgitate my bastard message and leave, warning him that I'll kill him if he comes near me again. I lock the vision of Samuel's warm mouth in my mind and imagine smashing it.

I press the white mark at the back of the toilet. I hit it. Again and again, I try to find the door. With the violence of my thrashing against the wall and the whiskey in my veins, the floor lurches and I fall to the floor, hitting my jaw on the urinal. I pray it doesn't bruise. Ilnok is knowledgeable of which marks on my body are the result of his entertainment and which are not. The scratches on my neck and ass and inner thighs are his. A swollen jaw is not.

After another wave of gut-clenching nausea, I stand, remembering the boy I brought here last. Young, hairless, perfect. I have to remember what I did to make the wall open.

I close my eyes and picture the boy, shirtless, eyes leaking large, slow-moving tears. The image swims and I'm picturing my brother, Kenny – not the boy. Maybe I never saw the boy. Maybe I acted to save my kid brother. This would explain my inexplicable actions. I don't like that it relieves some of the blame I want to shove squarely down Samuel's throat.

Kenny. Again, rage. Rage over the fact there was nothing I could do to save my family. Mother, father, brother. Gone. Rage that I didn't die then too, that I'm here and not with them. Rage that I'm too much the coward to join them. I don't want to think of these things. I don't want to remember. Not for the first time, I wish they had wiped us all out at once, like they did with Asia and Europe. Why did I have to be left in this half of the world?

I pound at the wall again and again until the strength drains from me, and I slip to the cool, damp, muddy-yellow floor. Am I doing something wrong? Or has Samuel closed me out?

I go to the bar and order whiskey and a beer. I glare at the tender, daring him to speak. Daring him to kill me for my failures. He brings my drinks, doesn't look at me, moves away.

I'm thinking of the patches in my pocket again. I'm picturing pulling one from my pocket. I wrap my left hand across the front of my throat in a parody of self-strangulation, covering my jugular with that hand, keeping my right hand from slapping on a patch. My right hand fiddles with the patches in my pocket.

I can't. I have to find Samuel. I have to stay clear enough to find Samuel.

CARAPACE

Ilnok is finished with me. I'm tired. I'm sore. I have to sleep. I'm afraid I won't be able to move. The need to be away from Ilnok and his group helps me jerk my aching muscles into action around loose and painful, over-stretched joints.

Ilnok pushes the bowl of patches toward me, already engaged in some kind of almost silent conversation with another of the ants in the high-walled, red-trimmed room. I grab a handful, although my pants pocket is still full of them.

I allow myself one patch to endure my time as play toy for this crowd of monsters. It was my ritual, the application of the patch at the end of a session, but I can't. I have to have the strength Samuel accuses me of having. I have to remain clear.

I have to find Samuel. This is my chant as I drag my pants over my sticky legs. The pants cling to the moisture and I feel raw as the fabric grips my skin when I pull.

I move to the street, wanting nothing more than a drink and a patch on which to reach oblivion. But I have to stay clear.

I spend an hour dragging myself through streets — streets on which I know I've seen Samuel — and only twice stop for a drink. I don't put on a patch. I succumb to the nausea and puke once. I ache everywhere — elbows, knees, hips, fingers. My head pounds.

I don't put on a patch as I roll onto a dorm mat, curl toward the wall, and fall asleep.

I dream of my brother, mother, father. Gutted, throats cut. Long, tapered fingers missing from my mother's hand. My brother's arm, hand reaching toward me, resting on a table on the other side of the room from his body. Then I dream of Samuel smiling at me, my brother standing beside him in a small room, with others – humans. I dream of hope filling my brother's eyes.

"Kenny!" I shout, then realize I'm awake and have said it aloud.

I have a patch halfway to my jugular to wipe out the dream before I realize it's been a long time since I didn't have kaleidoscopic drug-hazed dreams.

I need the patch! I don't want to dream!

I return the patch to my pocket. I have to stay clear. I have to find Samuel.

Just as dawn breaches, my monitor lights and I hurry toward Ilnok. At least when I am with Ilnok, my entire mind is engaged in blanking itself out. And I don't want to think any more. Not about Samuel, not about Kenny.

It seems I can only obtain peace in the midst of abuse.

CHAPTER 16
FATCHK

I creep along the dark street, open to the taste of the night and the brothers around me. I cannot appear to hurry, although I am late to my meeting. Refuse swirls around my lower limbs as I search the street and taste the scents again.

I believe I have lost the two brothers who have been trailing me. The clumsy human members of the ant corps that attempted to follow me were lost due to their blind inability to taste the street, but the two brothers were harder to lose. To do so, I needed to move with haste through two separate hive-groups in order to dissipate my scent, but not with a speed that would raise alarm, all while masking my anxiety with a purposeful concentration on things pleasant.

I dart down an alley and then curve back toward the meeting place.

Ketann is rising to leave the private eating room when I enter. I close and lock the door. Ketann sinks back to the blue and green cushions, exuding a mixture of concern and irritation over my tardiness. The irritation is fair. We both endanger ourselves through our efforts to help the human rebellion.

Registering the décor – all themed to the sea, oceanscapes, sailing vessels, this world's underwater creatures – I join Ketann and we embrace in greeting, identification, and sharing.

"Apologies," I click. Flavor-scent of sincerity. "Very dangerous." Slight crimson smear of fear. "I am being watched."

Ketann exudes his own slight red blossom of fear in response, recognizing this meeting is now more dangerous for himself as well.

"I have not been able to meet with my human contact, Samuel," I continue. Sight-scent of the human tints my words. "I have attempted to send a message regarding potential use of Nestra."

Scent-identification of the queen's Shame Receptor fills the air around us, along with the unmistakable soft gold flavor of my admiration. Nestra is strong, so full of duty to our mad queen, yet so much the epitome of all that is good in our people. I long to share with her, to show her the depths of my esteem.

Ketann's yellow-green scented question comes after a long moment. "How can I assist?"

"Can you meet with others at court?" Warm flavor of hope tints the sour of the question.

Ketann discharges more red fear, then with a small shudder and the unquestionable scent of loyalty answers, "Yes. I, and others of my bond-group."

My hope rises and I bathe my brother in warm satisfaction.

"Dev'ro," I say, transmitting the scent-identification of the queen's favorite.

Bright crimson burst of fear from Ketann. "Hazardous!"

This is true. Dev'ro is as sick as the queen, infected by her, perhaps unredeemable. But we must take the chance. If he can be turned...

"Yes." A bare acknowledgement of his statement. "And Nohj'sem," and again, I evoke the scent-identification of another courtier close to the queen's court.

"They are both sick with the queen's contamination. Much risk." The room is thick with Ketann's fear now. I cannot fault him. If I could come close enough to make these connections, these efforts, I would do so. I cannot. So, I look to those brothers who might. Even so, I understand and forgive Ketann's fear.

I force myself to calmness and exude comfort and consolation, all four upper limbs locked around Ketann in empathy. We sit in silence for a time, while I secrete compassion and dark warmth.

After some long moments, Ketann slumps against me with a small click of thanks and clears the air with the color of his determination.

"Dev'ro," Ketann repeats, "Nohj'sem."

I transmit my gratitude. "Yes."

"Others?" Ketann asks.

"Your discretion. The two I have identified are closest to queen," I answer.

"Those farther from the queen may be easier to convince, to win, and may still be helpful," Ketann says, flavor-scent questioning his own judgment.

"Your discretion," I repeat.

"Dangerous," says Ketann again, but this time with only a flicker of fear. Again, he tastes of determination. Then comes the flavor-scent questioning the necessity of this perilous foray into the queen's courtiers.

"The time draws near for the humans," I respond to the unstated question. "The queen is nearing the full complement of brothers. Mere months, no more." I pull my two right limbs away and nestle back in the cushions in thought. "Nestra may be unwilling to assist," I continue, although again the soft gold of my admiration for Nestra belies my willingness to believe such a thought.

"We must risk much," Ketann says with sincerity and more determination.

"Yes." Comfort, consolation, warmth, well-wishes.

"Must you go now?" Ketann asks.

"Yes." As much as I would like to relax and wordlessly share comfort and strength until the room is bright with confidence, I am suspect amongst some of my brothers. I would not endanger Ketann by lingering here.

CARAPACE

When I emerge from the private eating room, I spot one of the brothers who followed me earlier this evening. Perhaps I was not as clever as I hoped in eluding him. He stands at the entrance of the main dining hall, antennae twitching, head swiveling. I move further down the hallway of private eating rooms and let myself into another – which is thankfully empty.

Watching through the cracked door, I see Ketann leave the room in which we conferred. I close-focus on Ketann, apprehensive he will meet with trouble, guilt oozing from me that I will be the cause. Instead, he is greeted by a brother and led to a table in the main dining hall.

The brother trailing me does not appear to take notice of this and my breathing relaxes. I watch for a long time as Ketann orders and consumes a meal with his bond-brothers. I wonder if he has prearranged this rendezvous, or if luck is with him.

After a time, the brother who was following me leaves the hall. Even so, I leave from a back entrance, well-wishing sent in Ketann's direction although he will not detect it in this crowd.

I cannot relax during my navigation to my home. Cannot stop a twitch of nervousness each time I turn a corner. I keep my antennae focused on everything and everyone around me, the entire time attempting to exude relaxed contemplation and serenity. Even though I arrive home safely, I worry I am as transparent as I feel.

CHAPTER 17
SAMUEL

From behind my desk and through a mud-streaked window, I watch the changing of the guard. I haven't fathomed the reason or the exact timing, but I have discovered at least once a week, all but two guards leave the factory and it's sometimes as long as twenty minutes before the replacements arrive. Now is the time.

I'm preparing the report of last week's production. The factory is producing well and although the quota keeps being raised, my workers meet the demand. My workers. These humans are pressed to the limits, and still they give me what I ask when I tell them I need more. I have to review the line process again, see if I can concoct another streamline to greater efficiency. I have to find a way to give back to them, to ease their load, if only until the next, higher, quota comes in.

Tamerak does nothing more than pivot his head toward me as he rises to greet the new guard supervisor at the factory entrance. It's still odd to me the way his body moves in one direction, while his head looks toward another. His eyes, unlike

109

ours, see to the side as well as to the front, but I humanize Tamerak. I expect him in his apparent love for me to become like me.

I bend my head back and expose my neck to him. He doesn't take the opportunity to run his mandible across my neck in the gesture which, between us, I have come to equate as a pat of affection. When he pats me, he's gentle and tender, his antennae tapping against me, smelling me, while the smooth outside of his mandible runs over my skin. It is a macabre game we play – I, offering my life, and he, sparing it by failing to rake his mandible into my jugular, my windpipe. It's appropriate to the circumstance.

I wait until Tamerak is outside the factory entrance receiving whatever communication they have for him, delivering his report, before I leave the gray metal walls of our office. I stand against the railing looking down at the production line. No one looks up at me. I stroll the length of the catwalk and confirm there are only two ant-guards on duty on the floor.

I walk to the hanging metal steps that lead down to the floor. Simon glances up and – after making sure the guards' attention is elsewhere – I give Simon the barest of nods.

He turns his grinder off, puts a final timing gear into the full cart at the side of his workbench, and begins rolling the cart toward the back wall of the factory – all as normal. I can barely hear the squeaking of the overloaded cart wheels over the rumble of machinery.

Today is the culmination of Simon's plan. If it works, it'll revolutionize how we smuggle parts out, reduce the personal danger to each thieving worker and let us take as many parts as we want — so long as we still meet quota. Failing to meet quota comes with its own penalty.

The bins at the back of the factory open both ways — into the factory so workers can load them, and out of the factory into what used to be a passage with a conveyor belt for moving the parts to the loading dock. The conveyor passage is no longer used now that human labor is so abundant — and, until two days ago, was inaccessible.

By working through a maze of ductwork, Simon located the conveyor room and made short work of breaking the lock on one of the bins — an unallocated, unused bin. All Simon has to do is get a couple of gears into that bin without being caught and by midnight, we'll be that much closer to having a couple more trucks ready to roll.

Despite the genius and apparent ease of Simon's plan, the sweat on my forehead increases with each step he takes toward the bins. My fingers grow cold as though all blood is draining from them. I cast my eyes in random pattern over the factory floor, determined not to be caught focusing on Simon or the guards.

Just as Simon reaches the bins, one of the ant-guards begins moving in his direction. My stomach lurches toward my throat and I tighten my fingers around the railing. My arms shake.

Jan jerks her head up from her work, looking first toward Simon, then at the guard moving toward him. Our eyes meet in a shimmering moment of despair. I see on her face the instant she makes the decision.

She yells to be heard over the tooling machines. "I said stick it up your ass, Caveman!"

She slams the metal shaft she is finishing on the metal workbench. The people around her feign deafness and continue filing, sanding, assembling, trimming – eyes fixed on the work before them. They want no part of the trouble that will come from this.

I am overwhelmed by Jan's bravery.

Eli – "Caveman" – turns to her, swollen blacksmith's arms hanging loose at his sides. With no enthusiasm for the role he is about to play, he lifts a shaft in one large dark-skinned hand and bangs it on his workbench to add to the noise. His normally iron-curtain face droops with pity. His lips move as he mumbles something. I know Eli. I can't hear him, but they are words of sympathy and compassion.

"Screw off, man!" Jan yells. "Think you can call me names and get away with it because I'm a woman?" Jan is loud. I can see from her face she hates his pity. She is strong enough for this. She slams the shaft on the workbench again. "I ain't afraid of you."

"Get back to work!" Eli yells the words, deep voice rumbling, but there is no anger in his face, no force other than that necessary to make himself heard above the machinery. Again, he

112

bangs the shaft twice on the workbench. The metallic clang rings through the open area of the production floor.

The guard who was heading toward Simon pivots and heads toward Jan and Eli. He doesn't hurry to reach them. There's no need. They're only humans and he'll mete out whatever punishment has been earned. I am relieved when the second guard moves – with the same complacent slowness – toward them as well. I spare no glance to Simon – he'll make use of Jan's distraction and I don't want to draw attention to him.

Jan flies at Eli, landing a glancing punch across his massive flat nose. She stays in close, punches him in the gut several times.

Eli grunts and grabs her. He twists her sinewy muscled arms behind her. He turns her so her back is against his chest and traps her there with one arm.

"Damn you!" She slams her head back into his colossal chest, and then again. She is angry, but not at him. Not at him.

Eli pulls her arms up behind her. She yelps and stops the head butting. He won't hurt her – both because they are friends and because he'll be punished if he damages a worker.

The first ant-guard is almost to them. Jan and Eli can stop the exhausting work of fighting soon. I'm ill with what will come next. I'd like to go back into my office rather than watch the punishment, but I have to observe so I'll know – and be able to tell others – how best to treat Jan's injuries later.

"Release her." The words click and whistle through the ant-guard's shiny black mandibles. The speaker at his shoulder amplifies his words so they are heard across the floor. Jan kicks at Eli's shin with her work boot as he pushes her away. She looks menacing but I notice her boot doesn't connect.

"Who is responsible." There's no inflection to make the phrase a question. The guard's top two arms weave before him, while the bottom two point laser pistols at the two humans.

"*He* is," Jan spits. "He insulted me. Called me a *man*."

The guard doesn't respond or change position, except that his arms continue the odd weaving motion. The second guard appears next to the first. He removes a pistol from the holster slung in the middle of his chest. I scan the floor to assure myself again there are only two.

"I don't guess you androgynous brother-humpers would understand, but I'm telling you, I was provoked!" Her hands are tight knots. It is a show of anger, but it's also a mark of her fear.

The first ant-guard's top limbs stop their slow dance. His attention and his weapons are now fixed upon Jan. The second guard has a weapon trained on Eli.

Through clicks and rasps, the ant tells Jan, "I have determined that even if this was said, this is not sufficient provocation for battle."

Here it comes. I brace myself in anticipation, hands wringing the railing, elbows locked, feet frozen to the floor.

The ant gestures to Jan with his gun. "Step forward." Jan doesn't move, fear now evident on her face. The ant says, "The man will assist me."

An alarm sounds announcing pending punishment. The humans stop their work and shuffle toward Jan's workbench to watch. The machines power down from a whine to a low rumble, and then to silence. We'll all be able to hear the blows connect and the grunts as air is pushed from Jan's lungs. If Jan were inclined to scream when she was beaten, the screams would echo through the near-silent factory. Jan won't allow herself to scream.

Eli holds Jan while the ant beats her from collarbone to shins with an old spring-style billy, pausing to administer additional beatings at her breasts and thighs. Eli's dark face is stone. He doesn't protect her because he knows this will gain her additional punishment.

Jan falls to the floor retching when Eli releases her. She curls into fetal position at his feet. The sting of the guard's electric prod convinces her to try crawling to her workbench.

I want to kill the guard. He was unnecessarily hard on Jan. Jan never listens to my speeches about taking it easy but I'm already planning another gentle chastisement. We can't afford to lose Jan and she can't take another beating like that soon. Perhaps the pain she's suffering now will make her more receptive to good sense.

As she drags her herself along the cement floor, Eli's guard turns away and crosses the floor, heading back toward the entrance. A beast roused from slumber, the machinery rumbles to life with a building roar.

Like Eli, everyone is back to work, eyes lowered to the job before them. Eli's large hands move over his workbench with purpose, but they're shaking and he's still watching Jan.

Jan's guard moves the prod toward her as she hesitates in pulling herself upright on her workbench. She stands and picks up the unfinished shaft. The ant-guard turns away to join the other.

I watch Jan until Tamerak comes back in. My jaws ache with the grinding of my teeth. She coughs and works at a slow pace, concentrating on the labor. She and I know if she doesn't pick up her production, she'll be punished once more. She winces as she bends into her bin again.

Eli shuts his eyes, suffering for his part in Jan's pain. The muscles in his arms flex and dance as he works a shaft into its receptacle and crimps the ends. He wipes at his nose with the back of a massive hand and leaves a streak of blood to his wrist. I am sure he believes it fitting he should bleed at the hand of Jan, although he and Jan understand the greater good they served today.

As Tamerak reaches the bottom of the stairs, my eyes seek out Simon. *I hope Jan's pain bought us something.*

Simon glances up at me from under his furrowed brow. Seeing me watching him, he barely nods. Despite his success, he does not smile.

CHAPTER 18
NESTRA

Sunlight dapples and dances on the earth around the stool as I sit, rigid, under my favorite tree in the queen's garden. My tight posture is not due to stiffness in my limbs or any feeling of physical infirmity – I feel better physically than any time in recent memory. My tension is, in fact, due to my well-being.

For the last ten days, I have been regaining my health. My guilt lies in the reason behind my new-found soundness.

Despite my resolutions not to take any of the queen's strength during the fugue state necessary for off-loading, I find my unconscious self is hungrier and more insistent upon self-preservation than in repentance. Time and again I have lapped at the sweet wellspring of the queen's strength. Even now, as I chastise myself, I cannot stop feeling pleasure at my renewed energy.

I sigh, air rushing in gusts through my files and scrapers, sounding a low moan across the garden. As I push the elongated breath out, I slouch back against the tree trunk, and the scrape of the rough bark of the tree up my back adds a small scratchy echo.

CARAPACE

No brother to wipe the scratches from my back, I think, more as an internal lament at my inability to share than as any complaint at having to maneuver to wipe my own shell.

I try to clear my mind of the argument between my conscious self demanding my own death would be better than stealing from the queen again, and my unconscious self screaming for life. I feel divided between the two selves, and then feel also a third self: the self that like a teacher over newly hatched brothers demands cessation of argument and commitment to harmony of the whole. I force my attention to the garden, distracting myself with patterns of light, the fragrance of the pungent white flowers, the colors of the ball-shaped blossoms, and brilliant climbing, flowering vines. I listen to the voices of the garden – wind sighing through leaves, the grate of branch on branch, the hymn of the many insects. I also notice through the symphony of sight/scent/sound, the flavor of humans and the monotony of metal shears scraping slowly open, quickly closed, slowly open, quickly closed.

I focus on the taste/sound and glimpse the two humans working at the far end of the garden, trimming the opposite side of a hedge. Ever since I approached them, they have either been absent from the garden or working at a great distance from me. They are afraid of me. I cannot resent their fear, given the fate of most humans in the queen's court – and out.

As I catch brief snatches of the humans through the loose hedge, I recall why I had approached them. They had appeared to be sharing. I am again fascinated by the idea, and envious of their ability to share and their clear enjoyment of touching.

Ridiculous. I am so obsessed with the desire to share, I attribute senseless human behavior with meaning and find myself envious of these mush-soft beings.

Curiosity compels me to focus on what I can see and taste of the humans through the dark leafy hedge. I try to turn my attention back to enjoyment of the garden and stand to walk among the loamy paths, to feel the sun's warmth on my shell and move among the flower fragrances.

The scent of the humans draws me and before long, I realize what had seemed random wandering has taken me rather close to the far end of the long hedge upon which the humans labor. I step to the backside of the hedge. The humans have not noticed my presence. The shock of their postures freezes me.

The taller brown-haired human clutches shears in its hands and stretches its face to reveal white teeth as it trims the ragged offshoots of new growth from the hedge. The smaller black-haired human stands behind the working human with arms wrapped around its middle, body pressed against body, head resting on the taller human's back, face turned away from me.

Sharing! I cannot imagine what else to call it.

The smaller human disengages from its embrace, moves around to the side of the taller human – back still toward me – and, trailing an arm across the back of the taller, lifts its head. The taller human stops the clipping and presses its mouth to that of the smaller. My legs weaken and I must utter some sound, because the taller human glances at me and the smaller human spins to look at me. Neither move. The smaller human retrieves clippers from the earth near its feet, then both turn toward the hedge, and commence clipping. Both steal occasional glances toward me. Their attitudes show fear.

I take two shaky steps toward the humans – for what purpose I do not know. The humans stop clipping and dart around the far end of the high hedge, clinging to each other.

Sharing. A shudder of pain courses through my abdomen.

When I have collected myself enough to move again, I wander the garden with labored steps, searching for the flavor of the humans, wanting to watch them. They are gone.

***

I eat in the solitude of my rooms. The tinkling of bells as a breeze moves through the window and sways the branches of the homeworld tree in the corner does not sooth me. I know the queen will be calling me soon, and the negative chemicals produced by my sharp-toothed guilt melt into my already dark mood and make it heavier.

A subtle dread slows my already hesitant reach for the terminal as I hope for a different quotation. Each time I have touched my terminal in the last three days, the same quotation has appeared.

Gather your strength from those whom you serve.

The same quotation. I growl in frustration, recognizing the circular manufacture of negative chemical production leading to negative reactions, thus creating additional negative chemical production.

I will not! I will take no more strength from the queen! I can control myself! I, too, am strong, or I would not have lasted this long!

I fling myself from the terminal and into my bed-pit, vowing never to ask the terminal for another quote of benediction. Instead of benediction, it has become a taunt, a curse.

In my bed-pit, I loosely tread the cleansing mantra. I do not fall into the light trance which will make it truly effective, but instead drape it as a rote filigree over my tumultuous thoughts.

I am an addict, I admit to myself, chanting the mantra as a background song.

The queen is being affected by my theft. I click through terse thoughts as though composing a list.

I am committing treason, I add to my list.

I will cause no more hurt, I demand of myself, and the part of me that demands the queen's strength adds, *except unto yourself!* I wince at the cowardly addition and continue my list.

I should be, will be — am! — the most loyal of the queen's subjects, and will never betray her again.

Satisfied with my fervor and sincerity, I fall into the solace of the mantra and only rise when summoned by the queen.

***

Fugue state. I lower myself in the cushion of the protective mantra, but do not relax into unconsciousness. I am determined to maintain control enough to keep the queen safe from the self who lusts to rob her again and again. I float the colored scents and sounds that keep me safe and separate from the venom and contagion flowing into me, but because of my refusal to succumb to the trance, the poisonous bile burns me, testing my ability to endure. I straddle between sweet mantra and pain.

Indeterminate time. Indeterminate, not because of the trance, but because of the apparent elongation of time through agony.

I endure.

I follow the mutable, wending path of the mantra, knowing where I long to go, where I will not allow myself to go.

The mantra leads me down and, as I knew it would, spirals me toward the beautiful, magnetic, irresistible, glowing dewdrop of the queen's strength. I wrench away, insides twisting in pain, but determination burning in me as brightly as that strength which I lust for and refuse to take.

I resist, and do not take, although the path of the mantra refuses to flow away from the golden prize.

Soon, too soon, the firm knowledge settles that I am beyond what I can safely accept from the queen.

No more. The thought bubbles up through the viscous thickness that infects me and I hope the queen will relent.

The mantra twists away and out, and I crawl, holding to tendrils of light until the red light of the queen's bedchamber washes over me.

Awake.

Bent, cramped, sick, but awake. Awake, and the victor, and ill beyond any recollection of illness. I lie without moving for some time, eyes failing to pull the collection of visual images through my various lenses into a coherent whole.

"I don't allow for lazy, languorous workers, and certainly not in my bedchamber." The queen's words are strongly delivered, too loud and laced with cruelty.

I will myself to move, but merely manage a jerking spasm of limbs.

The queen's cruel laughter lances through the room and echoes from the walls, from the rapiers dangling from the ceiling toward me, from the ceiling itself.

"Go!" shouts the queen, and her cool pincers close on my throat, squeeze in threat, and then release. She laughs again.

I gurgle as I struggle to the side of the bed-pit, barely managing to drag myself to lower elbows and knees, and crawl toward the door. I am almost to the door when I regurgitate the remains of my last meal along with a glutinous black acid onto the floor. Somehow, I manage not to fall forward into the filth.

The queen roars in anger and kicks at me, knocking me to my side on the floor, limbs draped through the spew.

After screeching to a brother to clean the mess, the queen lifts me to my feet and slams my head against the wall in the hallway outside the door. My ever-present escorts draw back.

"You grow old, Nestra," the queen spits, mandibles pinched into her fierce smile, as if my decrepitude pleases her. I hear the threat behind the words.

Without the strength to open in the ritual bow to the queen, I drag myself along the wall toward my rooms. I hope I can get to my rooms without crawling.

As I near the end of the corridor, the queen bellows, "Pull yourself together. I'll need you again soon. You didn't do half your job!"

***

I crawl the last distance to my rooms. I struggle to my bed-pit, ignoring the vomitus still clinging to my limbs. As I fall, helpless, to the cleansing mantra, the small voice of my inner self speaks up in taunting tones:

Certainly the queen is better off for your sacrifice. But how do you fare?

CHAPTER 19
KHARA

I've fallen into a new pattern. Not so different from before – still Ilnok and loathing and nausea, still sleep and food, still time in bars – but beer instead of whiskey and beer, and patches only with Ilnok. I have discovered a self-control I didn't believe I possessed.

I've reclaimed Refugio's as my own. I walk the streets, those places near Refugio's where I know I've seen Samuel in the past.

No ant has spoken to me again, not even the tender at Refugio's. I'm again just a pet. The fear of death for failure to deliver my message has lessened. My pattern, my search for Samuel has taken on a purpose of its own, which I don't analyze or understand, but continue to pursue.

In searching the streets, I've learned others have patterns. I've learned to recognize certain humans in their hopeless meandering, learned it may not have been as hard for Samuel to track me streetside as I'd thought. Before now, the patch obscured so much. So blessedly much – attraction and repulsion at the thought. My new awareness of my surroundings has shown me I'm not the only human in pain. I'm ashamed that this helps.

I pause in the street, back to a rough, grimy wall, and watch humans and ants push by. I can't picture Samuel – nothing but his thick, warm lips – and hope I'll recognize him if I see him again. Ilnok will be calling me soon – *repulsion/patch bliss* – and I watch the street partially hidden behind a sweetmead vendor.

A man turns the corner toward me, and I'm struck with a jolt of recognition. Big man, large lump of nose, thick mouth, high collared shirt which hides a monitor like my own. He's taller than I remembered. The mixture of relief and buried anger freezes me. I'm not as angry as I expect to be, want to be.

His eyes meet mine; his mouth grows taut and pulls down into an expression of anger. At me? At himself for letting me find him? I know now he has been hiding from me. He crosses the crowded street moving away from me, no longer looking at me, but keeping me in his peripheral vision. This is too much.

"Samuel!" I cry, incautious as this may be. "Samuel!"

He slows. He finishes his crossing of the street and stops, turning to look at me. I walk to him, willing him to stay, anger rising in me again and overriding the relief. That he would try to avoid me! He's the bastard who first approached *me*! *He* got me into this!

He waits, watching me approach, a look of unhappy resignation crossing his face before all expression flees his features. His mouth is not the warm, soft mouth of my memories.

"What do you want?" he asks as I stop before him. His voice is a monotone, neither angry nor kind. His eyes dissect me, looking from my face to my bare arms, to my feet, and back to my face.

I'm so surprised and angered at his apparent indifference to me I can't speak.

"You've cleaned yourself up a bit," he says. Still monotone.

"Fuck off," I say, angry. Angry!

"You have a limited vocabulary," he answers. Before I can say anything more, he says, "You told me to leave you alone. I have. What do you want?" His eyes are locked on mine, but my own eyes move from one eye to his other, to his mouth, in a repeating triangle, trying to read his non-expression. Why am I standing here with this man?

My silence leads to a lifted eyebrow, and a wry twist of his thick lips. He says, as if I'm stupid, with a slight pause between each word, "What. Do. You. Want?"

"I have a message for you," I say. I'll end my new pattern. I'll deliver the message and retreat to my old pattern of patch and patch and patch. This idea both repels and attracts me.

"I see," he answers. "What is it your ant friends want to tell me?" he says, and I'm confused. He continues: "Decided to join the ant corps, have you?"

My anger at his insinuation flares, and I only recognize I've moved after the flat of my hand has dashed across his face.

Samuel's head rocks a little under my blow. His face doesn't show the anger in his narrowed brown eyes which, if possible, bore into me even harder.

"Not my ant friends," I whisper between clenched teeth. "Yours." I take a deep breath, hoping I'm remembering the name right. "Fatchk."

Samuel's eyes open and round, but with no delay of surprise, his strong hand grasps my upper arm and he begins walking, dragging me in tow. It's several steps until I think to yank my arm from his grasp and stop.

"Don't touch me," I hiss.

Samuel turns toward me, smiles at me – there is the mouth I remember! – and says, barely moving his lips, "we should walk." He moves a hand toward the small of my back but doesn't touch me and motions ahead of me with the other hand in a chivalrous gesture. His eyes flick up and around at the humans and ants nearest us, and then back at me. He's still smiling.

I begin walking and he walks with me.

"Where did you hear that name?" he asks through his smile. The smile hasn't moved to his eyes.

"From your friend," I say.

Samuel doesn't answer and I wonder at the betrayals he's imagining. Wonder at the betrayals in which I may now be taking part without even knowing it.

"Message," he says. It's not a question, but a command for performance. Irritation flashes in me. First he attempted to cajole

128

me into his hopeless rebellion, then abandoned me, and now seeks to command me. But I want to be rid of this burden.

"Nestra. Shame Receptor," I say. I pause. "I don't have any idea what this means or if it means anything. I think I'm remembering it right."

"Continue," Samuel says. Irritation flares in me again. For several steps I say nothing more.

"Please," Samuel says. The gentleness in his voice makes me look up at his face, and his eyes are soft as he glances toward me.

"Nestra wishes to share, will share with humans, and this will weaken her loyalty to the queen," I say, in one breath. "That's all." Another couple of steps, and I ask, "Is this Nestra an ant?"

I wonder at my question. I'm not interested in Samuel's rebellion. I don't care about his cause. He's rebellious and will die. I'm compliant and will live.

Samuel doesn't answer. We continue to walk. I don't know why I stay with him.

My monitor tingles against my throat. Ilnok calling me. I pull at my collar and the red glow shines out. I'm sick to my stomach. These two worlds don't mesh.

Samuel stops walking, turns to face me, eyes fixed on my monitor and filled again with suspicion. His mouth hardens.

"I don't know what you're talking about," Samuel says. "I don't know what kind of joke this is."

"Wha...?" I start. It's more breath than word. My mouth hangs open in surprise unable to conclude the truncated question. I've lived for days on end with this nonsense rolling around in my mind, and with fear of reprisal for not finding Samuel, torturing myself, and now I find there was no point?

"I don't know how much of your drug you earned playing your stupid joke, but I don't think it's funny. Hope it was worth plenty to you." He turns and begins striding back the way we came. The set of his massive shoulders is rigid.

"Samuel," I say. Surprisingly, he turns toward me. Not surprisingly, his anger shows on his face. I pull my hand from my pocket and throw a handful of patches into his face. Most scatter at his feet, one landing in his short, sandy hair before slipping to his shoulder and then to the street.

I want to scream at him, but I don't dare. Too much attention streetside is always dangerous. "I don't need them, thanks." I say. I wish I could feel satisfaction in addition to the betrayal and anger.

His mouth twists as he answers. "I can see that."

"Fuck off, Samuel," I say as he turns away. I can't tell if he's heard me as he walks away. It's moments later I wish I hadn't said those words. I hear again his cutting voice telling me I have a limited vocabulary.

"Fuck off, Samuel," I say again, to myself alone, as I make my way back up the street behind him, toward the sweetmead vendor.

I hate Samuel and his rebellion. More than having a self-protective desire not to endanger myself with foolish dreams, foolish risks for an ungrateful man, I'm now angry and determined not to become involved. *Bastard.*

I hate that in these past days I'd come to believe in the softness of Samuel's mouth. In the gentleness of his eyes, his hand on my face in a dim, blurred room. I realize again the truth that I can trust nothing and no one but myself.

I hope never to see him again. I won't look for him. I'll avoid any place where I might see him.

Asshole.

CHAPTER 20
DEV'RO

I am sated. The dead and dissected human at the base of the cushions I have been occupying is being cleared by lesser brothers attempting to keep the lounge somewhat unlittered. One brother gathers the small parts – fingers, toes, ears, nose. Does he count to make sure he has gathered them all or does he just pick up all the pieces he can find? Might there be a leftover nubbin under a cushion? The other brother lifts the body and the mangled head flops backward showing my handiwork. My sigh of satisfaction gurgles as air bubbles from my pores through the thin human blood. I reach for the light, sweet fruit juice that contrasts so pleasantly with the bitter iron of the red fluid.

Excellent toys, these creatures. Almost a shame to exterminate them. What will we do for entertainment then? In thinking "we," I refer to the queen and myself. She is the perfection of our people. Through my close association with her, I have learned to appreciate her cravings, to feel them myself. And she, I believe, has learned to value me. I have worked hard to acquire her favor and intend to keep it.

I laugh to myself, mandibles drawn into the twisted smile that terrifies so many. I perfected the expression by watching my queen, having almost absorbed the ability from my frequent contact with her. No other courtier is as graced with her touch or brief sharing embrace as I am. My chemical contact with her fills me with such feelings of power. My greatest satisfaction comes when I slake my lust for supremacy with blood – whether obtained in a slashing frenzy or through slow torture. I want to be with her now to share this sensation of hunger temporarily fulfilled. The queen's tastes are as voracious as my own, and she would enjoy the brief feeling of being sated.

A brother enters the small lounge and moves to sit near me on the cushions as I continue to watch the pieces of human body being removed. I tap my antennae against the brother's in the barest of greetings. This is Ketann, one of the lowliest of courtiers, a wall-hanger, no one important. I know little and care not at all about him, but am careful to remain princely in my manners, if only to emphasize my power at court.

The brother smells of greeting and of awe and – yes, I relish it – of fear. This is appropriate. I pinch my perfected smile toward the brother.

"Pitiful creatures," the brother says. The brother's comment is tinged with the flavor/scent meaning pitiable, rather than connoting pathetic or contemptible.

I respond by deepening the flavor and sharpening the meaning toward the latter tones. "Yes." Again my mandibles draw together into a smile bearing the sharpened edges.

"Do you not think . . .?" says the brother, now deliberately shading the flavor/scent toward pity and perhaps even compassion. He brushes his slim fingers against my arm and I can taste him with utmost clarity.

I do not hesitate. With both upper pincers I throw back the head of the other and snap out his throat with a sharp crushing clamp of my powerful mandibles. The decapitated head falls into my upper pincers. With my lower arms, I push the body from the cushions as thick yellow blood flows over the shell of his shiny black thorax. I kick the body toward the brothers just now finishing with the human detritus, and toss the head among the still twitching limbs.

I know better than most the consequences of tasting, when touched by the queen, as this revolting brother did. Shuddering with the thought, I order another human brought forth. I take my time with this one, removing the digits from its limbs, then smearing its face with its own blood before forcing it to swallow the small pieces. I remove the ears and tongue before slicing into the body cavity, savoring the screams and denying the human even the comfort of their drugs. It does not die until I have removed half of its viscera.

By the time I have finished, the flavor/scent of the traitorous brother is impossible to recall. I go to my meeting with my queen flush with self-satisfaction.

CHAPTER 21
SAMUEL

I've been at this bar for some time hoping for news of Fatchk. As I sit here, I realize hope is not a strategy. I have to move now because I can't sit here without drinking and I can't drink any more without endangering my equilibrium and blurring my senses.

None of my normal contacts has been able to put me in touch with Fatchk. They haven't indicated he is dead, but I haven't been able to gain any information as to where he might be, nor what danger might be keeping him from meeting with me. I can't entertain the thought that he's no longer a part of the rebellion. Ants, I have learned, are either for us or against us, although many refuse to be involved with us outside of following the queen's dictates. Humans are the same: those with the rebellion, those with the ants, and those too afraid to be involved either way. My confusion regarding where Khara stands is distracting – logical distrust battles against intuitive attraction. I shake my head in a physical effort to get her out of my mind.

I don't like it, but I have to take the risk, and approach an ant whose loyalties are not altogether established with me. I have seen him with Fatchk. But he also met with Tamerak once regarding the business of the factory. I rise and walk to him. He's alone.

"Do you wish to dance?" I ask. I have seen this approach from the more pathetic of the humans – those in search of favors and willing to sell themselves for an evening or a dance. Under normal circumstances, this tactic is accompanied by an opening of the shirt to reveal the soft flesh of our chests, but I can't do this without revealing my collar.

The ant raises an arm as if to wave me away, but I say, "My name is Samuel." This shouldn't raise suspicion because the ants know we identify each other with names, not by scent, and often identify ourselves to ants in this manner in the hopes of being remembered later, for perhaps another evening of favors exchanged. I believe they can't often visually distinguish between us, just as we struggle to differentiate one ant from another.

The ant pauses and then rasps out, "Samuel?"

"Yes," I answer. "Do you wish to dance?"

The glittering eyes of the ant focus on my face. My armpits prickle with sweat, both at the danger of trusting this unknown, and at the idea of what this ant may want to do during our "dance." I can't allow it to harm me in ways Tamerak will notice, but I may not get the choice.

"Sorm'ba," says the ant. It's telling me its name. "I will dance."

Instead of moving toward the dance floor, as I expect, Sorm'ba guides me to a dark hallway which leads to small private lounges. I balk at entering the hallway. "I only wanted to dance," I say, hoping to back out of my mistake.

"I am brother to Fatchk," hisses Sorm'ba. "He has spoken of you. Come, Samuel."

The relief that floods through me is tempered by my lingering caution. I want to believe this means he is close to Fatchk and shares Fatchk's ideologies, but all ants refer to each other as "brother," and it's their apparent ability to taste or smell the nuances behind the word that lend it different meanings.

He has spoken of you. I decide to take the risk. I follow Sorm'ba as he leads me to a small lounge, opens the door, and enters the oil-black darkness. I follow and Sorm'ba closes the door. I hear the door latch, but don't move in the perfect blackness. The hair stands on my neck and legs as I wonder who or what else might be in the room.

A dim red light glows from the ceiling and I'm relieved to find Sorm'ba the sole occupant of the small room. He moves to cushions, gesturing to me to join him.

"Much danger," says Sorm'ba. Given the nerve brightening panic of my last few moments, I find this understatement almost comical.

"Fatchk is watched," says Sorm'ba.

"I received a message from an untrusted human," I say. "I do not believe it is from Fatchk. I believe it is a trap, but I don't understand the trap."

"Message?" says Sorm'ba.

I repeat Khara's message. The fact of whether or not the message is from Fatchk, this brother may not know. However, perhaps the ant will be of some help in understanding the purpose of the message.

"Message is from Fatchk," Sorm'ba answers. "Must try to subvert Nestra's loyalty. Humans can help."

I can't breathe as I recall my last meeting with Khara, my reaction to her, my insults to her, when she was telling me the truth and risking herself to do it.

"I don't understand," I say. Sorm'ba tells me what I already know about ants "sharing" their chemical message through touch, and then explains Nestra is the queen's Shame Receptor. I tell him I don't understand this reference.

"The queen is sick," says Sorm'ba. "She has illness. She should not have survived."

"Survived what?" I ask. "Survived the voyage here? Survived the illness?"

"Survived," he answers with finality.

I still don't understand. I don't say anything because I can't think of how to sort through this misunderstanding between us.

"Queen is infection," Sorm'ba says at last. "Queen makes us sick. Our people are not sick without a sick queen. Sick queens are not permitted to survive."

"You mean she should have been killed?" I'm afraid of injurious insult with the statement, but I can't manage to interpret his statement in any other way.

"Yes," says Sorm'ba.

"You are fighting to kill the queen?" I ask. I'm incredulous.

"Yes."

I allow this thought to spin through my head until a gust of laughter escapes me. "Then why don't you?"

"Queen is infection. Those closest to queen are infected. Those infected infect their brothers. Sickness spreads, but weakens with distance from queen. Those close to queen taste like queen. They will not kill her. Those without sickness are killed if they approach."

I think I'm beginning to understand. The queen is the apex of a pyramid. Those immediately under her are sick, and in turn, those under them are sick, perhaps to a lesser degree, but infected. Any bottom layer ant that attempts to get to the queen has to get over the infected layers under her, and can't. Over time, the infection spreads down the line.

"You don't want to be sick?" I ask.

"No."

"Okay, who is Nestra? What is this Shame Receptor?"

"Infection weakens queen. Negative chemicals. Shame."
Sorm'ba waits while I nod. "Nestra digests negative chemicals.
Nestra saves queen."

Again I'm flailing for understanding.

Sorm'ba continues. "Queen orders none can share with
Nestra. Nestra desires sharing. If loyalty of Nestra can be tainted,
perhaps Nestra will turn against queen. Hurt queen."

I like the idea, but I'm still not making the connection.
"Nestra is saving the queen. Does this not mean Nestra is very
loyal to the queen?"

"Nestra is not sick," answers Sorm'ba. This doesn't make
sense to me if Nestra is the one who takes the queen's sickness, but
I move on.

"The message said Nestra could share with humans. But we
don't communicate with chemicals," I said.

"You do not perceive chemicals. But your bodies release
them. The taste of your fear was very strong." I'm embarrassed. I
feel somehow naked in front of this ant – although actual nudity
wouldn't have embarrassed me. I wonder at what Tamerak has
smelled on me from time to time and either ignored or
misunderstood. "Nestra wishes to share," Sorm'ba continues.

"I have humans who will share." I think of Diane and
Tanner and what I'll soon be asking them to do, but I also know
they'll do it. "What happens if this is accomplished? What happens
if the queen is . . . ," I want to say "killed" but can't bring myself to
believe in such a possibility, "hurt . . . by Nestra?"

"Infection will ease," Sorm'ba says. After a pause, he says, "Our people are not sick." It seems important to this ant I understand this, but I don't.

"And then what?"

"We will generate new queen," Sorm'ba answers.

"New queen? A healthy queen? Why can't you do that now?" I ask. What in the world have we been fighting for if they can just make a new "not sick" queen?

"Queen cannot be generated except by queen or at death of queen."

"New queen," I say, more to myself than to Sorm'ba, trying hard to digest this enormous amount of new information. "Then what happens to humans?" I hold my breath after this question.

"We ask forgiveness. We repair."

I want to scream and call this ant a liar. It's too much to hope for.

"Our people are not sick," Sorm'ba repeats.

"You are not sick," I say.

"No. I am not sick." Sorm'ba pauses and says, "I am shamed for my people."

My breath is quick and harsh. Our plan for striking at the ants includes a widespread attack, lots of trucks, lots of foci. I've coordinated with four other rebellion pockets in Douglasville, Stone Mountain, Forest Park and Lithonia and they have a similar number of outside contacts. It's a sparse net, but we have a plan. We hope that in another year we can...

142

But, if I've understood this ant, our assault can be far more focused, aimed at the center, at the queen and those closest to her. I've thought for a long time that things seemed worse in this city than others – then dismissed the idea as self-centered. But what if it's true? What if it's because we're at the hub of the infection? Hope surges through me and my mind races through new alternatives.

I have much to do!

I jump up, and say, "Thank you. Most sincere thanks. May I be dismissed?" The energy that flows through me could keep me moving for a week.

Sorm'ba says, "I do not dismiss brothers. You are free to go when you wish."

I'm out the door before I register his statement. Humans – brothers? Even then, the import of his statement barely gives me pause.

I need to call a meeting.

I need to talk to Tanner and Diane.

My heart races as I leave the bar in slow steps and move down the dark humid street, thinking of the other thing I need to do.

I need to find Khara.

CHAPTER 22
NESTRA

In the war I fight within myself, self-preservation has won. Or perhaps not *won*, since concessions have been made between the conflicting drives that govern me.

Following the session that almost killed me, I was summoned to the queen's side for another session too soon and without sufficient cleansing. The repentant, honorable, loyal aspect of myself was too weakened for personal control. The aspect of myself that fights for life lapped with hunger at the rich dewdrop of the queen's strength. I awoke to a quiet and subdued queen, but with at least the strength to remain on my own feet to return to my room.

I fight with my own conscience and conflicting instincts, vacillating between the opposing ideas of taking my own life, and preserving it, even at cost to the queen. The compromise I convince myself is best is to taste minutely of the queen, since my survival is essential to her own. Unless and until she allows another Shame Receptor to be prepared, my death will damage the queen. I vow that should a new Shame Receptor be prepared, I will then end my own life . . . perhaps even confessing all to Queen Tal and accepting the killing blow from the queen herself. I think this just. I do not focus on the inconsistency of failing to suggest to the queen that a new Shame Receptor be prepared, thus allowing my thievery to end all the sooner.

I sit in the garden, knowing myself to be alone in the world, and believing myself deserving of my solitude. I sit before a blank canvas, painting supplies gathered around me, and find I cannot summon the loose serenity that will allow imagination to grow into inspiration.

Refusing to allow frustration to build, I push my painting supplies to a jumbled pile near the base of the easel and turn on my stool to face the grandeur of the private garden. Colors, scents, plays of light and dark as the sun settles toward late afternoon, combined symphonies of sound wash over me. I drink it in and force calmness upon myself, letting myself descend into the lightest of trances.

I am drawn from my dreamlike state by the sharp snap of a twig nearby – a sound which does not belong to the slight breeze through the leaves or the purring of insect wings. There, quite near me, the two human gardeners squat pulling weeds from a bed of mixed flowers. They do not look at me, and I wonder if they can have failed to notice me. The humans have not been this close to me since I first approached them.

I determine not to move, not to alert them to my presence, so I can once again observe them. I am sure this time, if I watch, I will find an explanation for their previous appearance of sharing which will defy the meaning I have assigned to it.

I wait. I watch.

For a brief time, the humans work, weeding, near to each other, but not touching. Disappointed, I suppress a sigh that might have been loud enough to arouse them. Then, the larger human, the one with lighter hair, stops weeding long enough to wipe its brow with the back of one dirty hand. It leaves a smudge of dirt on its wet forehead. The smaller, dark haired human looks up at the other, then pulls a rag from a pocket and, with slow, gentle motions, wipes the other's forehead. The taller human pulls the smaller closer and they touch mouths. It is intimate, visceral. Not quite the intimacy of sharing palpus to palpus, but then these humans do not have palpi. I shudder, with a pang of ecstasy and torture combined.

Either my slight movement or some small sound it produced causes the humans to look toward me. I brace for the feeling of rejection which will come with their withdrawal, but neither human moves. One reaches for and clasps the hand of the other, soft dirty fingers intertwined, but they do not rise, do not flee. They continue to look toward me. The various facets of my eyes focus on the touching hands dangling between the two crouching humans, creating a visual tunnel that includes the humans and the plants nearest to them, but all pivoting around the hands layering imperfectly in the center of my vision.

I raise myself from the stool, all four arms held out in a posture of supplication. I take several long steps towards them. Still the humans do not flee.

"I will not hurt you," I say, realizing again the humans cannot understand my words, and hoping the sound of my speech will not frighten them and cause them to leave.

The smaller human stands first, pulling the larger human to its feet. Still clasping the other human's hand, it moves its other arm out in a mirroring posture of supplication and says, in my own language, "I will not hurt you." The voice is high and watery and weak, and the accent is strange, but the human has repeated my words.

I step closer, keeping my arms out, and repeat, "I will not hurt you." I wait for the moment when my approach will cause the humans to withdraw, but step after step I approach and they do not flee. Even after I am close enough to tower over the two small humans, close enough to reach out and touch one of the soft creatures, they stay. I can taste the rich scent of fear emanating from the two.

Again, I say, "I will not hurt you."

The larger human releases its hold on the other human's hand, then pulls the smaller one closer and wraps an arm around its shoulders. The smaller looks to the larger, which nods its head without taking its eyes from me. The smaller human looks back to me.

Very clearly, it says, "You will not hurt us."

Not a repetition this time. An acknowledgement. In my own language.

"You speak my language!" I cry, my surprise raising the volume of my words above the low level I have used thus far.

The humans flinch, shuffling backward. I glance toward the garden entrance where my escort waits, but cannot see the entrance from where I stand with the humans.

I throw my head back in the gesture of absolute subservience and repeat, "You speak my language. I will not hurt you."

When I bring my head down to gaze again at the humans, the smaller has moved a step closer. The scent of fear that blossomed at my outburst is dissipating.

"I learn your language," the smaller human says. "You will not hurt us?" This time the second phrase is formed as a question.

"No."

I find the idea of humans speaking my language almost distracting from my focus on the two beings touching each other. My surprise leaves me with nothing I can think of saying to the humans and for a time we three stand, unmoving. The humans lower themselves to the ground, and, again clasping hands, look upward at me.

Delighted, I fold my long limbs, amidst small cracks and pops, until I am seated in the warm grass before the humans.

"You share," I say. My words are more a statement than a question.

"I do not know 'share'," the small human answers.

"You touch," I say, and move my high right pincer to touch my lower left pincer. The humans do not flinch away at my movement.

The small human shows its teeth in what must be their equivalent of a smile, and says, "Yes, we touch. We are . . . ," it seems to be searching for words, "hive brothers."

Again I am surprised, delighted.

The taller human speaks for the first time. "Hive *bond* brothers," it says. Its accent is terrible, but it is clear the addition of the word is important.

"Bonded hive brothers?" I ask, and wonder how humans with no discernible hives can have learned this distinction between business relationship or other relationship and bonded friend.

"Bonded hive brothers, yes," answers the smaller. The flavor of fear is almost gone and the warm flavor of my curiosity seems enhanced by a similar scent from the humans.

"We touch," says the smaller human, demonstrating by moving her hand to the arm of the taller. Then, with hesitation, "I touch you?"

The taller human says something quickly – sternly? – to the smaller in its own language, but the smaller seems to ignore it, not answering or turning, but continuing to gaze at me.

Despite my curiosity about these humans, I find myself repelled by the idea, both because the soft creatures are vaguely repellant, but also from the ingrained dictum that no one touch me, under penalty of death. I do not move, do not answer.

The smaller human moves its hand toward me. My curiosity stays my instinct to pull away. After all, the queen's order does not include humans. The soft human hand comes to rest on my lower arm, well above the pincer.

The flavor/scent of curiosity heightens with the contact, laced with a tinge of fear. It is not true sharing. There are no vague images that pass from the human to me, but even so, the increase in the intensity of emotional content is pleasant and yet jarring. I do not move, but focus my attention on what I am receiving, hoping to expand the sensation.

After minutes, the taller human reaches for me, hand coming to rest on my other lower arm. The flavor difference between the two puzzled me – both curious, both a bit frightened, and yet the difference in scent is clear. Almost as if the two are of different species, or of different divisions within species.

"You are different," I say. I color my words with the visual scents of my meaning, knowing even as I do there will be no true communication outside my simple words.

The smaller human bends its head to one side, as if listening to strange insect song, or perhaps even catching a small bit of what I attempt to share. Then it shakes its head and says, "I don't understand."

I do not know how to explain further and so remain silent. I focus on the flavor/scents the humans exude.

"You communicate in this way?" the small human asks.

"Yes," I answer. "We share."

"I don't know 'share'," says the small human again.

"Exchange meaning, emotion, insight, identification," I say, hoping the human understands at least some of my words.

The taller human makes a small noise and both smile at me. The smaller human asks, "Do you 'share' humans?"

"I taste your curiosity, I smell your fear," I answer. "Not much fear," I add, hoping not to elicit more fear and thus cause the humans to leave.

"Do humans share?" I ask. The humans look at each other, but do not answer. "You touch mouths," I continue. "This causes great sharing in my people."

The humans smile again, and without removing their hands from my arms, lean toward each other and touch mouths to each other, not briefly this time, but for a prolonged moment, mouths locked together as if they indeed have palpi. The warmth and velvet purple-blue emotion that flows over me causes me to droop in my posture. The rasp of my rough breathing sounds as the two draw apart and gaze again at me. The sour scent of questioning comes from both, colored with concern.

Concern? These humans feel concern for me? Confusion boils in me as I sit torn between an expanded feeling of loneliness, and a desire to keep the humans with me always. Crush them to me.

"Powerful emotion," I say. "You share powerful friendship."

"Yes!" Both humans respond together and the flavor of concern fades, blended into peacefulness and quiet. The bright red scent of fear is now undetectable.

After another several moments during which I focus again – these humans are difficult to taste – I enjoy the lapping tides of emotional current of the two . . . confidence, triumph, curiosity, and under it all like a deep underground spring, the velvety purple-blue passion ripples serenely.

The smaller human breaks the silence. "I am named Diane," it says.

The taller human adds, "I am Tanner."

"Nestra," I answer.

"We are hive brothers? Friends?" asks Diane. "We share together, and are friends?"

"I would share with you again," I answer, ashamed I am so desperate for sharing, yet treasuring the experience. I know if I never see these humans again, I will always remember the trust and kindness shown me this day.

152

Without releasing its hold on my arm, Diane reaches with its other hand up higher than the level of its head, toward my mandibles. "Share with mouth," Diane says, and brushes my mandible.

Bewildered, but willing, I extrude my palpus.

"Feel my happiness," Diane says. It closes the covering over its eyes, and smiling, reaching high, places its palm against my palpus. It is not the banquet it might have been with a brother, but still, a sweet bouquet of peace, happiness, friendship, trust.

Tanner stands. "We go now," it says. "Night comes."

Diane removes its hand from my palpus and stands with Tanner. Their heads are on level with mine as I sit, their soft eyes squishing as they blink their covers open and closed.

"We will come again," says Tanner, "hive brother."

I am unable to rise until after I have watched the two depart, again clasping hands. Just before they move beyond my vision, they touch mouths again, and I feel a resurgent glimmer of their passion in my chemical memory.

I return to my room, tranquil, quiet, and ready for sleep.

CHAPTER 23
KHARA

I'm lost. My routine, my safe existence, my oblivion has left me. I wander, wanting to crush my head against a wall, against the pavement of the street, but know this'll give me no peace. And the damned patches don't help either.

After seeing Samuel I returned to the patch, hoping to recapture the blankness that overrode the blackness inside me. Three days of masking my anger in the wash of the drug led me to a feeling of failure, disappointment, a yearning for the purpose that had illuminated my days as I searched for Samuel. Memory of my temporary consciousness defeated my grasp on oblivion.

Damn Samuel.

I still don't want Samuel's rebellion. I want life before the invasion. Or I want the amnesia and nonexistence of the days since. Yet each day calls to me now from a direction I can't see, a path I can't find.

I have abandoned my old haunts, both wanting to avoid Samuel and determined not to be a conscious person in the places where the ghost of myself once lived. I don't want to face that memory of myself.

I bathe myself more often these days, eat more often. Lost in new-found clarity and wakefulness, I wash others as they sprawl in the dorms, half-human, as far gone in their escape into the oblivion of drugs and alcohol as I was. I feed those too weak to move.

I endure Ilnok and his associates. I choke down sweetmead and prepare my body for violation, prepare myself to act as drinking vessel and toy. I behave.

And yet I'm lost. I'm conscious now and lost. And angry.

***

I'm leaving Dominique's, leaving Ilnok, empty and raw. The last of the session was unbearable because I didn't renew my patch. It was a red, red end of the session – red light in the dim room, red flashes behind eyelids squeezed shut, red revulsion as the palpi entered me, red menstrual blood on the table, on my legs, under my buttocks. The ants don't seem to care. This stickiness is on my legs now, different from the sweetmead, or the other fluids that often bathe my lower body. Away from Ilnok now, I want to wash. I want a drink.

I don't know if I can stay awake that long.

I move away from the entrance to Dominique's determined not to limp, although my hips and knees seem loose. One step. Another. I'll go to a dorm first and then a bar. If I have the strength.

I haven't gone far when I am supported by a hand taking my elbow. I jerk away from the touch, stumble, and catch myself on a graffiti-painted rough brick wall. I straighten and begin walking again. I don't know who touched me. I don't care. I care only they don't do it again, but I'm sure my reaction will have cured any intentions to help me. One step and another.

"Khara." I stop. A human voice. Deep. Gentle. I don't know anyone who would speak to me. An ember of fear ignites in the emptiness of my middle. And a small glow of hope. I lean a shoulder against the wall, hoping I've imagined my name in my exhaustion.

"Khara." Again. I squeeze my eyes closed and roll until my back is against the wall. I open my eyes.

It's Samuel.

"I won't touch you again." His brown eyes are soft, pitying; his mouth is the warm mouth of my dreams. "You need help," he says.

I turn away from him and back onto my shoulder, then push away from the wall and begin walking again.

"Khara," he says, and his voice has a note of pleading in it. I want to laugh at him, but I don't have the strength. Samuel pleading with me. I remember our last meeting and want to tell him to fuck off, to exercise my limited vocabulary. I don't. I keep walking.

"How'd you find me?" I say, unsure whether he's still walking with me, not sure I should care, but I do.

"Dominique's." A pause. "I thought you were dead. I couldn't find you anywhere. But then I learned where your master . . . goes," he says. I wonder which word he didn't use. Plays? Tortures? It doesn't matter. "I waited for you," he finishes.

"Fuck off," I say, and an aborted chuckle escapes my mouth. I take several more steps, sure I've angered Samuel again. I take satisfaction in this thought.

I stumble to a stop and turn to see if he's still with me. If he hasn't given up on me already, I want to see the anger in his face.

Samuel is smiling at me. Smiling. I'm confused and dizzy. One strong arm reaches up as if to support me again as I sway. I flinch and he stops himself, lowers his arm to his side, with small twitches toward me as if determined to catch me if I fall, and sure I will. "You are one tough lady," he says, still smiling.

His smile is crushing. I want to cry. I'm flayed.

"Go away, Samuel," I say. "I'm tired." I turn and stumble toward the dorm that is nearest. Just one block and I can rest. I'm alone again in the crowd.

***

Samuel is there when I wake. He has a bowl of steaming water, and a clean rag. He offers them to me with a lift of one heavy eyebrow. I look at him and then away, toward the stained wall. He doesn't move. I turn back to him and take the bowl, not understanding why he's here or what he wants, but the water's warm, the rag's clean, and I want to wash.

"You need food," Samuel says.

I pull the rag from my face, shove it under my shirt. "What the fuck do you want now?" I ask. "Why are you here?" I'm angry again, but I don't know what I'd do if he just left.

"I came to apologize," he says. He looks around at the sprawled human bodies around me and says, "Can we walk? I'll get you some food."

"I can get my own damned food, thank you very much," I answer. I want to sound forceful, but my words are pathetic and childish.

"I think we can help each other," Samuel says. Before I can respond with a question or a demand for him to leave, he adds, "Can we take a walk?" Again, he glances around, but this time with eyes widened to indicate he wants to be away from listening ears.

I want him to go away. And yet I don't. A huge sigh gusts out of me.

"I guess I can eat," I say. I sound like a child. "I know a good place," I add, hoping to counteract my peevish tone.

Samuel leaves so I can finish my washing. I meet him outside the dorm and lead the way to the shop that serves rice and fish. As soon as we're walking, Samuel takes my elbow and starts to talk, but I jerk my arm away from him again.

"I'm not going to hurt you!" He seems angry I'd think this of him.

"I . . . I don't think you're going to hurt me," I say. I'm ashamed, but I want to explain. "It isn't you. I get touched enough. I don't like to be touched." I can't look at him.

"I'm sorry," he says. We walk for a minute with no words. Then he says, "I'll try not to touch you again, but no promises."

I think of several responses, all of them rude, but I don't say anything.

"Thank you for the message," Samuel says, not looking at me. He's walking very near me, but appears to be making an effort not to jostle me.

I'm angry again – angry for getting the message in the first place and the burden it placed on me, angry at his reaction when I delivered it. But I say nothing, not knowing what response he's expecting, or why he's here.

"It was helpful," Samuel says. Still I wait, walking, not believing he's just apologizing, and wanting to hear what he wants of me now – if only so I can refuse him.

"Don't talk much, huh?" he says, and I can hear in his voice he's smiling again.

"I have a limited vocabulary," I answer, almost smiling myself.

"Look, I'm sorry for the way I treated you. I was . . . an asshole, as you would say." He spits out the curse word as though it doesn't fit right in his mouth.

"Agreed. It doesn't matter," I answer.

We walk for a time, and as I step toward the entrance to the rice shop, he says, "Let's keep walking for a bit. I'll buy your meal, to make up for prolonging the time when you can eat it."

I'm hungry now and tired of waiting for Samuel to tell me what he wants. I have credit enough from Ilnok for a hundred meals. For some reason, I step toward him instead of into the shop.

"We can help each other," he says, walking again.

"I don't need your help," I answer.

"You're strong. You're angry, and you already have helped me. Helped us. And in so doing, helped yourself," Samuel says. His eyes wander over me and he says, "You've cleaned yourself up."

"I...," I begin. I don't know what I want to say. I don't need his help? I don't want to help him? But the feeling of lost purpose that's been haunting me chokes off my response like a noose.

"Help us fight, Khara," he says. "Join us. We can offer some small protections, but that doesn't mean it won't be dangerous for you. It will be." He takes several quick steps to move past me, turns, and places himself in front of me. He walks backwards now, glancing over his shoulder every once in a while to see if the path through the crowded street is clear. His brown eyes are soft and caring, his mouth is relaxed, neither smiling nor tight with anger. He comes to a stop, eyes fixed on mine. His tongue licks at his lips and I'm mesmerized by the wet pink thing. I jerk my eyes from his face and stare at the cracked cement between our feet.

His hand approaches my chin as if he would lift my eyes to his face again. I raise my head to avoid his touch and he drops his hand.

"You need this. You've already taken great risks. You did so for reasons of your own." His eyes move back and forth between my own and I feel like a snake, innards coiled, ready to strike, but hypnotized into motionlessness. There are flecks of gold in the brown.

I drop my gaze to the sidewalk again. My defenses drop with my eyes. "What do you want me to do?" I ask. I still have the ability to refuse, but I do want to hear what he says. I don't understand his effect on me.

He doesn't answer and I look up to see him smiling again. His teeth are small and straight, with sharp incisors. I like the smile. I like that I have earned it.

"Eight o'clock. Outside Refugio's. Meet me. We'll talk about what you can do, what you are willing to do. It'll be up to you," Samuel says, still smiling.

He's giving me choices. It's been so long since I've felt I had choices. I'm stunned, feeling buoyant, released from something somehow.

"If Ilnok—" I say, and he interrupts, "I understand. If you can't, then same time next night, okay?"

I nod my head and look down at the cracked sidewalk again.

"Come on, let's eat," he says, and takes my elbow to turn me back toward the rice shop. I jerk my arm away from his touch and am sorry in the same instant. Not because I want him to touch me – I can't bear it – but because of how he must interpret my reaction.

"I'm sorry," he says. "I'm really sorry."

Somehow I feel he's not apologizing for touching me, but expressing sorrow for something bigger than this lapse.

I shudder. Samuel represents a danger to me. Not because he'll ask me to risk myself physically, but . . . .

I can't finish the thought. I'm scared and excited, and for the first time in a long, long while, alive.

CHAPTER 24
SAMUEL

Khara and I move through the back alleys and dark spaces that are my pathways. When I can, I whisper to her, teaching her the ways of stealth. Where to watch, what to look for.

It's remarkable how observant she is for someone who so recently lived a lifestyle of oblivion. Her ability to move in silence is a testimony to the depths of her self-preservation. Against my will, I am impressed with her brightly burning core, so strong and fierce. I can't let that incandescent kernel seduce me. I can't allow emotion to interfere with my duties and responsibilities. Even so, I'm smiling, stomach jumping with each step we take toward this culmination of a months-long effort to wake Khara up, to get her involved. She'll be an asset to the rebellion.

The closest of my squad are at the meeting. Silence cottons the room as we enter and Khara's anxiety is evidenced by her effort to hide behind me. I turn to pull her forward, and then remind myself not to touch her. She moves beside me at a gesture.

"Mmm, que bella," Jan says in an aside to Bell with an appreciative grin, and Bell, stone faced, whispers something into her ear. Not like Bell. He must be troubled by some new crisis. I'll ask him when we're done here.

Bell's eyes meet mine and now he smiles. He winks.

I narrow my eyes with an odd pang of possessiveness and then almost laugh picturing the unhappy response they'll get from her if either of them touches her.

The group shuffles chairs to make room at the round table, and Khara and I sit between Rex and Diane, Rex almost dumping his own chair over backwards in order to pull Khara's chair into position. Khara looks at Rex – his face is stretched into a huge smile – but says nothing, and I wonder if she recognizes that this is the boy she rescued from slaughter. I run my eyes around the table and stop on Jan, who says, "Eli couldn't make it." Before I can express concern, she says, "He's fine."

My squad eyes Khara, although they know of her through my reports, and Khara stares at the center of the table. It would be easy to mistake her anxiety as anger.

"Introductions," I say, and Khara jerks her head up. I start with Rex, who grabs and shakes Khara's hand, profuse in his thanks. Khara can't mistake him now. I wince, waiting for Khara's explosion at Rex's grasp upon her hand, knowing this reaction won't be understood by my people. Khara doesn't jerk her hand away as I expect, or yell, or shove herself away from the table. She looks long into Rex's eyes and, as an awkward silence descends and Rex's face reddens, she says, "You remind me of someone I used

164

to know a long time ago." There seems much behind her quiet statement, but she doesn't elaborate.

Diane and Tanner wave in unison as I introduce them together. Jan half stands to reach a hand across the table to shake, but Khara keeps her hands in her lap and says "Hello," eyes flicking from the extended hand – as if it were an insect – to Jan's face. Jan leaves her hand out and looks at me. The expression on her face is poisonous.

"It's me," Khara says. Jan looks back at Khara, and Khara says, face coloring, "It's me, not you. I don't like to be touched." Khara keeps her eyes on Jan's, and the strong muscles in Jan's arms bunch and release, but then Jan pulls her hand back across the table and says, "Okay, I get it, my bad." She smiles and says, "Welcome."

I am thankful I have such good people.

Bell stands, bends in a small bow and introduces himself. I expect him to flash his trademark smile, make some suave witticism. Instead, he sits again. His expression is pleasant enough but his eyes seem locked on her, as though he is looking for something from her, some response.

I turn to Khara. She nods to Bell with a nervous smile, acknowledging his introduction, then looks to me. No explanation there.

"Khara," I say. "I've already briefed everybody on your general background as I know it, but is there anything you'd like to say about yourself?"

Khara shakes her head, and says, voice low. "No thanks."

"There are some things we need to know," I say. "For example, I've tracked you long enough to know who your master is and where and how you spend your days, but I may have missed a thing or two. Do you have any contacts? Any human friends you talk to and trust?"

"No," Khara says. It's the answer I expected.

"Any humans who might become suspicious at a change in your patterns?"

"No."

"Which ants do you come in contact with besides your master?" I ask.

Khara pauses, nonplussed. "Whichever are at the club at the time . . . ," she answers.

"Do you know any by name? Do you have dealings with them outside of Ilnok's presence?"

For the first time, Khara loses her timidity. Her mouth drops open and a short burst of breath escapes. "Of course not!" she answers. "Why in the fucking hell would I . . . ? would I . . . ?" She sputters to a stop, takes a deep breath then lets it out, regaining her composure. "I don't want anything to do with them. So, no." Another deep breath.

"Do you have any business contacts? Shop owners? Ants you are on good terms with?" I ask.

After a pause, Khara says, "Bartenders, I suppose." Bell laughs at this, but Khara doesn't react. "I don't speak to them, or have a relationship with any. But they know me, I guess."

When I look at Bell, his head is lowered, perhaps contrite at this ungracious response to Khara. I'm surprised at his behavior. Khara is new and raw and scared, and Bell is usually much more supportive. And flirtatious.

Into the silence, Khara asks, eyes glazed and introspective, "Can anybody really have a good relationship with these monsters?"

"Not all ants are bad," I say.

Khara snaps her head around to glare at me. "Not *all* ants . . .?" Her voice is raised and her hands are clenched into fists.

"Fatchk didn't hurt you," I say, hoping to break through to the rationality behind her instant rage. "Did he?" I can see Khara is thinking, evaluating.

"It's true," Diane adds, before Khara can flare again. Tanner nods his head beside Diane.

"Do you know their language?" Diane asks.

Khara seems confused at this tangent, then shakes her head as if clearing it, and says, "No. I mean, not more than a couple of words here and there. And I don't even know if I'm right. I can't explain it, but I get feelings or meanings, sometimes, like I'm at least getting the gist."

"Would you like to learn?" asks Diane. She leans across me toward Khara as if she would like to reach out to comfort and pet her, but she doesn't move her free hand at all. I admire her control, her form of reaching out with body language, without touching. I determine to practice and learn this method, if only in respect for Khara's comfort.

Khara cocks her head, perhaps considering Diane's question: whether it would be better to avoid all things related to ants, or be better to understand them, even if she never speaks to them.

"Yes, I think so," Khara answers.

"Would you like to meet a nice ant?" Diane asks, as gently as if she is speaking to child, although they are about the same age, in their early twenties at the most.

Khara guffaws, something between a belch and a snort. "Fu-u-u-ck . . . ," she says, elongating the word into an obvious expression of incredulity. "As if."

Diane is cajoling now. "We know an ant," she glances over her shoulder at Tanner to include him in the statement, "and it's nice. Gentle, I mean. It doesn't want to hurt us or use us. It wants . . . well . . . to be friends, as crazy as that sounds."

Khara snorts again.

"Hey, man, it's true!" adds Tanner. "It's the weirdest thing! It's actually pretty cool!"

Khara stares at the two of them and Diane continues. "Are you afraid of getting close to ants?"

Khara's expression sours. "I don't get a choice."

"If you had the choice? Could you do it?" Diane asks.

Khara doesn't answer, but shudders.

Diane looks at me. "Samuel, look, we could use the help. We're only let into the garden to keep it up, and it's a big garden. We're falling behind and you know the queen. She's famous for getting rid of 'useless' humans. Nestra wants to share all the time. Khara could maybe take over some of the gardening duties . . . ."

Tanner takes up as Diane trails off. "Yeah! She could help with the work, we could help Khara with the language, you know, and . . . Yeah, this could totally work!"

I can see the benefits of what they suggest. Bell, Jan, and Eli work full days, Rex can't go near ants – not that he'd likely be recognized, but we can't take the risk; his computer skills are fantastic and he can't be lost. Tamerak needs me at the factory. Khara could slip in and ease the danger to Diane and Tanner by taking over some of their gardening duties.

"Khara?" I ask.

Bells raps knuckles on the table, a light staccato, for my attention. "She admits she doesn't have any other skills or contacts, Mate. This would be perfect," he says. I widen my eyes at Bell, chastising him without words for the negativity. Khara seems to hear the slight in his comment and her eyes dart to him before she looks down at her hands.

"Khara?" I ask again. She looks up at me, agony and pleading written on her face.

"It would help?" she asks.

"It would help," I answer.

After a moment she whispers, "What can I do?"

There is a release of breath around the table, as if the decision has been made, as if Khara has passed some test.

The rest of the meeting is spent with me explaining what I understand about Nestra, and Diane and Tanner explaining the odd form of sharing they engage in. Diane tests Khara's vocabulary and is incredulous at how much Khara understands. Even Khara seems pleased with her knowledge. Despite the lack of practice in speaking the ant's language, according to Diane, Khara's accent is excellent.

"She should be the one sharing with Nestra, not us," Diane says. "At first I thought she could help with the gardening, but... wow." Turning to Khara, she continues, "Girl, you are good!" Khara graces Diane with the most genuine smile I've ever seen from her. It's nice to see.

Diane gives Khara a few additional words to practice and the meeting breaks up, Diane and Tanner heading for privacy, Jan announcing she's headed for a bar.

"I'll join you," Bell says, surprising me. I expected him to stay, to welcome Khara, talk to her, charm her, try to put her more at ease. Or to talk to me about what's troubling him. I glance at him and he's looking at me. Despite his cheerful tone in offering to join Jan, his expression is grim. I cock my head, asking a question with the gesture. He shakes his head like he is disappointed in me and then flashes his eyes at Khara. Now I understand. I remember our last conversation about Khara, his warning she's not to be trusted. I've had a change of heart — of mind, I correct myself — on the subject, but it's clear he hasn't.

I'm not worried. He'll see, in time. I'm right about her. I smile and his mouth stretches into a lopsided grin, chagrin evident but unable to maintain his seriousness. After a moment, his smile becomes sincere and he raises a hand to his forehead in a mock salute before turning to take Jan's elbow to escort her from the room.

Rex stays, grinning at Khara, until I tell him he should go home. He leaves drooping like a disappointed puppy.

"Stay safe," Khara says as he's leaving, and Rex grins and blushes, taking the comment as encouragement of some kind.

Khara looks at me and I am, for no rational reason, uncomfortable at being alone with her.

"Do you know how to get back?" I ask.

"I don't think so," she answers. Bell's warning pops into my head and I can't help thinking she's saying this so I feel safe she couldn't find her way back here again, a double agent playing her part.

No. I'm right about Khara.

I lead her through the darkness to a street near the dorm where I met her yesterday and, with nothing more than a long glance at each other, we part ways.

All the way to Tamerak's home I think how much better Khara looks than when I first found her. How the lamplight glowed on her loose curls and youthful skin as I left her. Khara is beautiful – intense, scared, strong, . . . and beautiful – and I can't seem to keep myself from noticing the fact.

CHAPTER 25
KHARA

I'm wearing gardener's overalls like Diane and Tanner. We approach the small guard shack that leads to the queen's private garden, but I'm not as nervous as I was a couple of weeks ago when we first tried this. The ant-guard seems to have accepted there are now three humans working in the queen's garden.

Nestra's not in the garden, so I work alongside Diane, pulling weeds and raking. They haven't allowed me to trim hedges and trees, or to move and replant certain plants, since mistakes would be spotted and might cost the two of them their lives. I'm satisfied with the monotonous work they've assigned me. It lulls my mind and body.

Diane leaves me to speak to Tanner. I can't hear the words, but don't imagine they're about anything important. I think they can't go long between speaking, touching, kissing, and whatever the current conversation, it's just an excuse to be together. I glance toward them, and yes, Diane is looking up into Tanner's face while her hand brushes up and down his chest and stomach. She doesn't seem aware of the contact. It's a need she's fulfilling. Tanner's hand rests on Diane's shoulder. They smile. They kiss. As Diane turns to rejoin me, their hands each trail along the outstretched arm of the other, sliding from elbows toward wrists, from wrists across palms, until their fingers part. Tanner darts toward Diane, catches her hand and spins her back for another quick kiss. They laugh.

In the days since I have been watching them, I admit to a growing fascination. I've spent so long hating the idea of anyone touching me, cringing at the thought of a living creature contacting my skin. Even the odd street dogs that rub against passing legs, that humans stop to pet and feed – ugh. But days with Diane and Tanner – it's almost one name for one entity, Diane-and-Tanner – have awakened the notion in me not all touch would be bad. They take – and give – comfort with their small touches, caresses. I don't yet have the imagination that'll allow me to picture flesh against my flesh, but I admit to at least allowing the idea to intrigue me.

Diane smiles at me as she returns to my assigned patch of garden, leans toward me, and asks, "How's it going?" She's not leaning toward me to whisper, but seems to use the brief proximity to show closeness and friendship.

"Fine," I answer. I like Diane. I suppose she is a friend. Strange thought.

An hour later, Nestra enters the garden and I'm startled as I am each time at its size. For several minutes, Nestra sits under the large oak it likes. Diane and Tanner move toward each other and wait at some distance from Nestra, out of sight of the ant-guards that always escort Nestra to the garden. Twice I've joined Diane and Tanner in "sharing" with Nestra. This time I'll meet with Nestra alone.

Nestra approaches them, taking a meandering path through the garden to reach them, and they talk. Diane and Tanner each have a hand on one of the ant's lower arms. They're explaining the danger of not keeping up with the gardening. They're suggesting I'm not needed for the gardening and I'm willing to share alone. A small, insecure part of me wonders if Nestra will find this satisfactory. I believe Nestra would rather have Diane or Tanner if restricted to sharing with only one of us. I'd rather not touch this huge ant again, although it's proven to be as Diane and Tanner described and not like Ilnok.

I no longer shiver when the moment of contact comes. I no longer wish for the patch Samuel has asked me not to wear when I'm with Nestra — not that he needed to.

The three approach me where I wait.

"Nestra understands," Diane says to me in the ant language. "Nestra is concerned for us." Diane still holds the arm of the ant. She looks up toward the ant. "Nestra does not wish to endanger us."

"No," rasps the ant.

Diane and Tanner release Nestra and return to their work. The giant and I continue to stand where they left us. The extreme height of this one is intimidating, far outside the normal variations I've seen.

"Will you share, hive brother?" Nestra asks.

"I will share," I answer. I can't make myself put a hand on its arm — *his*, I correct myself, *hive brother* — as he leads me to a part of the garden farther from his ant-guards. We settle in the trimmed grass near a high back wall covered with fuchsia and white bougainvillea blossoms. We're facing each other, me sitting Indian-style, and Nestra sitting in the complex equivalent. Our legs almost touch.

Nestra looks to the flowered vines and says, "It is beautiful." He doesn't reach to touch me, doesn't force the sharing on me.

"Yes," I answer, turning toward the wall. A lizard runs a horizontal path along the wall behind the vines as I watch.

I can't put this off any longer. I'm here to establish trust and gain information. I can't do that if I'm reluctant to share.

With a deep breath and a suppressed shudder, I reach both hands toward Nestra's two lower arms. Contact.

"Your fear is less," Nestra says.

"Yes," I answer. "You are my friend. Hive brother."

"You still have distaste," Nestra answers.

"It is not for you," I answer. "You are my friend."

"Your master is sick," Nestra says, and I almost laugh with the immensity of the understatement.

"Yes," I say. I can't suppress a shiver thinking of Ilnok.

"I am your friend," Nestra says. "I am your friend," then repeats it a third time. His chanted words come with a feeling of comfort, soothing my trembling.

"Thank you," I say, and I'm thanking him both for his words and the feeling that accompanied them, although the feeling was my own.

"You taste. Diane and Tanner do not taste," Nestra says. "I share, you taste." Nestra's antennae dance toward me.

I don't understand what he's saying, so I don't answer.

Again, Nestra says, "I am your friend," and again I'm soothed by the words. I close my eyes as Nestra repeats his words, and – distinctly, this time – comfort washes over me.

"You are . . . ." I don't know how to phrase what I want to say. "You are . . . giving comfort!" I say.

"Yes. I share. You taste," Nestra answers.

I'm speechless. I think back to the times I've thought I understood the gist of Ilnok's conversations with his associates.

"You are surprised," Nestra says.

"Yes!" I answer.

"You are questioning," Nestra says. It's as if he's showing me what he can taste on me.

I take a deep breath, try to calm my bizarre excitement.

"I have questions," I say.

"Ask," Nestra says. Again, the wash of comfort. It doesn't seem to course through me from where my hands touch Nestra, nor do I smell or taste anything, as Nestra often refers to the process.

"You talk, you communicate this way," I say. I'm establishing what Nestra has already told us.

177

"Yes."

"Why with humans? You say Diane and Tanner do not taste. Why do you share with humans? Do you share with other humans?" The questions tumble over one another.

Nestra chitters with laughter, and it doesn't sound the same as when Ilnok and his companions laugh. It is delighted, although directed at me.

I smile and realize as I do I've never smiled in the presence of an ant before.

"You are my friends," Nestra says, sober again. Guilt washes over me, and I assume it is my own guilt for the duplicity of my relationship with Nestra, before I realize it comes from him.

"You feel guilty?" I ask. "Why?" I blurt before thinking that maybe I shouldn't ask this question.

"I am not permitted to share with my kind," Nestra answers. I'm sad for him. Or is that sadness from Nestra again?

"Why not? I thought this is how your kind communicates," I say. I'm confused.

"The queen has ordered this," Nestra answers. Before I can ask if this is some sort of punishment – it's clearly distressing to Nestra – he continues. "I am Shame Receptor. No one must taste this."

Shame Receptor. I remember this was part of the message I carried to Samuel.

"You never share?" I ask. I'm incredulous. This expanded communication is fascinating and speeds understanding, and it seems to me being forbidden would be crippling to a species that uses it — like being deaf or blind.

"I share with you. I share with Diane. I share with Tanner," Nestra answers, and again I'm awash in guilt.

"Why do you feel guilty?" A small spark of fear ignites as I wonder if maybe Nestra is being as duplicitous as we are.

"I am your friend," Nestra answers, and douses my fear in the wash of something warmer.

"Why do you feel guilt?" I ask again.

"It is wrong. But I desire to share. I desire to share very much," Nestra answers, and this time I'm rinsed with the familiar feeling of addiction . . . the desire for the patch, the knowledge that it's wrong for me to lose myself in it — the *ache* for it — and the near impossibility of resisting that desire. Almost I release Nestra's arm to reach for a patch in my pocket. I stop myself and press my fingers harder against his arms.

"I understand," I say. And then with a very real desire to comfort Nestra, I say with true emotion, "I am your friend."

A sigh gurgles out of Nestra and he leans his head back in the posture of subservience I have so often assumed with Ilnok. I find this inappropriate — that an ant should assume such a posture with me — then remind myself this is slave mentality, and discard the notion. Nestra is complimenting me with his trust. In that instant, I vow to keep his trust. I hope he tastes this, too.

"Hive brother," I say, and for moments we sit together, saying nothing more. I close my eyes feeling better than I have since before the invasion.

Nestra says a word I don't understand. I'm bathed in a feeling of confidence shared.

"I do not understand this word," and I repeat the word in his language.

Nestra repeats the word. Then: "Not brother. Not male."

"I thought all your kind were male except the queen," I answer. "All brothers."

"I am like the queen, but changed," answers Nestra.

"You can breed?" I ask. I'm not sure what this information will do for us, but I'm sure Samuel will be surprised and eager to hear it.

"No. The queen changed my egg. I am sister, but not queen," Nestra answers. "A brother could not accept the queen's Shame."

I don't know what to say. I don't know what this means.

"I am a sister," I say. "I am female."

"You are sister . . . ," Nestra sighs. Comfort, friendship, security wash over me. "This is why you taste. This is why we share," Nestra says.

"No," I answer. "Diane is also sister." It can't be that I'm female.

Nestra says nothing for some time. If his — her! — mind is anything like mine, the new information we've exchanged is swirling in small eddies, looking for a place to settle.

My throat tingles, and the red glow of my monitor splashes across Nestra's shiny black shell. I jerk my hands from Nestra's arms, panic coursing through me as if I've been caught here by Ilnok. As if he knows where I am.

Nestra raises her arms toward me. "Share," she says.

"I have to go," I say, planning the route to Dominique's in my mind.

"Share," Nestra says again.

I put my hands on her arms, impatient to go so I don't anger Ilnok. Comfort bathes me again. Even through my impatience, my muscles relax. I sigh.

"Remember comfort," Nestra says.

"I will. Thank you," I answer.

We stand and move toward where Diane and Tanner work.

Tanner sees the glow of my monitor and says, "We can go now, no problem." We don't know how the guard will react if just one of us leaves the garden. I pull my collar high over my monitor so the guard won't question why a human with an owner is in the garden.

"Come again soon, sister," says Nestra.

Diane looks a question at me, and I whisper in English, "sister." She looks startled, but knows I don't have the time for explanations.

"Sister Diane," says Nestra. "Brother Tanner." Diane's eyebrows rise.

"Sister Nestra," I say, and hear a small sound of choked surprise from Diane. "Friend Nestra."

We leave the garden, and Diane and Tanner accompany me to a sweetmead vendor near Dominique's.

"Be safe," Tanner says as I order the sweetmead. His face is full of concern.

"Let's talk soon!" Diane says before the two of them move into the crowd.

It's not until I'm raising the sweetmead to my mouth that I realize I can still feel the warmth of Tanner's hand on the back of my own.

I hadn't even realized he'd touched me. How strange.

CHAPTER 26
NESTRA

The small antechamber off the throne room is darkened. I am aware of this fact despite my trance state as I accept the poisonous Shame from the queen. The queen has become so erratic in her behavior over the last lunar period that I, in fear for myself, have adopted the habit of not descending into the full depth of the trance that keeps me safe during downloading. It is a measure of the queen's increased insanity that I fear the queen more than the poisons that invade my body.

I lap at the shimmering globe of the queen's strength, little tastes only, and concentrate the dew-like glow toward strengthening the wall between my own sanity and the filth that courses into my body. I turn my thoughts away from any kind of measurement of how much more of the queen's strength this small diversion requires. Having already succumbed to taking from the queen during every session to maintain my own health, the small addition required to compensate for the lightness of the trance seems insignificant.

I would not have registered the scratch at the door to the antechamber but for the internal fire of the queen's explosive rage that follows it. The queen does not disconnect from me to respond.

After a second scratch, a brother enters, and – this surprises me – the queen's rage abates instead of erupting at the unpermitted entry. I lighten the level of trance even further in my curiosity, until I recognize the identification of Dev'ro in the queen's chemistry. I deepen the level of trance again at the sudden weakening of the wall within me as the flood threatens to overwhelm me. I am aware Dev'ro reports something to the queen, but am not aware of the contents. I can sense the report pleases the queen.

Without warning, the queen breaks from me. It is only the now heightened level of the trance that keeps me from drawing my palpus back in surprise.

"Do it," orders the queen, and then, without focusing on me, extrudes her palpus and connects again.

I do not know if this is a normal occurrence during downloading sessions, as I have always been at such a deep trance level only the queen's purposeful withdrawal and dismissal revives me to consciousness. I do recall there have been downloading sessions that ended with a brother present who had not been present at the beginning, or a brother missing who had been in the presence of the queen when downloading started. I have also had downloading sessions in the throne room with courtiers present, although not often. Through the dim swirl roiling inside me, I wonder how much business of the court has occurred without my knowledge or understanding during these sessions. I chant a level lower to hide the budding fear that rises in me at the thought that, had I not deepened my trance just before the queen disconnected, I might have given myself away by retracting my palpus. It is clear the queen expected she could break and speak and reattach without awakening me.

Dev'ro finishes his report but does not leave the chamber. I vacillate between deepening and lightening my trance with an uneasiness that tastes bitter with danger. With this newfound knowledge the queen conducts business during these sessions — and in private sessions such as this one — I do not know what to expect, and fear the queen will taste my uneasiness.

The trickling off of the flood coming from the queen comes again and realize this same lessening had come before the queen broke from me last time. Bracing myself to remember to keep my palpus extruded, I lighten my trance to listen. The queen breaks from me.

"It seems the end is almost here," the queen purrs and, through our connection, I can feel her pleasure rising.

"No more than another lunar period before enough brothers hatch. We can dispense with the final humans then," Dev'ro answers.

The blood lust that rises in the queen at the thought of wholesale slaughter makes me want to curl in upon myself, but I do not move my limbs from their awkward angles, do not shudder as I wish, do not draw my palpus in. Only a small part of this continent still contains humans, but I thought – given the queen's proclivities – she would save these alive. I think of the comfort I took from the humans I shared with – especially the human Khara – and used the memory of that comfort to calm myself. I refuse to focus on the thought of those humans gone.

"We will no longer be . . . inaccurate . . . when we report to home planet that this planet which is so perfect for colonization contains no intelligent life," Dev'ro says, with the rasp of a laugh. "Although I will miss my pets." Again the rasp of laughter.

I contain my surprise at the mention of the home planet none of us have ever seen – since all but the queen and the crew of the ship have been hatched either in orbit around, or on this planet.

"I would make a gift of yours for you to keep, if it were not so dangerous to leave any alive," answers the queen, and again, the blood lust that rises within her threatens to sicken me. As much as the queen enjoys her daily ritual torture of the soft unfortunate creatures, the prospect of unrestrained slaughter excites her even more. I deepen my trance to relieve my queasiness, as well as my mounting confusion and fear. While she will not likely react to the queasiness, fear will alert the queen to my wakefulness. The realization of this fact causes me to flee even deeper into the trance. Deeper, deeper, until I have almost achieved the unconscious state normal to downloading in the past. I am not aware when the queen fastens again except through the sudden renewed flood of blackness washing through me. I am not aware when Dev'ro leaves the chamber.

I float back into awareness at the queen's command. She is as subdued as she always is since I started stealing her strength, but she also exudes a satisfaction that is frightening. I push the swirling information I have learned – that the humans, as a race, have not long to live and a deception of home planet is involved – into the back of my mind and hope to be dismissed to cleanse myself and think. I push myself up from my reclined position. I refuse to focus on the queen while waiting for the words of dismissal. I balance on trembling legs and clear my mind, waiting for the blessed words.

"Come," the queen says. I am startled and jerk my attention to the queen, fearful she has detected something.

"The throne room," says the queen. "I am tired, but I must, and you will stay with me. I will need you again."

I almost sigh with relief at the mundane order. The queen has detected nothing. "Yes, Majesty," I say, and hope yet again my anxiety is not detectable. I hope my practice of separating myself from the queen will now help me isolate and suppress my inner turmoil.

***

As usual, I stand to the side and behind the throne. While I never focus on the business of the court because it does not interest me, this time I deliberately unfocus in an effort to maintain a light trance which will keep me from sorting my thoughts into their frightening constituents and keep me from exuding my fear and confusion.

The audience comes to an end. The queen has raged at more than one courtier, but this is ordinary now and I expect it of every audience. As the queen becomes more unstable, the frequency of her rages increases, and the reasons for the rage are more obscure. I cannot concentrate on pitying any of the courtiers today. In my opinion, most are as twisted as the queen.

Dev'ro leads the queue of courtiers toward the queen as they sort themselves into order according to their current ranking. I rouse myself. Queen Tal raises herself from the throne with obvious effort and moves to the front of the dais for the dismissal of the small gathering.

The queen's exhaustion is showing.

I wonder if this is as evident to any of the courtiers. For once, I cannot bring myself to feel guilty about the theft that leaves the queen less than powerful before these diseased flatterers.

Starting with Dev'ro, one by one the queen touches the courtiers in the ritual of dismissal. After the queen touches Dev'ro, he steps aside to allow the others to move toward the queen. Each of the remaining courtiers leaves the throne room as soon as they are dismissed. I do not doubt several are happy to be escaping with their lives.

A brother four from the end of the line touches the queen. The queen, instead of gesturing toward the rear of the room as she has for each of the others, jerks her arm up and closes her powerful top pincer on the throat of the brother. Yellow body fluid starts to ooze down the front of the headless courtier before the body crashes to the floor. I am the only one present who utters a sound, and it is a barely suppressed scrape of surprise.

Dev'ro steps forward and gestures to the guards for the removal of the body. The three remaining courtiers do not move or otherwise appear to react until the body has been dragged to one side. Then, each after the other approaches the queen with every appearance of confidence and, as though nothing has interrupted the ritual, accepts the queen's dismissal and leaves the room. None move with unusual haste, although I am sure each wants, with my same desperation, to be quit of the queen's attention.

Dev'ro slides to the queen's side. The movement is a question in itself, but I can also smell the strong sour green-yellow flavor of the query. Dev'ro has been as surprised as I am at the execution.

"Traitor," the queen hisses. Then, "*Traitor!*" she roars. After a brief moment of stentorian breathing, the queen says, "Dev'ro, he reeked of treachery. *In my own court.*"

Dev'ro does not react despite the cacophonous rolling screech which follows her words.

Once the queen has quieted, though her breath puffs and rasps, Dev'ro says, "I had heard a rumor of treachery." He pauses, and then continues, "But I could not believe such a thing could occur."

I do not know what response Dev'ro was hoping for, but it cannot have been the response he receives. The queen's head snaps around, both eyes fix on Dev'ro, and her pincer flies to his throat. I am sure the fluids of a second body will soon join the smeared fluids of the first. I wish I could close flaps over my eyes as the humans often do to obscure their vision. But the queen's pincer does not close.

Without dislodging the queen's pincer from his throat, Dev'ro leans his head back and opens his arms in total subservience. He says, "I am your servant, Majesty."

For the space of several breaths, neither moves. Then the queen lowers her pincer.

"I wish to hear of such rumors in the future," hisses the queen.

Dev'ro maintains his subservient posture, but answers, "Of course, Majesty. It now seems they have credence. As your most trusted servant," – I wonder if this is still true – "I will take care of it."

"And kill every brother in that traitor's hive. Today." The queen whirls away from Dev'ro even before he answers, "Yes, Majesty."

I have started to follow her when she, without turning, yells, "You are dismissed, Nestra!" and disappears into the antechamber behind the throne.

Dev'ro stands looking at me before leaving the throne room. His mouth is pinched into his usual frightening smile, but I

190

know he cannot be as confident as he appears. I am sure if I was nearer Dev'ro, I would taste the unmistakable aroma of humiliation and fear.

As I move down the corridor toward my quarters, I realize the queen will be even more dangerous after today, seeing treachery in every gesture, every scent. With my new knowledge and the resultant confusion, I might not live much longer than the pitiable humans left on the planet. If that long.

CHAPTER 27
QUEEN TAL

Another long day and I remain reclined on the cushions after dismissing Nestra from the latest session in my bed-pit. I watch as she creeps from the room, looking old and tired in her careful, pathetic, weak movements. She is full – I know – from the latest downloading session. The sight of her is disgusting.

If I had any strength, I would leap up and kill her right now.

The thought is followed by an involuntary, weary sigh. I should rise instead of allowing the brothers moving at the edges of the room to see me still languid after the session. Even so, I do enjoy the constant perfume of their fear as they work to avoid my notice. I snap a pincer toward a brother who passes too near me and inhale the delicious aroma of his reaction. A grin splits my face. I am too tired to move.

I am never tired. I am strong!

Still I do not rise.

I am never tired, comes the thought again as I raise myself to two arms, *except after my sessions with Nestra.*

This connection comes with a burst of fury that provides an energy of its own. The sudden power propels me from the bed cushions, and I leap on the nearest brother, expending my murderous rage in a furious ripping, slashing, and tearing which leaves fluid and body parts strewn around the room. The rich perfume from the remaining brothers thickens. With the combination of the intoxicating aroma and the pleasure of the kill, I am almost recovered.

After a brief pause during which I direct a vicious grin at the remaining brothers – *Let them worry they are next!* – ecstatic in my bloody release, the brothers begin removing the delightful, gruesome scraps.

The soft whirring of applause sounds from the entrance to the bedchamber. I spin to see Dev'ro, mirroring my smile with a twisted smile of his own. Then he bends, head back, and says, "I am here, as requested, Majesty."

Fury again courses through me as I scent Dev'ro and realize he, too, revels in my bloody performance. I want to jealously guard the pleasure for myself. I want fear surrounding and smothering me, not this smile. For a heady moment I picture adding his fluids to those gracing the walls of my room, and I stride toward him. Then the scent of his own blood lust and confidence reaches me and I feel the pleasant flush of being in the presence of a similar, hungrily destructive soul. I am tempted to turn and devour another brother, this time for his pleasure as well as mine. Weariness washes over me at the thought.

Damn Nestra!

"Come," I say, and move past Dev'ro into the corridor.

As we stride toward the throne room, Dev'ro walking to my rear, I turn and say, "Order a new Shame Receptor prepared for me. I will come to the breeding room and start it after this audience. Nestra has outlived her usefulness."

The flavor/scent of understanding and obedience which wafts toward me is strong enough that no response from Dev'ro is necessary. It comes to me with a taste of his pleasure which must be caused by imaging how I will dispose of Nestra. Perhaps I will let him watch.

In just a matter of weeks, I will have a new Shame Receptor and again will be strong. I vow never to keep a Shame Receptor as long as I have kept this one. Perhaps the weakness in them is contagious.

I am so pleased with my decision that I want to kill something. Celebrate.

Later. When I am not so tired.

CHAPTER 28
KHARA

I'm hurrying to make the meeting. The session with Ilnok was blessedly short although this does leave me in the now-unusual position of trying to navigate the streets in patch-induced stupor as the one patch I use for the sessions hasn't worn off yet. I shouldn't go in my condition – covered with fluids, reeking of my own pungent sweat, exhausted and stoned. But I look forward to my meetings with Nestra as salve to Ilnok's version of "sharing." I need to make this meeting to find out if anything has changed before I join Diane and Tanner in the garden later.

In my meandering path streetside, it seems less crowded with humans than usual, and with far larger clots of ants.

I stop outside a bar and I'm sure I can smell whiskey and beer through the open door. I can't go in. I won't allow myself, although it smells of home. I shake my head in an effort to clear it, but the faces that move past me blend together. In the aggregate features, I see despair.

When I look up again, I'm lost, buildings tilting, street twisting. I hope I can find my way to the meeting. I hope I'm not being followed. I have to stop and clear my head. In the blur and gray-brown-gray fog of my surroundings, I'm being careless. It's better that I miss the meeting. I need to eat.

I sit on a cement stoop that grinds at my ass bones through the thin cloth of my pants. I push Mexican rice and bits of chicken into my mouth with my hand. Watching and waiting, I measure the slow return of my awareness for over an hour. I feel better with the solidity of food where earlier only sweetmead filled me, and then was emptied from me. My head is clearing. I look at my surroundings again.

I'm not far from the street I should be on, but I would never have found the meeting through my haze. I move through pedestrians again aware of their sparsity, if only because I don't need to twist and step to avoid them. I'm late, but I hope my friends aren't gone.

When I enter the back room of the small bar, only Samuel and Bell are there. I've missed the meeting. Samuel raises an eyebrow and gathers in my sorry appearance with a practiced eye. He says nothing. His face is tight with worry. I wonder what new crap has come up.

"My dearest Khara. Please take my seat." Bell jumps from his chair and offers it to me. It isn't necessary. There's another chair.

Bell is being so much more pleasant to me now – not like he was when I first joined the rebellion. Then, he was always watching me, waiting for I-don't-know-what. Now, he treats me with the same charm he uses on everybody else. Even so, I don't like Bell. For some strange reason, he reminds me of Ilnok.

"Diane and Tanner will be back in an hour. Can you be ready to go with them?" Samuel asks. He is asking if I can be washed by then. The softness of his eyes doesn't condemn my condition, but I shouldn't go to the garden like this.

I nod and drop into the offered chair next to Samuel, and Bell pulls another to my other side. I rest my head on the table for a moment before I ask, "Anything new?"

"Electronics factory, State Street," Samuel says. His thick lips stretch tight and his forehead furrows between his eyes. "The humans were taken from it two days ago. Mid-shift. None have been seen again. The three that were with us who were at the factory haven't reported in."

I'm confused. Why would the ants close a factory? I wait.

"It's staffed with bloody ants now," finishes Bell. "Like they don't bloody need us anymore." His words indicate concern but his manner doesn't. It's one of the things I don't like about Bell. He's too damned cheerful all the time.

Now I understand Samuel's concern. I put my hand over his as it rests on the scarred brown tabletop. It's how I would share with Nestra, comfort her. I realize, as my hand rests on Samuel's warm hand and callused knuckles that I don't need to pull away. Samuel looks at me, startled but seeming appreciative. He doesn't pull away. I can comfort Samuel this way, too. This pleases me.

Bell says, "We'll get them. We'll beat the ants."

When I look toward Bell he's watching my hand rest on Samuel's. Then he looks at me and mimics my gesture, putting his hand on my free hand. I jerk my hand away and stand up from the table.

"Don't touch me," I say. I keep my voice low, and pray the venom isn't obvious. I don't say this because I don't like to be touched, but because I don't want to be touched by Bell. There is something about his suavity that just rubs me the wrong way.

Bell raises his hands to the sides of his head, palms forward, as though I'm pointing a gun at him. He smiles, chin ducked and head cocked to one side, trying to look charming, I guess.

"He didn't mean anything, Khara," says Samuel.

"Certainly not, dear lady. I simply forgot myself." He lowers his hands and holds out one for a handshake, then remembers and pulls it back toward his chest. "Would you allow me to make it up to you? Perhaps dinner...?"

I'm such an ass. Bell is a good guy.

"Sorry, Bell. Just touchy." I try to smile but I'm not as good at that as he is. "You don't need to make it up to me. My fault totally."

"Very well," he answers with one of his signature bows that only involves the head and shoulders. "My invitation remains open." As he walks toward the door, he says, "Got to run, Mate." Just as he's passing through the door, he turns and looks at me. His face is blank. Not angry, not smiling. When Samuel looks up, Bell's teeth flash at us in a brilliant smile. He says, "I wish a good evening to you both."

Something happened there. Something. But I can't put my finger on what.

*****

I wait for Nestra in our usual meeting place, at the back of the garden near the flower and vine covered wall. I'm sitting cross-legged, leaning back on my arms, enjoying the coolness of the shade. I should be helping Diane and Tanner, but I'm tired and they're patient with me. I'm watching them through the trees. They meet for a brief kiss and for a moment, I imagine the comfort of that same warmth on my lips. I'm startled my imagination has progressed this far. I stand, deciding to join them, if only to distract myself from this confusing thought with the monotony of weeding or digging in the cleanliness of warm rich-smelling soil.

Nestra comes. I'm again settled in our meeting place before she reaches me. I'm glad to see her. I can no longer imagine her as belonging to the species of monster that inhabits our planet.

"Sister," I say, smiling, and am struck again that I can consider an ant a friend and enjoy our meetings so much. Nestra settles to the ground without speaking. I reach for her lower arms but she pulls them away and out to her sides.

"Sister Nestra?" I'm confused.

"You are my friend," Nestra says. "Trusted friend?"

"Of course!" I answer. I can't imagine the purpose of this question. "I would never betray your trust. I . . . ." I want to say, "I love you," like a child to a beloved grandmother surprising as this revelation is to me – but I don't know the words. If she would let me touch her, she would taste this on me. "I . . . we are . . . bond-sisters." I'd reach for her again, but I can't disrespect her obvious desire not to be touched.

"I will trust, sister," Nestra says after a pause. She sighs as if she has decided something burdensome. She brings her lower arms together in front of me.

I fill my thoughts with trust and affection and place my hands on her arms. A panicked fear fills me and I pull my hands back in my fright. It takes me a moment to realize the fear is Nestra's and not mine.

"You're scared!" I almost shout the words. I take a deep breath and release it through pursed lips and then ask, "Why are you so scared?" It occurs to me that when I first started sharing with Nestra I would have feared for myself, but I can't bring myself to distrust Nestra. We've shared so much.

"The queen," Nestra says. I understand fear of the queen, but Nestra has always been near the queen without this level of fear.

I wait. When she doesn't continue, I reach for her again, filling my mind with memories of shared comfort and thoughts of calm. It is hard to maintain this with Nestra's fear coursing over me, but I inhale deep breaths and try.

Nestra sighs, but can't shake off her fear.

After several minutes like this, she says, "I will confess." Again I wait. Guilt, fear, trust wash over me from Nestra and I battle to overcome the negative emotions while reinforcing the trust. After another minute, she says, "I . . . steal from the queen."

"What?" I'm not asking her to repeat herself, but what she has stolen. Nestra will feel the intention behind my question.

"Strength," she answers.

"I don't understand," I say, although I'm sure she can sense my confusion.

"Strength. In fugue state. I take strength from the queen."

I can't begin to imagine how this can be done, but there is much about the communication between ants I don't understand.

"That's good, isn't it? I mean, for us?" I'm referring to Nestra and me. "If she's weaker?"

"No. She is more unstable. More angry."

I now understand Nestra's fear. "Did she catch you? Are you in danger?"

"All are in danger near the queen," Nestra answers.

My thoughts swirl through the imperfect understanding that exists between us, as I attempt to continue to comfort Nestra.

"All humans will die by the end of the next lunar period," Nestra says. It takes me a moment to break from my spinning thoughts and register this next statement. My own fear courses through me with a jerking stab.

"What? Why?" I can hear my own panicked breaths panting from me. I want to run to tell Samuel, run to safety — although there is nowhere safe.

"No longer needed. Sufficient brothers will hatch." Nestra tries to wash me in comfort but our combined fear overwhelms her efforts. I can smell the cold sweat that has sprouted all over my body.

"Can you put the strength back?" I ask. It's ridiculous, but it seems Nestra's theft has caused this problem and maybe she can fix it. That we will not die if she returns what she has stolen.

"This will not stop the death of humans," Nestra answers. Sympathy and comfort. In my panic, they seem fruitless, an icing over putrid flesh.

"I will help humans," Nestra says. "I will help my sister." Affection, fear, affection — waves that crash against me.

Again, as if my brain is trapped on a speeding circular track, it takes a second before her words have any meaning. Then, "How?"

"My sister Khara will tell me," Nestra answers. Trust. Affection.

I have to meet with Samuel. There has to be a way. I don't want to die, but more than that, the idea of all humans . . . gone . . . is a tragedy bigger than my death.

"How will all the humans die?" The pit inside me opens with the question.

"This I do not know," Nestra answers. "My apologies." I am awash with her regret.

Great. If they use the same weapon they used at first, on the other side of the planet, we'll be just gone in a flash – disintegrated or whatever. No chance to fight.

I push my prickling fear aside and concentrate again on sending Nestra trust and love.

"I am a traitor," says Nestra. This snaps me from the whirl of panicked thoughts overlain by my efforts to transmit friendship.

"No!" I say. "The queen is a traitor. You are my sister!" This seems to appease and comfort Nestra, and I feel a wash of relief, as if I had granted absolution of some kind.

"I must go now. I will come again," I say. I haven't told her I'm part of a human rebellion – not because I don't trust Nestra, but because I have Samuel's trust and won't betray it – so I can't tell her I have to meet with him to discuss this.

As I turn to leave, I say, "One lunar period," more to myself than to Nestra. One month.

We have one month to win and live. Or one month until we die.

CHAPTER 29
SAMUEL

I've gotten a message from Fatchk. It came through a trusted source, but he got the information through dubious channels. It could be a trap. Yet, I have to take this risk.

It's been weeks since Fatchk contacted me, which only adds to my anxiety. With the shocking information Khara's gotten from Nestra, there's no more time for planning, no more time for building up our resources. We're not ready, but we have to act. I've passed this on to my outside contacts in Lithonia, Stone Mountain and Forest Park but have heard nothing from Douglasville. It's as if all contacts from there have disappeared. I hope that doesn't mean what I think it means.

Based on what we've learned about the queen's "sickness" and how it's spread, I've changed our local plan from joining in the generalized attack to a focused assault on the capitol complex. And Fatchk may have information that will make the difference between probable death and certain death.

Khara offered to come with me. I need a woman for the meeting, as it's to take place in an ant club under the cover of supplying male and female humans to a patron. If this isn't a trap, the patron will be Fatchk. I planned to take Jan, but she can't get away from her factory dorm for this meeting. Khara volunteered. For some reason, this makes me uneasy.

"We are to enter the club as a couple," I explain, as we hurry toward the meeting. She doesn't answer, so I explain further. "We link arms." I pause, waiting for the injunction against touching to be raised. Still Khara says nothing. "We don't allow any other patrons to separate us. We say we are borrowed as a favor between brothers." Our monitors will help with this ruse. I open my collar.

Khara nods, concentrating on my explanation, as she matches my movements and opens her own collar.

I'm exasperated at what seems to be a failure for her to understand my point. "We will need to be always touching. Arms linked at least. Perhaps other touching." I watch her face for reaction. I hate that I'm pleased at the thought, but there it is.

"I understand," Khara answers. She isn't looking at me now. She seems amused.

"Can you do this?" I ask.

A faint smile touches her lips, and her eyes flick to mine and away. "I think I can handle it," she says. "I'm touched by Ilnok every day and live through it," she says, then continues with added vehemence, "even when I'm sure I can't stand another fucking moment."

Her words come with an internal stab that Khara feels she needs the same endurance to tolerate her master's abuses as to link

205

arms with me, and then I'm angry with myself for my ridiculous desire that she feel different toward me.

"Not that you're anything like that monster," Khara adds, "I didn't mean that."

The adolescent elation that flurries through me at her statement angers me further. I can't allow myself this distraction. The stakes are too high. In my self-directed anger, I increase the pace of my stride.

After a minute, Khara's hand clutches at my elbow, then closes around my arm. "Hey!" she says. "Slow down, I can't walk that fast."

I look down at her hand and through a weak smile she says, "See?"

I slow my stride until Khara can keep up with my brisk walk. She drops her hand from my arm.

Inside the club, we're escorted to a reservation book, and then to a room on the second floor. My worries about the difficulty of getting to the meeting room were over-blown. Khara clings to my arm throughout the procedure, and I don't tell her this now seems unnecessary. Her breast brushes my triceps as we stand outside the appointed entrance, and the prickle-skinned pleasure that warms me causes me to vow I'll never again touch Khara outside of this one mission.

Our escort scratches at the door, opens it, waits until we enter and then closes the door behind us. Fatchk is there, alone. The relief that torrents through me clears my head.

"This is Khara," I say. He's met with Khara — the last message I received from Fatchk was through Khara — but even Fatchk has difficulty recognizing differences between humans with whom he is unfamiliar.

Before I can say more, Fatchk gestures at the four walls and ceiling as though a king displaying his castle, and says in haughty, loud tones, "I do not need names, creatures, I need drink, I need pleasure."

In an instant, I am alert and worried about what Khara's reaction might be. My eyes dart toward Khara, expecting fear and distrust.

Khara's face is placid. She bows her head back, spreads her arms wide, and says, in a cool monotone, "We are your servants." I'm impressed at her frigid reserve and perfection of reaction. She doesn't have my reasons for alarm at this most un-Fatchk-like behavior from a trusted comrade.

Fatchk gestures at Khara, and Khara walks, still open, to stand before Fatchk.

"Remove," Fatchk says, flicking a pincer at the front of Khara's loose shirt. Khara pulls her shirt over her head and drops it to the floor. I am horrified and excited. Even in my uneasiness over Fatchk, my eyes dart to the rounded profile of her young breasts. She points to her loose pants — an unspoken question — and at Fatchk's gesture, kicks off her sandals and drops her pants to a pile on the floor. She is nude. Too thin, but shapely. And beautiful.

At another gesture from Fatchk, Khara drinks a proffered bowl of sweetmead and lies back on cushions, head back. I am aghast at what I am watching, both because Fatchk is involved, and because of Khara's obvious complacency with the procedure. I have to find a way for us to escape from this apparent trap, but can't yet fathom how this might be done. I am . . . distracted . . . by Khara's nude body sprawled before me.

Fatchk dips his large head toward Khara, palpus extended. Khara pushes her head back and opens her mouth. The palpus writhes between Khara's lips. The excitement I am beginning to show in response to Khara's open nudity and prone form is doused by my revulsion at this scene. I'm frozen. Even my thoughts are frozen around the bare determination that I have to get Khara out of here.

Fatchk removes his palpus and leans again toward Khara's face, mandibles clicking, head nodding toward one of Khara's ears and then the other. If Fatchk clips or hurts Khara . . . . I step toward them.

Fatchk glances up at me and Khara rises from his lap. She is expressionless, although her eyes lock with mine from the moment she begins to rise until she is beside me, turning way, turning back to face Fatchk.

"Remove," Fatchk says to me. I don't move, other than to clench and unclench my fists, confused at the point of this trap.

"Go," Khara whispers through lips that don't appear to move. "Go," she repeats, and there's urgency in her command.

I remove my clothing. I drink the sweetmead offered. I recline. I open my mouth. I hope to mimic Khara's acceptance of this, but Tamerak has never asked such things of me and I don't know what to expect. Fatchk's palpus moves into my mouth. It is dry and scabrous, like the tongue of a cat. I prepare for the gag reflex that must come as the palpus moves toward my throat. But the palpus stops just inside my mouth, and I feel a slight – almost provocative – suction against my tongue, nothing more.

When Fatchk removes his palpus and begins moving his mandibles toward my head, I understand.

"Nestra . . . ," Fatchk breathes toward my left ear.

". . . must . . . ," as a breath toward my right ear.

". . . discover . . . ," toward my left ear.

". . . who . . . ," toward my right.

Fatchk pulls back and centers his head over my face, and with the faintest click, I am sure I hear, "Friend."

I don't understand this scrap of a message, and hope Khara will have more to add. I can't ask for clarification. Fatchk has gone to a vast convoluted effort here and I can't betray that effort with stupidity.

Fatchk releases me, reclines backward in a human attitude of boredom, and with the back talon of a foot, flicks the small pile of Khara's clothes away from the cushions.

"Bring me drink and then go," he says, without looking toward either of us. "I now wish rest."

Khara, naked, lithe in her movements, brings Fatchk a drink and then dresses.

I feel the self-consciousness pulling my clothing back over my body I didn't feel in removing them.

As Khara and I leave the room, I look back at my friend. I fear for Fatchk, and am confident we are not betrayed. Given how short a time we humans have left and the danger to Fatchk that necessitated this charade, I'm certain this is the last I'll ever see of him.

Back on the street, Khara releases my arm. She has lost the languid fluidity of her movements through the club and the glassy look in her eyes. She seems bursting with pent energy.

"Human traitor in rebellion," she says. "What did he say to you?"

I don't answer, feeling the shock of Khara's statement in my gut and groin. Fatchk must believe the human is high in the organization to have risked this meeting just to ensure the information got to me.

"Nestra must discover who," I answer. "Will she do that?"

"The question is *can* she," Khara answers. I sense defensiveness in her answer. "I'll ask her tomorrow, if I can."

"Tell no one," I say. Khara doesn't answer but throws an exasperated look at me to say she's not stupid.

At the next intersection, we part, Khara heading toward a streetside dorm. I have to arrange another meeting of my cadre. I have to determine how to ferret out a traitor without announcing that I know. Betrayal is black within me.

***

Khara is with me again. I try to suppress the question within myself of why she has volunteered to help me again, whether it's an indication she . . . . No. She's trying to help the rebellion. She trusts me and is confident in my abilities. As I am in hers. She's shown a cool capability in all she's attempted. Our meeting two days ago with Fatchk could not have been handled better.

The thought of the meeting recalls a vision of Khara, nude, splayed over the cushions. I move an inch or two farther from Khara as we walk, to avoid touching her arm by accident. I *must* clear my mind of Khara if I'm to remain effective. This mission may cost us our lives, and this unwanted emotional – and physical – reaction Khara arouses in me can't be indulged.

Tonight, we commit outright theft. Breaking and entering. Rash, and not to be considered, except for the fact we only have time left for rashness.

We round the corner at the back of the old warehouse that, if our information is correct, is now a weapons cache. With only a month left, our careful stockpiling of trucks, gasoline, food, medication has become moot. We need weapons.

We'll keep walking, feigning drunkenness, if the ant-guard is still at the door.

There's no guard. The bulb above the door is broken and the far end of the alley is in blackness. Although this is as planned, I'm uneasy at what may be hidden in the shadows.

Khara and I walk to the far end of the alley. The depth of the darkness there makes it difficult to search, but I take one side of the alley as Khara walks in silence against the wall of the other side. We meet at the far end. She shakes her head to show she found no one lurking behind dumpsters. We walk back up the alley in the same way. We wait in the shadows.

A human figure turns the corner and staying close to the warehouse wall, moves to the darkened door. After a moment, and a piercing metal clang, the human walks back the way he came. Again we wait. No alarm is raised.

Khara and I emerge and walk to the door. The lock and chain are on the ground to the side of the door. The door hangs open a mere crack. There's darkness beyond. I pull the door mere inches and both of us squeeze through the opening, the broken glass of the light bulb crunching beneath our shoes.

In the pinhead of light from a laser pointer, we move through crates upon crates of machine pistols and automatic rifles and other weapons confiscated by the ants. I locate the boxes of ammunition and begin marking the boxes to go with the weapons we'll take. Khara begins moving the heavy metal ammo boxes toward the door, one by one. She is preternaturally silent as she moves.

The screeching brakes of a large truck sound through the warehouse. This will be the garbage truck with empty dumpster mounted to the front that my people are bringing. Trash trucks are the only vehicles the ants allow on these streets – and not often enough – we wallow daily in garbage. I turn off the laser pointer and wait. I don't know where Khara is in the darkness.

The door shrieks open, and a voice yells from the doorway, "YOO-HOO!" I am certain the booming shout can be heard for blocks around this building. I move behind boxes. I can see the dim outline of a human body standing in the open door. I can feel the pulse in my neck, hear the pumping rush in my ears.

Laughter sounds. Light gleams from a flashlight in the hand of the man at the door.

"Come on, Mate, transport has arrived. Where are you?" Bell's voice. My breath bursts from me in relief and adrenaline anger.

"Bell . . . Jesus," I say, loud enough for him to hear. The light beam flashes toward me.

"Asshole," Khara whispers from behind me. At the moment I agree with her.

In minutes, my people have loaded the dumpster to the top, and Bell leaves me with a clap on the back and another laugh. "Be back soon, Mate," he says as he switches off the flashlight before going out the door. I hear the trash truck move away down the alley, picture my people hanging to the outside like infant marsupials.

Khara and I go back to marking ammo and moving boxes toward the door.

The door screeches open again. I can't hear the trash truck outside. Again, I kill the light and duck behind boxes, although I half expect another of Bell's jokes.

"Halt!" grates the unmistakable voice of an ant.

Through the pounding pulse in my ears comes Khara's calm whisper.

"Fucking hell."

CHAPTER 30
NESTRA

It is evening when I am called once again to the queen's bedchamber. The halls are quiet and empty except for the small scrape of feet against carpet – mine and that of my ubiquitous escort.

In the past, I would have preferred this setting – the silence, the darkness, the lack of courtiers and public nature of the session. I would have used the setting as an additional calming factor to help ease me to the trance. This evening I regret there will be no court audience, no courtier in private meetings with the queen.

I need information.

Sister Khara has asked a favor of me, a favor I am only too willing to accomplish, despite the personal risk.

Sister Khara has told me of a human resistance, a group of humans who hope to survive the annihilation planned by the queen. I have long sensed the underground river of resistance in sister Khara, the secrecy, and now I understand. I, having already betrayed my queen, have no trouble siding with the humans in their efforts. I know humans and my people can co-exist in peace, as evidenced by my bond friendship with sister Khara, and to a lesser degree, with Diane and Tanner, the humans first courageous enough to approach me and generous enough to share with me. And now there is a human traitor – a wash of guilt coats the inside of me as I remember that the word applies to me as well – who threatens this life-preserving effort. Sister Khara wants to discover the identity of this human.

This will be difficult, as humans cannot be identified by the scent/flavor visual/voice patterns that allow my kind to accomplish sure identification. However, even brothers refer to certain prominent humans by their names for this reason. I must discover the name. And to do this, the queen or a courtier must reveal this information during a downloading session upon which I can eavesdrop.

This quiet night session will bring me no information.

Indeed, the queen has been summoning me more and more often in the evening. I do not doubt this is so the queen can rest after being depleted by me – another wave of guilt – instead of needing to proceed with the business of court. As such, my failure to help sister Khara is caused by me, which causes another surge of guilt.

This is no way to approach a downloading session. I push my thoughts away from my negative ruminations and began the preliminary treading toward fugue state.

Bright light glares from the opening to the queen's bedchamber. For a moment, I think there might be an evening meeting planned after all.

The scene that greets me as I step to the doorway sickens me and breaks me from my efforts at tranquility. The razor spears bursting down from the ceiling above the bed cushions glint with the recessed bright lights that shoot down through them. Impaled on several of the centermost is a human, one long knife stabbing through the back of its head and emerging through a torn eyeball. Blood is still falling, in slow droplets, down onto the bed cushions, and onto the queen, who lies there enjoying the mild suffocation induced by having her pores blocked by the sticky thin red substance.

"Majesty," I croak, wishing to turn away from the sight. The required bend of my head backward only brings the dead human into better sight. Perversely, I focus one lens on the drop of human blood growing fat at the end of one of the rapiers before it falls to the bed cushions.

"Come."

When I lower my head, the queen is gesturing to a long cushioned lounge to the side of the room. Cruelty pinches across her face as she again gestures away from the bed, as though she is punishing me by failing to allow me to wallow on the foul bed cushions. I hold back a sigh of gratitude. Let Queen Tal believe she is being cruel.

CARAPACE

I fall into the trance that prolongs my sanity. I fall deeper into it than I thought to allow myself, craving the unconsciousness it brings me during downloading. I feel little guilt as I sip at the queen's strength.

Then the climbing swirl from unconsciousness at the end of the session. It must have been a long session as the bedchamber has been cleared of the human debris. The body no longer hangs impaled, floating in the silver teeth. I suppose the queen's workers are quite practiced at cleaning such things with efficiency.

A groan grates from me as I move to stand, a groan which is echoed by the queen. For the first time ever, I think I catch the red scent of fear from the queen, but then decide it is merely trance-confusion of the scent with the visual of red blood still covering parts of her shell.

After an initial flail of effort, the queen rises with a jerk, and I am washed with the passionate black anger that pours from her on the heels of the fear. Before I can wonder at the cause of the queen's anger, she strikes out at me, throwing me to the floor at the side of the bed cushions. I lie without moving as she advances to stand over me. With another flashing movement, her pincer bites at the edges of my throat, scratching into my shell.

The crimson scent of my fear balloons through the room, and I know it to be my last sad excretion. I wait, motionless.

"No," says the queen. "I cannot... yet." Then she turns and moves toward the lounge we have just vacated, only now revealing exhaustion in her motions.

"Get me Dev'ro," she says, and a brother scurries toward the back entrance to the room.

Before I can finish my obeisance, the queen bellows, "Get out of my sight!"

The flavor/scent of fear remains fresh on me all the way back to my rooms.

CHAPTER 31
KHARA

I can still hear the echo of the ant's grating bellow of "halt." Samuel doesn't move. I don't move. I can't breathe. My heart seems to want to drown its own beating in the churning fluids of my stomach.

Samuel's hand touches my arm, slides down my wrist to clasp my hand. He pulls me with slow, quiet steps toward the back of the warehouse through the ebony darkness.

Piercing light blazes throughout the open warehouse. I close my eyes against the sudden brightness and stumble. Samuel pulls me along by my hand, strong fingers squeezing mine. I'm happy for the contact and for his strength.

We run, crouched, around towers of boxes. I hear the scraping and pounding of many ants entering behind us. I have no desire to stand and count the number of our enemy.

We're going to die.

Samuel crashes against a stack of boxes with a shoulder as we run past, and the tower topples and falls. The loud *zing* of a shot is followed by a ricochet of light as an ant fires toward the crashing sound. Samuel weaves and wends his way around crates and metal boxes like a mouse running a maze. My mind screams through an accelerated monologue of curses, but I don't voice them.

We're trapped at the back of the warehouse, a cinderblock wall cutting off any further escape. A vision flashes into my mind of Samuel and me, still clasping hands, being fired upon – firing squad fashion – against the impenetrable wall. I grind to a halt behind Samuel, but before I can gain my feet, he pulls me again along the wall to the left.

Samuel climbs crates, which teeter but don't fall. I stand at the base, abandoned, although I know I can't climb after him without bringing him down with the wobbling crates. I hear ants searching, but no speech between them. I can't distinguish how many search, or even how close they are to finding us.

At the top of the stack, Samuel stands before a mesh-wired window we can't break or open. He turns his back to the window looking over the whole of the warehouse. He shouts, an incomprehensible guttural roar, and then jumps down toward me. Several shots are fired, and through my panic that Samuel has been shot, the crash of glass sounds above us.

Samuel runs back the way we came, but as I race to follow he whispers, "Go back!"

I'm confused, but as I hesitate, he picks up a heavy metal ammunition box and turns to run toward me again.

"Hold this," he whispers as we reach the crates at the window, and "stay here!" He runs again. He runs farther this time.

Just before I lose sight of him among the boxes, he ducks his head and slams a shoulder into a tower of crates like a professional football player. The tower totters, and Samuel pushes again until it too crashes to the floor. Several more shots light up in that direction, but Samuel races toward me.

He grabs the ammunition box from my hands and again climbs the boxes toward the window, hampered only a little by the heavy container in one arm.

I know what he'll do. He'll be lased before he can do it.

Samuel doesn't hesitate as he reaches the top of the stack, but slams into the window, ammunition box held in front of him like a ram. The glass doesn't shatter, but breaks away from the rotting frame in a jagged flapping sheet. More shots, and now they're burning and splintering the wooden crates and cinderblock around me. Samuel is out… but is he alive?

I pull the lid off a nearby broken crate and reach inside. My hand closes on a pistol, which I pull out and throw as far as I can to the right of where I stand. Scraping of scurrying ant feet and more bright shots. I imagine the burning sensation of a laser blazing through me. I round to the darkest side of the tower of crates and climb with all the strength of my panic fueling me. Shots and more shots, light lancing around me, no longer spaced by brief pauses. As I reach the top, a searing burst of fire lances across my cheek.

I kick against the crates and throw myself over the sill, ignoring the ragged flap of mesh-wired window hanging from the top of the frame that swings outward with my passage. I'm still falling through the air when I hear the crates crash to the ground inside the warehouse. Samuel breaks my fall with outstretched arms and then I'm on my feet again.

"Thank God," Samuel says, before he again smashes my fingers in his grip and pulls me into a run.

A phalanx of ants rounds the corner moving toward us. I slam into Samuel as he turns to run in the opposition direction. The ants close on us with unnatural speed, the length of their legs and stride eating up ground. Samuel jerks left into an alley and my joints feel as if they'll separate with the strain at shoulder and wrist. Samuel pulls trashcans and broken furniture down to fall behind us. A chair hits my leg, but this doesn't slow me down.

Down alleys, across broad streets, more alleys, over walls, through buildings, again Samuel runs as a mouse in a maze. Samuel knows this maze as no other can, and the sounds of pursuit are no longer nipping quite so close. Samuel dashes into the entrance of a crowded bar. The loud music, blue and green lights, and dank close smell of other humans drown the smell of my own sweat, the sound of my breathing, the cacophony of my heart.

Samuel slows and moves with leisure through the crowd. His hand remains clamped on mine. Then we're out a back entrance, and Samuel breaths, "That ought to dilute our scent." We run again. I'm lost, but Samuel isn't.

We run, and continue to run. Samuel no longer holds my hand, pulling me along behind him. This makes it easier to run. I keep pace with Samuel, although I'm not sure whether that's because he's slowing his pace for me, or whether my panic makes up for his better physical condition.

I expect any moment for ants to encircle us. I know why Samuel continues to run – the greater the distance between the ants and their quarry, the more our scent will have dissipated.

The humans around us move toward their nighttime destinations – frames in a slow motion film. We run and leap past them, amongst them. They all ignore us. Defense mechanism.

Another turn and I'm in familiar territory, but am lost to Samuel's secret navigation of it. He dodges to the right up a tight alley just past one of the dorms in which I sometimes crash. We scramble and jump over piles of trash. He turns into a low doorway, which leads to another alley I don't recognize. The pace slows only when we round corners. The muscles in my legs burn. I need Samuel to help pull me over a chain link fence. His large hands are strong and sure with me. We run, and turn. And run. Again I recognize the neighborhood, but not the connection to the one we just left. Samuel understands the maze of this city with a clarity that is stunning, confusing.

My lungs ignite with a chill fire. I can't breathe. My lungs can't process the air I need. Samuel must have a destination in mind and I stop trying to anticipate it, concentrate only on continuing to move. My abdomen tightens into a knot that stabs and stabs with each step. Samuel doesn't appear to be slowing, nor to be in need of slowing.

"Samuel." The word comes between bursts of breath. "I need. To stop." More bursts of breath.

I need a drink. The thought comes unbidden and I don't like its intrusion. I recognize the cop-out it represents. Again, with pain and a stab of breath, "Samuel!"

"Hang on. Hang on, Khara. Hang on." Samuel almost sings the words in time to his steps. I marvel at his controlled singsong whisper.

As we turn another corner he reaches a large hand back for mine to pull me along. With his efforts to move me again supplementing mine, I risk a glance behind us. I don't see the closing black mass I've been imagining.

"They're gone," I gasp. "Samuel!"

He pulls me sideways into a brick alcove in the alley wall. His iron grip on my arm keeps me from smashing into the wall, but jolts my arm again. Pain shoots through my shoulder. The alcove is ten feet deep and ends at a large metal door with a large lock in the bar across it. I hope I'm right that they're gone. We're trapped.

Samuel pulls me to him, back and into the deepest shadows. With his arm across me, body pressed along my side, I feel protected. Samuel squeezes and rubs at my jolted shoulder while watching the mouth of the alcove. After a moment pressed against each other, both breathing in sharp bursts, Samuel creeps away toward the entrance. I have an almost uncontrollable urge to grab at him. I want his protection.

He moves against the brick. Despite his size, he melts against the rough wall. His fingers dance along the jagged surface, his feet move without sound. He controls his breathing until I can hear nothing but my own. I concentrate on slowing my own breathing, but my body still screams for air. My lungs are determined to snatch it from the night around us.

I hold my breath, listen. Breathe. Hold my breath again and listen. Nothing. I'm torn between my desire to melt farther backward into the darkness, and to join Samuel in gazing up the alley. He shifts, and I tense myself for running. He watches for another couple of seconds and then relaxes. He presses his forehead against the brick.

My God, we made it.

Samuel creeps back to join me. He puts his mouth close to my ear and whispers. "I don't think they've tracked us." He looks toward the alcove entrance again. "We can go soon." He touches the warm metal collar at the base of his throat no longer covered by his torn shirt. It rests in a mist of sweat on skin.

His eyes move over my face and he groans. "Jesus, Khara." I reach my hand up to the burning area on my cheek. "Here," he says and pulls my cheek toward his shirtfront. When I back away there is a red gash across his shirt. He looks at my face again and says, "I don't think it's still bleeding." He pulls my cheek toward the opposite side of his chest, and holds me there longer than the dabbing requires.

Through the tear in his shirt, Samuel's chest hair tickles against my chin. I'm torn whether to pull away or relax in this comforting warmth. I close my eyes. Even above the sound of my still loud panting, I hear his deep, quiet breaths.

I can't remember the last time a human held me. It flashes through my mind that I want to back away, put distance between our flesh, but I realize before the thought is done, that it's just habit. I like the feel of Samuel against me. I raise my hands and rest them against Samuel's back. It is broad and strong. I slide my hands across and down his muscular back, thin shirt wet with the sweat of his exertions. I breathe in the smell of his fear, his skin. He is delicious. I fight the sudden urge to lick his chest and taste the salt on him. The muscular pliant softness of his body – so unlike the ungiving press of ant armor – strikes me as weakness and yet arouses me.

My skin tightens into gooseflesh, but I'm not cold. I look up at Samuel and realize with a hot shiver I want to kiss him. I want his thick lips against my mouth where only hardened mandibles have ventured for months upon months.

He is looking toward the entrance of the alcove. We are pressed so close. My need for his mouth is an ache in my chest, in my gut. I wait for him to turn his face to mine, but he doesn't.

"Samuel?" I whisper. My voice is rough from the hard breathing and the running. He doesn't hear me. "Samuel?" Louder. I can hear the pleading in my voice and hope he can't.

He doesn't turn toward me. "Khara, don't." His arms are clenched at his sides. The muscles in his back are taut. He's fighting with himself or with revulsion. I'm frightened he'll push me away. I'm paralyzed wanting to clutch him closer to me and afraid of what his reaction may be.

"Kiss me, Samuel." I'm begging. I can feel my face flushing as I hold his body against mine. I want him. I'm terrified he won't do me this kindness.

After what seems an hour, he turns his face to mine. His eyes dart back and forth as he looks down into my eyes. He seems to want to ask me something, but I can think only of the unfamiliar, thrilling sensation of his body pressed against me, his warm breath on the skin of my burning cheek and on my lips. He doesn't push me away.

"Kiss me, Samuel," I say again. I raise myself onto my toes, pressing my body tighter against him as I lift my mouth to his. I'm braced for the intimate stab of rejection. I don't close my eyes. I need him as much as I have ever needed a patch or a drink. I'm shaking with need as my lips touch his.

His mouth is warm and wet and open. My hunger is returned with a fierceness that incites me. His massive hands are in my hair. His mouth devours mine. One hand closes on the back of my neck above my monitor, pulls me into him. The other hand moves to my back, pressing my hips to his. My fingers dig into the muscles of his chest, his thigh.

228

I push my body from his and lift my shirt, wanting it off. I want his skin against mine. His mouth doesn't release mine, so I can't lift my shirt over my head. I pull the remains of his shirt up. I press my bare chest against his. My flesh against human flesh in an electrifying moment, bodies slick against each other with the sweat of our exertions. My hands fly across his body, caress, pull at him, hungry for the feel of him. His breathing is no longer controlled.

My body is on fire, alive to the sensation of us. Pressed against the brick, I want to drag him into me with an astonishing violence. He sucks in a rough breath as I reach into his pants, tug down on his pants. In only a few frenzied moments my own pants are on the floor of the alley.

Samuel slows the pace. He cups my uninjured cheek in one hand and looks into my eyes. He smiles. We are both panting. Then he kisses me again, and with eyes closed, I'm only sensation, surrounded by strength. His large strong hands clasp my naked ass, and lift me on to him.

He is urgent, and gentle, and as hungry as I am. For a time that remains immeasurable, we are breathing each other, sharing each other. None of the humans or ants that pass the mouth of the alley appears to spare us a thought.

I'm beyond thought, intoxicated.

CHAPTER 32
BELL

I'm craving a ciggie. However, smoking is either a shared occupation – for those of us who have them – or a solitary endeavor. Given how few of us do have them, it is, under most circumstances, the latter. I'll have one when I'm done meeting with Samuel. It wouldn't do to appear to have an endless supply. My fingers twiddle at the pack in the front pocket of my trousers as my bum grinds into the wooden crate I'm sitting on.

"You're sure your contact can deliver that much gasoline?" Samuel asks from his perch on his own crate. We are meeting in one of our regular spots, what used to be a storage room, one with exits at either end – two exits, something we tend to like.

"I'm quite certain." I remove my hand from the temptation in my pocket. "When have I ever let you down?"

"Never, Bell." His eyes flash to mine for a moment of camaraderie, and he puts his big hand on my shoulder.

I like Samuel, I truly do. He is so genuine and warm, even though he spends most of his time trying to deny any human frailty.

230

His eyes return to the brief notes he's been consulting. "I wasn't questioning *your* reliability, but that of your contact. I'll have Eli coordinate the pickup," Samuel says. He seems distracted as he continues, finger flicking at the top corner of his notes, eyes running over the unpainted plasterboard walls without seeming to see them. "Keep your ears open for any caches of med supplies or weapons. Can't have too much of either."

"Always, Mate. I take it you think we have enough vehicles in working order? What do the numbers look like?"

"We'll never have enough of anything, but the cell directing the trucks is doing a great job. Nothing for you to concern yourself with," Samuel says. He tosses the answer off as if he's saying "don't worry about it," but I know Samuel. He never tells more than he needs to. Not because he doesn't trust me, of course, but for the safety of the rebellion. It's deuced hard to get information out of Samuel, which is a good attribute for the leader to have.

It's late and our meeting's wound down, so I stand and stretch. I've another meeting to get to and then later, a delightful lady to meet.

Samuel looks up at me as I stand, a strange expression on his face. He opens his mouth as if to say something, then drops his chin and shakes his head.

This could be interesting.

I settle to my uncomfortable seat again. "Samuel. What's wrong?"

"I..." He doesn't get any further.

"Samuel, Mate, this is me. Bellamy. What is it? Maybe I can help?"

"I shouldn't say anything."

But...? I don't push him, don't move. His shoe scrapes across the cement floor as he adjusts his position on the crate.

"But," he says. He glances up at the water-stained, buckling ceiling — it's almost an eye roll — then leans closer to me and says, "We have a traitor — a human traitor — in the rebellion."

"What?" My stomach flutters — my characteristic first response to danger. "Who? What do you know?" My hand moves to my pocket again, to the ciggies.

"I don't know who. Khara..." — sweat blossoms on the back of my neck during his pause — "When Khara and I met with my ant contact, that's what he told us. It's too dangerous for me to try to meet with my contact again, so Khara is going to try to get Nestra to find out more."

"I should bloody hope so," I say, because it is expected. But this is not good. I knew Khara was going to be trouble.

"Don't say anything to anybody about this," Samuel says, running a hand over his short-cropped, sandy blond hair. The hair on the top of his head remains standing — something that would look ridiculous on anyone else, but on this ruggedly handsome man only increases his look of determination.

I raise my right hand as if taking a pledge and put the other on my heart.

He sighs. "I probably shouldn't have told you."

I put my pledge hand flat on my thigh, rub it to remove the perspiration there. "Hey. Mate. This is me, Bellamy."

"Yeah. I know, buddy. See what you can find out, will you?"

"Priority one. It's our lives at stake," I answer. I need to get out of here. The air is too close. I put on my best chipper smile. "Got to run for now, but I'm on it."

"Yeah," Samuel says, gaze directed at the wall again. Now I understand his distracted and dejected manner. With this news, we all have reason to worry.

When I'm a block away walking through the darkness, I light a ciggie, inhale, then inhale again without releasing the first drag, let loose the double puff in a slow stream of smoke through pursed lips.

Khara.

When Samuel first wanted to bring her into the rebellion, I knew she'd be trouble. I tried – Lord knows I tried! – to convince Samuel it was a bad idea. Drug addict. But he didn't listen, did he?

My mind flashes to the first time he brought her to meet us. She was nervous, but no more than I.

I was sure she would recognize me. Samuel, despite his attempt to hide it, is so possessive of her, so attracted to her. What would he do if he knew I'd seen her in the buff, doing the disgusting things she does for her master? I've met with her master often enough while she was there. I thought at that first meeting she would out me in front of the whole group.

But she hadn't. She acted like she'd never seen me before. Those drugs of hers must be mind-blowing.

After that, I'd thought myself safe. I'd lightened up towards her.

Now... what to do?

I take another long drag and let the smoke trail out of my nose, letting it burn away the stink of the street. I look at my watch. Realizing I still have time before my next meeting, I slow to a stop, press my back against the rough blond brick between a supermarket and a restaurant. I have to think.

Khara. With her connection to Nestra she is more of a danger than ever. I take another drag.

She has to go.

I'm satisfied with the answer that floats into my mind as if it's not my own. I never liked her anyway.

But even with Khara out of the way, Samuel remains a danger. He will work with relentless determination to ferret out the traitor. Even without Khara.

Samuel has to go.

I'm less happy with this thought. I like Samuel, I truly do.

I stride across the pavement again, trying to escape this latest idea, wanting to find a different answer. Another deep inhale and then I toss the remains of the ciggie a good five feet in front of me so I can crush it out with my next step. Only half smoked, but I have more.

I push all thought from my mind for the few minutes it takes me to get to the back alley of the Westin Peachtree. I go in through the entrance that leads to the kitchen, ride a short way up in the service elevator and make my way to the bar.

"Brother Temsa'a," I say as I approach my contact. I slide onto the stool beside him. He pushes three packs of ciggies to me and I stand to put them away – one in each of my front trouser pockets and one in the breast pocket of my shirt.

"Credits?" I ask. I don't often ask but when I do, I get whatever I ask for.

He picks up the wand that sits in front of him on the bar top and I pull my credit ring from my watch pocket.

"Five hundred," I say and watch as my balance rises by the requested amount. More than enough to keep me in my nice little flat for another month, eating what I like instead of the mush so many of us are forced to live on.

"Tomorrow, at about this same time in the evening, the rebels will be picking up a large delivery of petrol," I begin. I give him the same details I have just given Samuel. I don't feel too bad about this as Samuel told me Eli will arrange the pickup. Eli is smart. He'll make sure his people are not captured when the transfer is interrupted. And if they are, whose fault but theirs?

Temsa'a raises a pincer and the bartender brings me a chilled vodka. I lift the glass in salute to my benefactor.

I like Temsa'a, I truly do.

CHAPTER 33
SAMUEL

My day at the factory ends after an eternity. The workers leave under the watchful eyes and occasional searching pincers without incident. I bow backward as Tamerak takes his leave of me. As with most evenings, Tamerak does not require me. I move through the streets in a manner I hope looks aimless, confirming I am not being followed. I have to meet with my people to coordinate the various deliveries of the goods and equipment and weapons we have managed to cache.

I hope Khara is there.

In the week since our robbery of the weapons warehouse, Khara has been a constant companion, if only, at most times, in my thoughts. Instead of confusing or distracting me, our sudden relationship seems to have clarified me, intensified my focus on the importance of our survival. In the random moments we have found to be alone together, her barriers against physical contact seem to have crumbled – in fact, inverted – and she insists on touching me, on me touching her. When we are with the others, her reserve returns, but I don't know if this is to preserve herself or to preserve decorum in the face of our relationship.

All of my top people are at the meeting: Bell, Jan, Eli, Rex, Diane and Tanner. Khara. The various deliveries are coordinated in short coded bursts – my people know their jobs well. They each report on the status of the planning for the first strike of the rebellion. From what Khara has learned from Nestra and what I've discovered through Fatchk, our attack is focused on the queen and those closest to the queen – those whom both Nestra and Fatchk have referred to as "sick" or "ill."

Our hope is that resistance will be negligible once these "sick" leaders are removed. If this isn't the case, then we'll go out fighting, which is better than dying as we do now, by an ever increasing rate of disposal. The streets are less crowded by the day and stories of mounds of dismembered human flesh abound. Jan, Eli and I work at the factory, wondering if each day will be our last as we are replaced by ant brothers. I look to Tamerak for signs of a coming purge, but don't know if he'd give any indication, despite his apparent affection for me, his pet.

Khara's monitor lights during Bell's report regarding our weapons cache and all eyes flick to her. She clenches her jaw and the red gash across her cheek squirms as she stares toward the middle of the table, unwilling to meet our eyes. Her hands on the table are clenched white.

"Fuck this," she murmurs. Her eyes rise to mine and she says, "I can't do this anymore. Not anymore." It seems our relationship has lowered her resistance to Ilnok, her acceptance. In this way, I've hurt her.

"It'll be over soon, Khara," I answer, pushing aside my concern for her, my regret at what the next few hours will bring for her. "Don't quit when we're so close. Don't get yourself killed right before we're free." *Free to be together without the torture you endure*, I want to say, but don't.

Khara's eyes are locked to mine, and I don't look away. I know what I'm asking of her and can't blame her for the anger evident in her rigid posture.

Khara rises from her chair, and the loud sound of the chair legs scraping away from the table fills the room. She steps around the chair, pauses, then lifts the chair, spins, and launches it at the wall behind her. Her scream of "Fuck this!" drowns the sound of the splintering wood.

Diane leaves the table and the room. As Khara stands there, breathing in heavy pants, Diane returns with a bowl of sweetmead and holds it out to Khara. After a moment, Khara sighs and takes the bowl. Diane leans toward Khara to whisper something I can't hear, placing a hand on Khara's shoulder. Khara doesn't shrug the hand from her shoulder, but nods, drinks the sweetmead down and leaves the room. She doesn't look back at me, and I am pained by my inability to reach out and comfort her. For long moments, I look at the dark hallway into which Khara disappeared.

"Well, that was dramatic," Bell says, bursting the bubble of silence in the room. Several of us chuckle in appreciation of the return to normalcy, although none, I would guess, find Khara's situation funny. Bell finishes his report. The meeting breaks up, and everyone leaves except Bell.

"Nowhere to be?" I ask. I had hoped to spend the rest of the evening with Khara, so I have no plans.

"Mate, I have information for you that you aren't going to like."

"The traitor," I say. It's not a question.

Bell nods, still serious, which is unusual but not unexpected given the topic.

"Sit down, Mate."

I sit. Bell sits. Still he says nothing.

"Out with it, Bell. We need to start figuring out what to do with this . . . this . . . ." I can't think of a polite word to use.

"Bloody bitch?" Bell finishes for me. I'm stunned at the uncharacteristic curse word. Then his statement registers.

"It's a woman?" I ask. My mind runs through women I know to be involved in our organization. I can't think of many, as we've compartmentalized as much as possible. It's impossible to suspect Diane or Jan.

"It's Khara," Bell says.

For long moments my mind can't fix on who Bell means with his brief statement. When it registers, a laugh bursts from me at the ridiculousness of the thought. I wait for the joke I know is coming.

Bell doesn't laugh, but looks down at his hands, his carefully manicured nails, still serious. "It's Khara," he says again.

I can think of nothing to say. I don't believe it.

"I'm sorry, Mate, really. I know you worked hard to get her in, I know you *trust* her, but it was all a ploy." His strange emphasis on the word "trust" seems unfair.

Now I'm angry. I trust Bell, I know from his manner this isn't one of his jokes, but I'm angry. I feel betrayed. I'm confused by the juxtaposition of two people I trust. I shake my head in denial, but then force myself to focus so I can determine what Bell knows. I can't afford an emotional reaction right now, although my instinct is to push Bell backward out of his chair.

"What do you know?" I ask. The quiet rationality of my voice is a feedback loop that calms me. He'll tell me what he knows and I'll be able to convince him he's wrong.

Bell explains – again – that Rex's apparent rescue was designed to provide an entrance into our organization. He reminds me of how much of the ant language Khara appeared to know at the beginning and how quickly she became proficient. He explains the interrupted robbery on the weapons warehouse was due to information passed on by Khara – "Despite overwhelming odds against it, you got away, right? With Khara?" He tells me that Khara's frequent "calls" by Ilnok are as often to report on the organization as to serve Ilnok's other demands.

240

It all sounds plausible. But I still don't believe it. I let Bell keep talking.

"I'm not trying to suggest anything, but...," he says. His voice is lower, confidential.

"Yeah?"

"After all that 'don't touch me'... She's given in, hasn't she? You're now... intimate?"

My mind goes back to my thoughts on the way to the meeting. Her complete turnaround. It must show on my face because Bell says, "I thought so."

He clears his throat. "Last bit," he says. I cringe. I don't want to hear any more. "Her master, Ilnok, has now been elevated to the queen's council." My fists clench. I want to hit him, but this is Bell. "Check it out yourself," he says. "You have contacts. What do you think that means?"

I jerk myself out of my chair. Nausea descends on me and I sit again.

"She joined them, Mate, as I tried to warn you before," he finishes.

My chest is in a vice. My relationship with Khara is a weakness. I'm angry I let her draw me in. Then a thought strikes me.

"What about Nestra? What about the information she's been getting from Nestra?"

"Probably lies, half-truths. Whatever they want us to know. You'll remember Khara only put up a token fight before getting into the whole sharing-touching thing with Nestra. Maybe she was trying to get Diane and Tanner out of the loop. Which she has effectively done, Mate." He pauses and finishes, "Maybe she likes what they do to her." For the first time since he began this conversation he smiles and I'm angry again.

"That's not true!" I say.

"Oh, really, Mate?" The smile is gone.

I don't know what to say. "I don't think she likes it. If she's with them, it's not because she likes it."

"No 'ifs' about it, Mate." A pause and then, "I don't guess there's any question what to do." He drums on the table, a rough staccato, with a sharp accent on his thumbs. When I raise my eyebrows at him, he says, "We have to kill her, Mate. By now she's given them all kinds of information about our plans. Thankfully, we haven't set a date yet and all the equipment stores were in code. You're the only one who knows where everything is, and how to get to it, and through whom."

I don't interrupt Bell's musings. I can't think past the fact that I have succumbed to emotional attachment and in so doing, endangered us all.

"We can't kill her," I say. Am I saying this because it's tactically sound or because I can smell Khara on me, feel her hands on me?

"I think we have to..." he says, but this isn't something I can think about right now.

"I'll work on it," I say interrupting him.

"Right," Bell answers, and rises from his chair. He claps me on the back and says, "We'll handle this, Mate. Let me know what I can do." He heads for the darkened hallway rubbing his hands together and saying, "Ah, the night is still young."

***

The next day, Khara waits for me outside the factory. She is across the street, sitting at a small white plastic table eating potatoes, but her eyes are on mine. She smiles as she puts another spoonful into her mouth. I feel sick to my stomach.

From two different ant contacts, I have learned Bell was right. Ilnok has been promoted to the group closest to the queen. This can't be coincidence.

I can't avoid Khara, and in fact, don't want to. I've decided how to handle her. Feeding her misinformation would be difficult, as all the rest of my people would have to be briefed on the misinformation so that any meeting Khara attended would be fraught with lies for Khara to take to her patrons. We have trouble enough finding time to meet and coordinate our plans as it is.

And I cannot bring myself to kill her or order her execution.

I approach her once Tamerak dismisses me. She still smiles, but is no longer eating. She stands as I reach the flimsy table, and rushes to me, throws her arms up and around my neck and raises herself on her toes in clear expectation of a kiss.

I remember her initial reticence at being touched and compare it to this behavior. In hindsight, the turnaround isn't believable. I turn my face away, and with hands on her shoulders, hold her away from me.

"Samuel?" she says. "What's wrong?" She tries again to lean toward me, pulling on my neck.

"Stop it," I say. My head is still turned away.

"Samuel?" she asks. She drops her arms.

Satisfied she is no longer trying to force a kiss on me – I think of the ease with which she allowed Fatchk to enter her mouth at his last meeting and shudder – I look down at her. Her eyes brim with unshed tears. "What's wrong?" she asks again, and this time her voice quivers.

She's very good at this. I have to push forward or find myself succumbing to her wiles.

"I know what you are," I say.

"What am I?" she says. Her voice is high and quiet, like a child's.

"You work for them. You're the traitor." I am not surprised by the anger in my tone, but Khara is. Her eyes first widen and then narrow.

"What are you talking about?" she asks. Her tone is no longer child-like, is not yet sharp.

"You're the one. You worked it quite well." I swallow. "Here's the deal. Don't ever come back. Don't ever try to attend one of our meetings. I'll kill you if you do." I want to tell her not to let me see her again, but I recognize this is for my sake, not the rebellion's, and refuse the confession of emotional attachment.

Khara looks dazed and flops down to the bench, knocking against and almost upsetting the plastic table. When she looks up at me again, confusion is written across her features and her eyes are pleading. She raises her hands toward me, palms up, a plea.

"Samuel, that doesn't make any sense." She blinks at some inward vision, shakes her head, and drops her hands to her lap. "Why would I tell you Fatchk said there was a human traitor? Why wouldn't I lie?" When I don't answer, she finishes, "If it was me? Why?"

"You weren't supposed to be at that meeting. Fatchk didn't know who the traitor is, so he gave you the message. You didn't know his message couldn't be checked on, so you told the truth." I take a deep breath, but keep from saying, *and then seduced me, so I wouldn't look to you.* "Or you told me so I wouldn't suspect you, of all people."

"No, Samuel!" she says. "I'm not a traitor." She stands, comes toward me, arms reaching for me.

"Don't touch me," I say, and recall how many times I heard these words from Khara in the beginning.

Khara freezes mid-motion, her mouth open with a small exhale of disbelief, tears welling and then rolling down her face, bumping over the welted scar forming on her cheek.

"Don't ever let me see you again," I say. "I don't care what you tell your masters — I don't imagine you'll tell them much if you don't want to get punished. Shoot, tell them you're still coming to meetings and lie to them about what was said. You ought to be good at that."

I turn to walk away. We'll have to be more careful on the streets now. Khara knows several of our hideouts and meeting places.

I've only taken a step when she says, "I trusted you." She sounds pathetic. She sounds like she's pleading although her words are accusatory. I am across the street when she yells.

"You fucking *bastard*! I *trusted* you!"

Without thinking, I turn to look at her. Her fists are clenched, her face is fierce. She's no longer pleading. She's angry.

She's no angrier than I am. Though whether I am angrier at Khara or at myself, I don't know.

CHAPTER 34
KHARA

Refugio's. I can't walk, so I can't leave. I can't close my eyes. When I close my eyes, the room spins and the bar tilts, and I know I'll fall off my stool. I look down and see my hands gripping the bar top. The vision of my hands twists in one direction and then in the other. The ant tender brings the bottle to pour me another whiskey, but I wave him away. I need to throw up.

No sooner realized than done. The tender cleans the foulness from the bar top while I fumble to find my pocket and another patch. I look down to help my hand find its way to my trousers pocket, as it is caught in fabric bunched in my lap.

I find my pocket, but no patches. I've stopped the habit of carrying handfuls of the patches and must have used up the few I just bought. It occurs to me I might have some in the other pocket, but after more fumbling, I discover that pocket empty, too.

I feel better, having puked. I'm sure I'll feel better still if I spew again. I don't have to think long of this possibility before the surging wave mounts and I throw up again over the still wet bar top. The room isn't spinning with as much fury, and I want to put my head down on the bar. I wait until the tender has finished cleaning my latest donation from the counter. I close my eyes and lower my head.

I wake with a foul coating on my tongue and teeth, and raise my head. I motion to the tender, and he brings me another whiskey. I use my first sip to rinse my mouth before swallowing.

Fucking bastard. I trusted him. He made me feel human, and only now do I remember being human hurts too much.

I need another patch. Each time the patch wears off my mind runs in the same furrowed circle. I want to forget. I want to stop the pain.

I slide from my stool, move across the bar toward the door. I have to go to the bathroom, but I need a patch more. I leave Refugio's in search of a vendor. I don't have to go far. Over the last month – or more? – the ants have made patches more and more available. Stores and street vendors are everywhere as if they want us to use as many as we want. That should tell us humans something, or at least those of us who haven't chosen oblivion as our new favorite pastime.

Pocket full of patches again, I slap another to my jugular. I begin the walk to the nearest dorm as the swirl of dim colored lights begins behind my eyes. I find a bed and sink into the twisting blankness that at some point turns to sleep.

**

I wake crying. I can't remember my dream, but remember I have reason enough to cry even without the dream. The fact that

I'm alive is reason enough to cry. I let myself sob and hiccup, let the tears and snot come. No thoughts.

When my tears start to taper off, my mind turns again to the pain that will help me continue, that will help restart the engine of my self-pity and anger. My mind turns to Samuel.

I slap a patch to my throat, hoping to wipe myself empty again, but before the wave can wash over me, I think, *Samuel was wrong to do this to me.*

I struggle against the drug with the next realization. *Samuel was wrong!*

I pull the patch from my throat and throw it to the floor. I'm not the traitor. Samuel now feels safe, and continues to plan and operate, but *there is a traitor.*

I have to find out who the traitor is – for me, for the human race. I'm angry at Samuel, I'm hurt, but I know him. He wouldn't have done this to me if he hadn't gotten bad information. He's gullible and stupid and... Anger wells up and the heavy, painful feeling in my chest comes crushing down again.

After washing and eating, I know I have to talk to Nestra. I've got to find out if she has discovered the real traitor. If she has, she's probably told Diane and Tanner, and then maybe Samuel will see . . . . No, at Samuel's instructions, I told her not to discuss the traitor with anyone but me.

It's up to me. I have to find the traitor, bring incontrovertible evidence to the rebellion – to Samuel – and prove he was wrong about me. If I don't, with the help of the *real* traitor, the ants will win. Despite the wish to escape the pain I'm in, I don't want to die, don't want all of us to die.

I go to the garden. Diane and Tanner are, in all likelihood, inside, so I can't enter. Hunkered into a recessed doorway, I wait, watching the ant-guard and the small unobtrusive street entrance to the garden. I'm shaking.

After three hours during which I have fallen asleep twice, Diane and Tanner emerge, holding hands. After a few steps, Tanner drops Diane's hand and puts an arm around her shoulder, pulling her close. Diane puts her arm around Tanner's waist as he bends to kiss her. I flash on a sensory memory of sitting atop Samuel's prone body, his hands on my hips, my thighs and knees wrapped close to his ribs, my body bent forward to kiss his mouth .
. . .

No.

I stand and walk to the guard shack as if I'm expected, hoping the guard won't stop me. He doesn't. I guess I came often enough with Diane and Tanner to be accepted. I pick through the garden to determine if Nestra is here. She's at her oak tree.

I creep toward her, keeping out of sight of her escort at the front entrance. She sees me. She rises and begins a slow and winding walk among the paths toward our usual meeting place. I turn and walk ahead of her to the spot by the flowered wall. I'm shaking in anticipation of sharing with Nestra, of receiving her comfort.

Nestra settles to the ground in front of me but doesn't reach for me. She's always waited for me to start the sharing, but today her failure to reach for me is a stab, another betrayal. For some time neither of us says anything, but sits, looking at each other. I'm afraid to start, but I have to find out if Nestra has uncovered the true traitor.

"Have you learned of the human traitor?" I ask without preamble.

"You are in pain, friend-sister Khara," Nestra answers.

Tears come to my eyes, and my lip quivers as I repeat, "Have you learned of the human traitor?"

"No," answers Nestra. "I would share comfort with you, sister." Her limbs don't move toward me. She won't force sharing on me.

I can't resist what she offers. I'm in danger of sobbing. My breath jerks out of me. I wipe at my tears and leaking nose before leaning toward Nestra and putting my hands on her lower arms. Comfort washes over me and I picture crawling into her large lap, like a child, allowing her solace to wrap me like a blanket. A conflicting vision of Ilnok, four arms around me, pulling me toward his palpus, keeps me from moving. This vision of Ilnok is wiped from me as I'm bathed in warmth, and feelings of trust, and maybe . . . love. I'm so needy I can imagine love from my alien friend.

After some time during which Nestra doesn't talk, I'm no longer crying. I sigh, but it is not wholly a sigh of comfort. I still have that lump in my throat as I remember the look on Samuel's face. Samuel has made a mistake that threatens everything.

"You are in pain," Nestra says again.

I don't know how to explain. I don't want to explain.

"I hoped you had discovered the traitor. It is important to me. To all of us. I thought perhaps you told Diane and Tanner of this traitor."

"You instructed me not to discuss this matter with my other friends, although I assured you they were not traitors," Nestra says. "They have not discussed this matter with me."

"I am not the traitor," I say.

"You are not the traitor," Nestra answers. "You are my bond-friend, my sister." Another wave of comfort rushes through me, and I feel myself flush with the warmth.

"Humans can't share like this," I say. "The humans do not trust me now."

"I trust," said Nestra. "I am not alone with you, sister."

A flash of anger surges through me, as I think of Samuel, of how he broke me out of my cocoon of aloneness only to throw me out unprotected by my shell.

"I don't need anyone," I say without thinking.

"You are my friend," answers Nestra, and I feel her sadness through her warmth. My careless statement has rejected her, too. I'm ashamed.

"No shame," Nestra says. "You are in pain. You are angry. You are . . . ."

"Betrayed," I finish. "Distrusted." I try to shake off my bitterness, try to relax into giving Nestra back some of the comfort and trust with which she has fortified me. Try not to think of Samuel.

"You care for your betrayer," Nestra says.

"No!" The surge of anger again. I don't want to talk about this.

"Yes. You care for your betrayer. Your betrayer was bond-friend, trusted by you. This is the cause of your anger and pain. I taste this."

Something is breaking inside of me. I don't want to think of Samuel.

"Attachment, devotion, affection," Nestra says. The tears come again.

"Love," I whisper in English. I don't know the word in her language. Don't know if she has the word in her language. Now that I've said the word, the pain washes over me anew. The anger recedes as I now admit the reason for it.

Loved, and lost. How clichéd. Sadness. Something tears inside of me. Nestra again bathes me in her warmth.

"I will continue to try to discover the traitor," Nestra says, breaking me out of my dark wallow, reminding me why I'm here. "It is difficult."

"Thank you, yes, please try," I say. I fill myself with trust and appreciation as I say, "Please don't endanger yourself." The loss of Nestra would be unbearable.

After some time of speechlessness in which Nestra battles my sorrow with her caring, I excuse myself and leave the garden.

I wander an aimless route, without purpose, waiting for the call from Ilnok. The physical yet almost painless torture he inflicts seems nothing, at the moment, compared with the anguish inside me from which I can find no escape.

CHAPTER 35
NESTRA

I pull myself toward my rooms, though I move without quite the sheer exercise of will I once needed after my sessions with the queen. This time, in addition to the queen's stolen strength to bolster me, I have the information I have been longing to learn. This time, I am sustained with the knowledge of the good I can do for my sister and bond-friend, Khara.

I know the identity of the traitor.

After meditation and a meal, I feel strong enough to venture into the garden, although my hope of seeing Khara kept my meditation ritual to a minimum. If the queen calls again soon, I will not be sufficiently purged to enter another downloading session without danger. I will meditate in the garden while I wait, if I have the opportunity, although such mediation will not be as effective as the complete submersion I attain resting in my bed-pit.

Diane and Tanner are in the garden when I arrive, and I am happy to share for a brief time with these friends. Their level of tension is high and I do my best to console them, but they cannot share as Khara can. My expectancy and impatience to see Khara leads me to ask of my friends if Khara will be joining them. The wash of concern and confusion which attends their non-committal answer that Khara cannot come today only increases my impatience. I do not press them by asking when they think Khara can visit me. The question might be interpreted as my displeasure with them, or might cause Khara problems I do not understand.

I stay in the garden until night falls. Khara does not come.

My meditation that evening is as much to complete the needed purge as to rebuild my happy level of anticipation at being able to help my friend Khara.

The queen calls me thrice the next day – twice from the garden and once in the evening. I am careful to take as little strength from her as necessary. I want to avoid causing the level of weakness that will lead to her fear, and thus to avoid another attack. The queen's distrust of me grows and I dread the consequences. I fear my time is short, but can think of nothing I can do to step from my current path.

Khara comes to the garden the following afternoon after Diane and Tanner leave.

"Sister Nestra," Khara says, and reaches for my arms. I can feel her exhaustion and muted sadness.

"Sister," I murmur and release the flood of affection and warmth which I feel at the flavor-scent of my human bond-friend. Khara releases her breath in what I have come to recognize as sign of relaxation and well being, although Khara is far from feeling well. Now that she is with me, my impatience drains away and the

256

anticipation is bearable. I wait, comforting and consoling until Khara warms with appreciation and friendship, sharing this easily with me.

"Have you discovered the traitor?" Khara asks, without hope that I have the needed information.

My happiness and excitement wash through her, causing her to shiver. Khara's eyes widen.

"You have! I can feel it!" Khara rocks forward. "Have you? Can you help me identify this person?"

"Yes," I say. "I have a name and physical description."

"Tell!" Khara says. I taste the flavors-colors-scents of Khara's question, shock, surprise. Khara rocks from side-to-side on her bottom to move closer to me.

"You may not know the person and may not be able to identify this person from the name and description I have obtained," I caution. I hope my information will be helpful, but my people cannot often distinguish one human from another. I do not want Khara's excitement replaced with disappointment.

"Tell!" Khara says again.

"The courtier who discussed this human with the queen referred to him as," and here I purse my mandibles and palpus into the difficult formation required for the human language, "Bell-mee." The word ends with a discordant click as my mandibles move back into place.

"Bellamy," Khara whispers. Disbelief, shock waft in waves.

"Bell mee," I repeat, because Khara's rendition of the word does not sound identical to mine.

Khara utters several words in the human tongue which I do not understand. The teal-violet flavor of Khara's shock comes with the new scent of anger. Khara does not move or speak further.

"His description was given as a human of good height," I continue, "and that his skin is of an appropriate tint." I know this is probably not a sufficient physical description to be very helpful, since it merely is a statement the human is tall by human standards and dark of skin, as almost half the humans of this city are.

"Bellamy," Khara whispers again, and again follows the statement with words of her own language. This time dark anger replaces the scent of her shock.

"You know this human?" I ask, sensing recognition amongst the black anger. "This is helpful?"

"Yes, oh *yes*, sister Nestra, I know this person. He is trusted. Beyond reproach. This will be difficult for my . . . friends . . . to believe."

"He is foolish," I say. "He believes he will be spared. He believes his life is important to my people."

"I'm so stupid. We've all been so stupid," and again words in her language. Bitter blackness thickens the air.

"He will assist in causing the death of the human leader," I continue. "I apologize, this human was not identified in the conversation. I cannot tell you a name or description."

258

"He . . . ," Khara says, then, "Samuel." She barely breathes the unfamiliar word. The velvet purple-blue I have come to associate with the passionate sharing between Diane and Tanner is evident, mixed with the soft gold flavor-scent of admiration.

"This is your bond-friend," I say. "This is your betrayer?" I regret my words, as renewed weariness and sadness flush the air around us.

"Yes, this was my friend," Khara answers.

"He will be called to the palace," I say.

"Samuel? To the palace? You mean here?" Khara asks. The sour green-yellow flavor of her questioning shows she feels she has misunderstood my statement.

"The human leader, yes, will be called to the palace," I answer.

Khara does not reply, but the flavor of questioning remains. I taste that Sister Khara now questions the possibility of this statement rather than her understanding of it.

"You will forgive? You will warn this human?" I ask. The combination within Khara of color-flavor-scents leaves me confused. However, my question clarifies several things in my friend.

"Yes, of course," Khara answers. Her emotions solidify from the maelstrom. "He is important to the survival of our race." The statement does not reflect the pulsating river which shows the human is important to Khara, personally, as well.

"You are a loyal friend," I say.

259

"You are a loyal friend," Khara responds. "Thank you for this information." Khara closes the coverings over her eyes and I can feel the concentration with which my human sister attempts to flood me with friendship, trust, affection.

"I must go now," says Khara.

As much as I want my friend to stay, I understand the urgency.

"Come again, soon, sister Khara," I say. The form of the word "soon" implies there is not much time left, but I do not know if Khara's grasp of my language has reached the level of sophistication to recognize this form. I hope my friend and I will live long enough to meet again.

CHAPTER 36
KHARA

I stand outside the factory where Samuel works, unable to ignore the churning of my stomach, the fear and hungry anticipation of seeing him again. He won't kill me in the street.

I knew if I went to the places where he meets with his people, if I found him that way. . . He said he'd kill me. A part of me doesn't believe this, refuses to give up hope. Another part of me remembers his narrowed brown eyes and his no longer warm mouth drawn tight as he said, "Don't touch me." The memory causes a stab between my lungs too real for me to believe it's psychosomatic imagination.

Jan and Eli come out of the factory at closing time with other humans. They are as quiet and subdued as the other humans around them. There is no beer-time camaraderie as might have been expected at closing time before the invasion. Jan and Eli don't appear to see me.

Samuel's not with the crowd leaving the factory, but I know from experience he'll leave last, with his master. They emerge.

261

Samuel moves his head from side to side, not seeming to focus on anything in particular, but I can tell from his sudden stiffening, from the pull of his mouth, he's seen me. His reaction to me is a punch in the gut. I can barely swallow around the sudden lump in my throat. My breath comes in shallow gasps.

His master speaks with him, Samuel opens and bends his head back, and his master moves away. He remains stone still, as though his master still occupies the space in front of him, before turning and moving away down the street. He doesn't look toward me.

I cross the street, but not running, as I want to. I don't want to endanger Samuel by drawing attention to him in this way. Once on his side of the street, I continue to walk, trying to catch up to him. As I draw near, my eyes roam over his broad back, the muscles of his bare arms, his solid buttocks and legs. I would be angry with myself, but I have given up on anger where Samuel is concerned. Now there's only pain.

"Samuel," I say, when I've gotten close enough to be heard. He doesn't stop or respond. I'm close enough to him to see the tightness of the bunched muscles in his jaw, the stretched tendons in his neck.

"I met with Nestra. I know who the traitor is."

"So do I," Samuel says without turning toward me, without stopping his walk. "We haven't suffered one raid since you stopping coming around."

"Can you at least listen to me?" I ask. I catch myself reaching out to grab his arm, to turn him toward me. Afraid of how he'll react, I pull my hand back to my side.

"I warned you," he says, with an ominous growl behind the words.

"I've stayed away. I'm trying to give you information that'll save your life. And maybe all of ours," I say.

He stops. He still doesn't turn toward me. I walk around to face him, careful as ever I was in the past not to touch him or brush against him as I circle him, although now for a very different reason. Remembering how I used to react to anyone touching me, I'm astonished by the hunger to touch Samuel that rises in me now.

"You aren't going to believe me," I say in a rush, and Samuel snorts.

I cringe, knowing how ridiculous I'm going to sound telling him about his most trusted friend, his second in command. There is nothing left to do but say the words.

"It's Bell," I say. His face twists with an incredulous look of disgust. That look, directed at me, threatens to crush me to the pavement, a blubbering mess at his feet. Around the tightness in my throat, I rush on. "He was identified as Bell-mee, a tall, black man. He's going to get you killed. I don't mean figuratively, I mean you, literally. You're going to be summoned to the capitol building. I don't know. Maybe the queen is going to kill you." Samuel's mouth opens to speak halfway through my speech, but I don't stop until I have all the words out.

He shakes his head in disbelief and the look of disgust intensifies with a further squint of his eyes. He says, "Are you finished?" The contempt in his voice pricks at my heart, and my eyes moisten.

"Yeah," I say, dropping my head, chin to my chest. "Yeah, I'm finished." Tears spill from my eyes, fall directly to the pavement. In this moment of exquisite agony, I crave Nestra's comfort as much as I ever craved the patch. I want so much to reach out to Samuel, to see him smile at me, to hear a kind word. I'm trembling in my need, my pain.

I see his feet as he takes a step backward, then begins walking around me, to leave me. I want to say something that will convince him, something that will stop him from walking away from me. I spin around to watch him go.

"Nestra says Diane and Tanner aren't traitors," I say toward his retreating back. He stops again. He doesn't turn around.

"Ask them. Ask them about me. You can trust them," I say. I take a step toward Samuel.

"I know I can trust *them*," he says, and then starts walking again. I don't move until he rounds a corner one block up and I can't see him any longer. I keep trying to be angry, but I can't manage it. It takes more energy than I can muster over the throbbing pain in my chest and my head, the choking lump in my throat.

CHAPTER 37
DIANE

We're sitting together on a lumpy sofa, legs intertwined, and I'm running my finger over Tanner's collarbone. "Do you think maybe tonight–"

Tanner interrupts. "Definitely."

My smile widens. We understand each other so well. It's dumplings for dinner then. I love that he remembers me saying I was craving them earlier, love that he's made the connection before I could even finish my sentence. He's the yang to my yin. I doubt either of us would long survive without the other – nor would we want to. The comfort of believing this so absolutely is the definition of heaven on earth. I'll thank him later in that special way he likes.

I'm leaning in for a kiss when Samuel comes in. His tight-jawed face is red and his fists are clenched into white-hot nuggets. His anger is radiating off him in razor-sharp spikes. There isn't much that would distract me from Tanner, but this does it. I've never seen Samuel so. . . I don't even know what word to use. Emotional.

"Samuel?"

Tanner turns toward Samuel. Samuel stops in his tracks but doesn't look at us. He looks like he wants to break something, like if his muscles were strung any tighter, he'd go pinging off the dark, wood-paneled walls like a golf ball.

"Dude," Tanner whispers. He's not addressing Samuel.

No kidding.

We have to find out what's wrong, to help if we can. Samuel is always so strong and clear-headed and I admire that. If he's this upset, it must be bad.

I stand and let go of Tanner's hand. I cross the threadbare blue carpet and close the door Samuel came through.

Samuel's jaw unclenches and he pants two quick breaths. His mouth closes and he breathes through his nose, nostrils flared and white with the long inhale, then relaxing with the exhale. His fists loosen their grip and he spreads his fingers wide before settling them against his thighs.

"Samuel?" I put my hand on his biceps, stroke toward his elbow. He's regaining control and I hope this will help. "Everything okay?" When he doesn't respond, I put a finger to his jaw and pull until he's looking down at me. "What can we do?"

His eyes don't seem to focus, and then he is here, he is with me. He shakes his head, and tries to smile but the attempt is a travesty.

"Is someone hurt? Did something—"

"Fine. Everything's fine," he answers.

Tanner is beside me now. "Tell us what we can do." Tanner pokes his thumbs to his chest. "We'll do it, man."

Samuel stays stiff for another moment, then exhales a breath that sounds like defeat. Ignoring the two ragged, overstuffed side chairs, he moves around the cheap coffee table to the sofa and collapses into the mismatched cushions.

"Khara," he says and my insides flutter with apprehension.

"Yeah, where's she been?" Tanner asks.

I've been worried about Khara. When she disappeared, Samuel was vague about her being on some mission. Now I'm afraid something's gone wrong. Khara's amazing – fragile as glass and tough as titanium – and I can't imagine her screwing any mission up, but these are dangerous times.

"Is she okay? She's not hurt?" I ask.

"No, she's not hurt," he answers, biting off the words. The anger is back.

"Samuel, what's going on?" I ask. I'm relieved by his words but not his tone.

When he doesn't answer, I go over to the private stash and poor a shot of vodka into a mason jar. Samuel prefers gin when he drinks – which isn't often – but we don't have any.

"Take your time," I say as I hand him the glass and settle onto the sofa next to him. "But, we're not going anywhere. Khara is our friend."

Samuel snorts and his eyes flash with anger again. Then, his face crumples into misery.

267

CARAPACE

Tanner sits on the other side of Samuel, one long leg folded under him. He smiles, at his most encouraging. "What works best for me," he says, "is to start at the beginning. Once we know what's going on, we'll figure out a way to fix it."

Samuel downs the vodka, sighs, drops his chin to his chest and starts talking at such a low volume we both have to lean in to hear him.

"I've got to talk to somebody." Neither Tanner nor I answer. Samuel will get to it in his own time. But, his tension and upset are contagious. I wish I could touch Tanner, hold his hand, curl up in his arms.

"We have a traitor – a human traitor – in the rebellion."

I want to gasp, want to say something in response but all I can think is that Samuel started this by saying "Khara." Not possible. I need to hear this out.

Tanner says, "Go on." He's not the exuberant boy everyone knows, but the quiet man that only rarely shows himself, and most often when we are alone.

Samuel tells us. First, what he heard about Khara from Bell, along with all the evidence. Then, what he heard about Bell from Khara, and about Bell being complicit in Samuel's betrayal and death.

Poor Samuel. His best friend and trusted lieutenant, versus the woman he loves. Even if he doesn't know how he feels about her, I do. When you're in love, you can see it in someone else.

268

"I..." Samuel says. He doesn't finish, but I know what he was going to say.

I don't know what to do.

"Samuel," I say. I move to my knees on the floor in front of him. I want him looking into my eyes. "We all trust Bell," I say. "There isn't one of us who doesn't owe him our lives at one point or another."

"I know!" he says and agony is plain in the twist of his mouth, the clamping shut of his eyelids.

"Tanner and I know and trust Khara. She's our friend and I don't believe she's the traitor," I finish. Samuel's eyes open in surprise.

"So. They are both accusers and both accused," I finish.

"Right," Tanner adds. He already knows where I'm going with this.

"Then, what either of them said doesn't matter. You can't choose. You can't know."

"But...," Samuel says.

"The important thing here is, one of them hasn't said anything about you and the other said your life is in danger."

"So?" Samuel can sense I'm leading to something but he hasn't gotten there yet.

"So, we act to protect you," Tanner finishes, slapping his hand on the orange cushion for emphasis. A dust cloud rises and hangs in the heavy air.

I pick up where Tanner left off. "Khara said you were going to be called to the capitol building – the 'palace.' What if you are? What if you are going to be killed there, like she says?"

"It's not going to—"

"But what if it does, man?" Tanner asks before Samuel can finish.

Samuel thinks for a bit. "There's nothing to be done. If I'm called, I go."

We can't lose Samuel. We can't. Not only is he a good man, but he's the head of our group, the one who keeps us all going in the right direction, who keeps hope in our hearts.

Tanner drums long fingers against his cheekbone. His hair hangs in his eyes as he thinks. "There's got to be something... If only we could send in a dummy. You know, like those manikins we set up once at that cell meeting that was gonna get raided?"

"That's it," I answer. Leave it to Tanner to come up with the answer. "We need a stand-in. We need somebody who can take your place at the last minute," I say.

"No." Samuel's answer is firm.

"Yes, Samuel," I say. "If Khara is wrong, we've done nothing. If Khara is right..." I let the thought sink in. "We can't lose you."

"If I get called to the palace, Tamerak will be called, too," Samuel answers. "So, I'm going, either way."

"Yes, of course. We'll have the stand-in ready for after you're there," I say.

"Nobody's going to take that risk," Samuel says but we both give him that you've-got-be-kidding-me look. We'd take the risk ourselves if we looked anything like Samuel.

Samuel sighs. "Tamerak would know the difference," he says. He's listening, letting me draw him the picture.

Tanner stands. He needs to move when he talking, planning. "So, we have this stand-in there. When Tamerak gets called by the queen, the stand-in moves into your place. Tamerak won't dare make a ruckus about the guy not being you. The queen'd kill him."

"This is stupid," Samuel says. "It's not going to happen."

"Then it doesn't. But we can't lose you," I say again. "We can't. You're our leader, our hope."

"Is there anybody else who can take over for you if Khara's right?" Tanner asks.

"Bell, maybe," Samuel answers and the agony is back in his face.

Neither of us says anything. It's time to let Samuel think. And while he's thinking, Tanner and I have to find a volunteer for the stand-in.

I trust Bell. I trust Khara. No wonder Samuel is so upset. Just thinking about this mess has me trembling.

I take Tanner's hand as we step into the tunnel that leads to the kitchen of a restaurant. I'm blessed that he is always there for me, warm, and steady – my other half.

CARAPACE

CHAPTER 38
SAMUEL

The information from Khara is right thus far. Tamerak and I have been summoned to the "palace." The queen ostensibly wants to reward him for the excellent productivity of his factory. I have to believe this is the half-truth which Khara hoped would lend her credibility. I can't believe the rest of Khara's ridiculous allegations. I've known Bell too long. Trusted him with my life too many times.

For all the strangeness of our summons, the walk to the palace is mundane. I walk in front of Tamerak, as though I'm his formal entourage. My sleeveless shirt is unbuttoned almost to my waist, with the collar thrown open to display my monitor. My rank is pinned to my shoulder and draped under my armpit. I walk with the curious skating motion that keeps me balanced and able to glide from side to side in the endless weaving dance that keeps me from being bumped and jostled by the other ants near the capitol building. It's an uneven, unmetered dance – slide, sway, doublestep, slide, slide, sway. It is a dance which the ants execute flawlessly and which I've come to enjoy. It's also one of the many ant

273

characteristics I am careful to adopt and display for Tamerak to assist his perception of my antlike – and therefore civilized – status.

A human stumbles in front of me whom I almost cannot avoid. Tamerak chirrups his displeasure. In this, Tamerak reminds me of the old barber who used to cut my father's hair. The old man never chastised the poor behavior of children in his little shop, but *tsked* to himself over every perceived offense. It strikes me that with this comparison I look for little humannesses in Tamerak, as he looks for ant in me. We anthropomorphize each other, thereby attempting to understand each other within the bounds of our relationship.

Tamerak touches the side of my neck with the long smooth edge of one upper pincer. It's a sign of affection. I don't know whether he's assuring me his chirrup was not directed at me, or whether it's more generalized – perhaps just a reflection of his pleasure at being summoned, and what a rise in rank or privilege might bring. I am too preoccupied with what else this summons may mean to take any pleasure or pride in the gesture. This all fits too neatly with Khara's prediction.

Paranoia. Khara's effect on me is dangerous. I've allowed my still unrelenting desire for her to cloud my thinking. My anger at her latest approach to me is in part because of the jump in my groin at my first glimpse of her.

Bell would never betray . . . . Before I can finish the thought, before I can outline the breadth of what and whom Bell would never betray, another thought comes to mind.

I never thought Khara would betray me either.

My thoughts circle each other, entangled. I'm tortured by the juxtaposition of the opposing beliefs. The very fact of this summons has me doubting Bell. The thought is dark and unworthy, but won't leave me – no doubt what Khara intended.

We arrive at the capitol building where the queen has made her home. My pace evens into a metronomic human stride as I march the few stairs to the main entrance. Tamerak stops to greet a triad and I stop too, rounding to his side and behind him, head thrown back in subservience. None of the group appears to notice me. Tamerak brushes me to signal the end of his meeting. I advance toward the main doors again, sick with adrenaline.

My shirt is marked with wide rings of sweat that start under my arms, spread up toward my shoulders and creep toward my chest. The shirt sticks to my back. I am struck with a flash of memory: Khara smiling, peeling my shirt from me, licking my nipple. Khara's eyes on mine as her hands roam, stroke...

We move into the crowded, almost silent throne room. The ants here don't touch each other. I've lived amongst them long enough to find this strange.

Queen Tal is not on the dais yet. Tamerak brushes me away and pushes toward a loose group that includes several ants I recognize as his friends. I search the room for clues, insights, scanning the humans.

I see Tanner with Diane. As planned, the queen's gardeners have managed to secure a part of the human/pet component to this strange audience. Diane stands behind a serious young man, her hands resting on his broad shoulders. She looks around the young man's shoulder at me. His eyes are unfocused and pointed toward the ground. She whispers something and he looks up.

On finding me, he raises his chin and his face burns with pride. My stand-in, should I feel it necessary, a volunteer here to risk his life for me and for the cause.

I'm crushed that he is so young, so willing. He raises his chin yet again and gives me the barest of nods, forcing me to acknowledge my debt. My hand rises to my heart, and I bow my head. I can give him nothing more than my utmost respect, and the solemn knowledge his face will stay with me forever – no matter what happens today. I turn away, looking for Tamerak. I have to be ready to rejoin him upon his signal.

Suddenly, Bell's face is in mine and he claps me on my back. "Mate!"

I am barely able to stop my expression of shock at his presence here today. I remind myself I know very little of Bell's routine, and perhaps it is not shocking for him to be present at court. As an unsponsored human, I wouldn't have guessed he would be. "Didn't know you'd be here," I say.

Bell speaks in the low voice required in the throne room – if only by the tense nervousness that laces the air, rather than by decree. He's smiling at me. "Just part of the crowd, Mate." He gestures toward the wad of humans to the side of the room.

"You clean up rather like a gent," he says raising his eyebrows and widening his eyes at me. He winks and smiles again, white teeth shining from his dark features. He chuckles and then sniffs at me, poking at the circles of sweat on my shirt. "You look fine, but," he inhales again, then leans in to whisper, "you smell." There is nothing unnatural in his manner.

I am rendered silent by my guilt. This man, this friend, wouldn't betray me. I smile and roll my eyes at him, then motion with my finger to my lips for him to be quiet.

"What? Is she coming?" he asks, obviously imagining I am motioning for silence because the queen has made her entrance.

I shake my head no.

"Bloody coward," he whispers to me. He wraps an arm around my shoulders and we stand together observing the crowd. Watching and looking for hints, betrayals, alliances, as always. I am disgusted with myself for believing Khara that Bell has betrayed me, that my life is in danger here today. I am furious with myself for allowing Diane, in desperation, to set up a stand-in.

I close my eyes. Bell's arm drops off my shoulder, and I open my eyes to see Tamerak signaling to me from his place at the edge of the crowd. Bell grabs my jaw and kisses me roughly on the cheek as he walks away to join the crowd of humans. This isn't like Bell and, despite my shame of a moment ago, a stab of uncertainty slides knife-smooth between my ribs.

I move toward Tamerak while watching Bell glide across the floor. He turns to face me from across the marble expanse. I expect to see him smile at me and wink again, or raise his chin at me in some private joke. He is expressionless, eyes like ghosts, staring. Then he nods at me, with a sadness behind his eyes. No smile, no joking manner. So unlike Bell. My stomach rises to my throat as the doubts that plagued me on the walk here begin anew.

Tamerak touches the side of my neck with the long smooth edge of one upper pincer. I lay my head back. He runs his pincer across my throat above my monitor. It is unlike him to show this level of affection in public. He must be extraordinarily pleased with me.

As I lower my head, I notice my stand-in is next to me. He doesn't look at me. Although he's about my height, he's not as solid as I am. We share the same cropped blond hair. He's wearing a white shirt like mine, my same rank. He is collared, like me, but is not standing with an ant-master. I wonder if his collar is genuine, or there as a prop for the mission.

I look to Bell, but he stands at attention, glazed eyes staring to the front. Bell's demeanor makes me ill. I am afraid the boy beside me will be needed – but for what? Khara's supposition that I'll be killed here today has to be wrong. The sweat circles under my armpits grow.

The room becomes silent as Queen Tal enters. She is a giantess of an ant. Most ants are only about a foot taller than me, but the Queen is a good foot or two taller than that. She's shadowed by another extraordinarily tall ant that must be Nestra, the Shame Receptor. The queen has no other entourage. She lowers herself into a large cushioned chair and begins to talk in a low clicking whistle that demands silence. I don't understand anything of what she says.

After several other audiences, the queen calls Tamerak forward. Without looking back, Tamerak reaches back to graze me with a pincer as he moves away, striding to the empty floor before the queen. My stand-in slides forward after I have received the touch. The boy's movement is small, casual, seeming accidental. I don't move, don't discourage the stand-in, don't whisper to him he's not needed. I haven't yet made my decision. Tamerak moves toward the queen, tall with pride, but with head thrown back in the proper attitude of deference.

"Step back, sir." It is the slightest of whispers from Diane, who stands behind me and on the other side of me from my stand-in. I don't move.

"Step. Back. Sir." No louder, but with a pause between each word which adds force to the statement. I shuffle backward, with a movement that mocks a shift in weight to accommodate sore feet. The queen speaks again, and now, now that I'm not standing with my master, Diane moves closer to me and translates from behind me and over my shoulder.

"She is pleased with production." I can tell from the slur Diane is trying to speak without moving her mouth. She is quiet, so quiet. "More words about good production." "Rewards are coming." "Inner strength important." "Strength leads to good production." Diane speaks in spurts. "Interdependence among brothers." Diane gasps before the next translated sentence. After a pause, she whispers, "Self-reliance from unnecessary human distractions." I'm struck with a chill at this latest translation. Diane slides into the next translation. "Again, importance of inner strength."

Tamerak opens himself to the queen. She motions to him, and he begins to speak.

"He thanks her." "He is unworthy." "Humans unworthy." This last proclamation doesn't bother me. Tamerak is making the necessary noises. Diane's volume lowers. I can barely hear her. "He's mentioned you, sir." Pause. "Good words, about you again, sir." She stops translating. Tamerak still talks, but Diane says, "Step back, sir." I am flush with adrenaline. My skin crawls at her whisper. "Step back, sir. Please."

I look to Bell. He glances away from me as my eyes reach his. He looks at the floor before his feet. He's been watching me, but now, won't meet my eye.

"Ssssssamuel." The word is sibilant, directed to the audience by the queen.

"Sir," whispers Diane. I can't look away from Bell. I will him to meet my eye. He doesn't. His face is taut; his eyes continue to search the floor at his feet.

"Ssssssamuel." The queen speaks louder this time, and Tamerak directs one eye in my direction with a slight turn of his head. Bell still doesn't look at me, and so I make my decision. I don't move forward. At a tap from Diane, the boy strides away from my side toward Tamerak. I am wounded by the boy's willingness to step into harm's way on my behalf.

Bell looks to the boy who should be me. His brow furrows with lack of understanding, and then his eyes dart to me. I watch his eyes widen with shock and fear. He knows the boy is in danger, sees that I know this. He looks from side to side, looking for an avenue of escape. He's in the front row, ready to be witness to whatever lies ahead for the boy – whatever was meant for me – and so can't escape without notice. His eyes return to mine. His complexion is gray.

My gut clenches and bile rises to my throat.

I turn away from Bell, sick with his betrayal, and look to Tamerak and the boy. The boy is kneeling, with his knees spread far apart, his arms thrown wide and away from his body, his head thrown back. In this manner, he shows deference to the queen, and then slides around on his knees to face Tamerak. Tamerak falters as he reaches toward the boy with a pincer. He must now have realized the boy is not me – the scent cannot match mine – but Tamerak also knows the queen will kill them both if something appears to be amiss. Tamerak slides his pincer along the boy's neck, just above his collar, in the same sign of affection he has so often shown me. I pray Khara is wrong.

The queen speaks.

"Oh my God." It's Diane again. I can't turn to ask her what was said. I take a shuffling miniscule step back toward her, hoping she'll understand this as a request for her translation. "Oh my God," she repeats.

Tamerak doesn't move. The boy doesn't move. Bell stares at the boy. The cavernous room is almost silent. Diane begins translating, but with a sudden roughness to her voice.

"Show inner strength." Diane whispers. "Take credit for your good production." Diane's voice breaks at the last word, and she releases a sharp exhale. Then: "Kill the worthless human."

Tears fill the wells of my eyes, which can't turn away from the sight of the boy, kneeling where I ought to be kneeling. My exterior is frozen, my innards are molten, my fists are clenched into rocks that may never open again. I'm afraid I'll be sick where I stand.

Tamerak doesn't hesitate – to do so would be his own death sentence. The queen's revolting test is a test Tamerak is determined to pass. He raises and opens his two large upper pincers and then slices them into the boy's throat. The boy never moves, as though he doesn't know it's coming.

Blood sprays in a thin mist as the head falls to the floor. After the initial spray, blood drains in a red flood over the boy's chest. The body falls backward onto the marble floor with a dull thud. A soft-bodied, unremarkable thud.

Diane vomits onto the floor behind me. I want to find Bell, but I can't move my eyes from the scene of my death.

Another debt. Another impossible debt.

CHAPTER 39
TAMERAK

I move down the stairs and out of the shadow of the palace. Stepping with the languid surety of a favored brother, I make sure my posture and gestures are those of pride. Though I cannot hide the scent of my confusion and fear, many of the brothers leaving the court taste the same. I make sure to avoid brothers who might, through their closer acquaintance with me, detect the subtler scents I exude and question me in their concern.

I did not find Samuel – my Samuel – before leaving the throne room. I cannot ask after my human, when in front of the entire audience, I have – to their knowledge – killed him. I curse myself for the conceit I felt at the summons from the queen and the pride I expressed for Samuel, since the queen's proclivities are well known. Foolishness!

Personal pride is the destruction of love for the society, I chide myself, the thought coming too late to be of any help.

Once I am well away from the palace and out of the constant crowds surrounding the area, I quicken my pace. I still keep a lookout for brothers who might attempt a brief streetside sharing, despite my desperate need for comfort and shared friendship.

My confusion over the actions of my Samuel tinge toward feelings of betrayal as I analyze and re-analyze the horrid situation. I am forced to accept the conclusion Samuel was aware of the purpose of the summons and arranged for another to die in his place. This hints at an organization among the humans of which I am unaware. It also suggests that as much as I care for my Samuel and attempt – feel! – true friendship for the human, he did not share this feeling to the extent of warning me or sharing his information. Confusion and betrayal and fear warp and weave through me as I walk, thoughts swirling around the terrible audience with the queen.

As I round a corner near my home, I catch a scent of my Samuel and pause, but then continue on, chiding my imagination. My imagination proves not to be at fault, however. As I approach the entrance to my home, my Samuel steps from the shadows at the side of the building. His scent is unmistakable.

"Master," Samuel says, and steps back into the shadows.

The brightness of the sunlight on the surrounding cement leaves me unable to see him in the contrasting black of the shadow into which he has moved. More confusion boils through me and for a moment I do not move. When I step into the shadows that have engulfed my Samuel, he is on his knees, bowing backward in respect, arms outstretched and throat exposed. For a brief instant, I think to kill him as the queen has ordered. I stand looking down at the soft human I have so relied upon and cared about. My Samuel does not move, quiet in his obvious respect. But then I wonder if I can trust that anything about my Samuel is obvious, given the day's events. I move a lower pincer toward Samuel's throat, unsure whether to slash or caress. The sudden image of the queen's cruel smile decides me. I do not touch my Samuel.

"Come," I say, turn, stride into the sunlight, and into my home.

The furtiveness with which Samuel slides through the entrance behind me renews my feelings of betrayal and confusion.

I have loved this creature whom I do not know.

I turn and go to my bed-pit, tasting the air to assure myself he follows.

"Explain," I say once I have lowered myself to the cushions. My command is abrupt with my uneasiness.

Samuel again falls to his knees and opens himself to me. He maintains the posture without speaking. I soften toward my human.

"Explain," I repeat, this time with the softened tones of resignation.

"I apologize, Master," Samuel says, bringing his head to the upright position and focusing his liquid eyes on me.

I sigh and stay my pincer before I can reach out and caress him as I wish to do.

"It was a human betrayal," Samuel continues.

"It was my betrayal!" I spit, surprised at the loud harshness of my reply. "You could have cost me my life!" Fear courses through me as I again consider the consequences of the queen's displeasure. The room grows thick with the bright scent.

"I was trying to avoid losing my own," Samuel answers, "although my life is yours now, if you wish it." He bends his head backward and opens himself to me. Again, I soften to my Samuel and, again, I sigh.

"How were you aware of the need for your actions?" I ask.

After a long moment, Samuel answers, "I, like you, have bond-brothers. Human bond-brothers. They made me aware." I can taste the caution with which the answer is delivered. This causes a renewed surge of fear/betrayal/confusion, and the sour green-yellow of the questions that form in my mind mix with the other scents in the flavor-laden room.

"Explain further," I order, frustrated with the need for verbal communication with the human.

Again, Samuel is slow in answering. After a cautious hesitation, he says, "I have explained, Master."

"And you will explain no further?" I ask, astonished by his reticence.

"No, Master," he answers, and again, opens himself in an obvious bid to soften his refusal.

I sink into thought, but can come to no satisfactory conclusion that will allow me to keep my Samuel. This saddens me, but not as much as it might if I were not swirling with feelings that he has betrayed me. I stand and approach him. I reach toward his throat and slide the edge of a pincer under the monitor collar.

A burst of fear explodes from him, but my Samuel does not move.

I disengage the collar and step back as it clatters to the floor.

"I release you," I say as I turn back to my bed cushions. My Samuel gives a small gasp but I cannot interpret whether this is a sound of relief or grief. The room is a cocktail of strong feelings, exuding from both of us. As I lower myself again to my cushions, I say, "You will be unprotected. Perhaps your human bond-brothers can protect you." I am ashamed as I recognize the brief flare of black anger that accompanies my thought that he will now have to rely on the bond-brothers he has trusted above me.

Samuel picks up the collar from the floor and rolls it over and over in his soft hands, as if seeing it for the first time.

"Go," I say with another deep sigh.

Samuel brings the ends of the collar together with a click, places the closed collar on the floor before him, and stands to go. At the entrance to the bedchamber, Samuel turns again, and with obvious concern, says, "The factory . . .?"

"It is to be purged in two days time," I answer, "Concern yourself not about the factory. A bond-brother of mine will be foreman, and he is capable of the job."

After a pause, Samuel turns and leaves the room.

"I would have kept you, Samuel, my friend," I finish, awash in sadness. I cannot be sure he hears me, but that is irrelevant now.

CHAPTER 40
KHARA

Sitting in my self-appointed sentinel post, my stomach is sour with fear. Samuel's not at the factory today. Were he and his master summoned to the capitol building? Is he dead?

I've found a spot from which I can watch the factory without Samuel noticing – at least I don't believe he's noticed me – and I've watched him morning and night, coming and going with his master since I delivered my warning. It's with a sick yearning that I watch him walk, notice the strength of his stride, the beauty and surety of his large muscular body in motion. I haven't followed him because I know he is expert at noticing streetside trackers. But I watch him move from the moment he comes into sight until he's gone. I close my eyes after he's gone and picture the warmth of his mouth, smiling at me, pursing to kiss me.

This morning, his master arrived without Samuel. This afternoon, his master left without Samuel. I'm stewing in an all-consuming caldron of fear.

Eli and Jan enter and leave the factory. Nothing in their manner is any different from usual, nor gives me any clues. I want so much to rush to them, ask them, maybe follow them to where they might be meeting with Samuel, or with anybody who can answer my agony. Instead, I wait until they're out of sight, then sneak down from my perch behind a greasy black chimney and head for the queen's garden. I have to talk to Nestra. I wait in the garden until nightfall, but Nestra doesn't come.

I don't sleep, and Ilnok's failure to call me makes the night ironically longer and more unbearable.

Samuel doesn't come to the factory in the morning. Jan and Eli don't come either. Only a small group of humans comes to the factory. Now I'm itchy with panic. They're gone. Dead, I know it.

Samuel, oh God DAMN it, Samuel! I need you!

My arms are clutched around me, hugging me, as I race again to the queen's garden. I'm willing to face Diane and Tanner and whatever danger that might bring, to talk to them or to Nestra. I need and dread the answer.

I enter the garden and walk through the bushes, and trees, and annoying bright flowers searching for anyone who can relieve my devouring need for information. Diane and Tanner aren't there. This only ratchets up my panic that maybe everyone is gone, dead. I sit on the grass next to a low bush where I can see Nestra's oak tree. I pull at the grass all around me, aware that enough of this will damage Diane and Tanner's careful work, but daring them to come and stop me.

Nestra comes. She sees me. I'm panting when she joins me in our secret meeting place.

290

"Sister Khara," she says as she approaches me, and in my imagination her tone seems mournful. I want to jump up and drag her slow moving body down to the grass and shake the information from her, but I restrain myself. I'm trembling as she sits across from me in the cool grass.

"Is Samuel dead? Is the human leader dead?" I ask. I realize after the words have tumbled from me that I haven't greeted Nestra with the politeness she deserves, but it's too late.

"Sister Khara," she says again, and now her tone is distinctly mournful. I cry out as I reach for her, clutching at her lower arms and pulling them toward me. I cry out again as her sympathy and love and concern flow over me. "No!"

No, please God, no!

"I mourn with you," Nestra says, and again the flood of sympathy. The lump in my throat threatens to choke me. I can't breathe. My cool tears strike my arms and I'm holding Nestra's arms to keep from fainting as blackness rushes over me.

"The human was killed in court, yesterday, in the morning," Nestra continues. I'm rocking forward and back. A low moan is coming from my throat, but I can't stop the sound. "I witnessed this. It is truth." Another flood of sympathy, love, friendship, commiseration. Nestra's upper arms touch my shoulders, touch my head, and I can't stop rocking and moaning.

"You must mourn in silence, sister-friend Khara. There is danger," Nestra says. My first thought is that I don't care. Her escorts can come kill me. Make this pain stop. But then Nestra, too, will die, and the thought of losing my last and only friend brings a measure of control.

After many more minutes of sharing, of allowing Nestra to fold me into her love, I'm able to find my voice.

"Was there much pain?" I ask. My mind shies away from her possible answer, but I need the nightmare visions floating in my mind to solidify into something bearable. I want to hear he died quickly and without pain.

"No pain. Quick. His master cared for him and is not very ill."

"His master? His master killed him?" I swear his master won't survive another morning going into the factory, even if tearing the monster limb from limb is my last act. As it will be.

"The queen ordered it," Nestra answers. Against my most fervent desires to destroy the monster, I find myself excusing him. A little. Then the pain rolls back over me and quenches my brief flare of anger.

Samuel!

Again, a flood of love and comfort from Nestra, battering at my pain, my self-pity. It's a measure of how much Nestra has helped me that I'm able to think of Nestra and regret I have nothing to give her in return.

"Thank you, Friend Nestra," I sigh. I'm in no hurry to leave her or the garden. I have nowhere in particular to go.

After another several moments, I think of Nestra again, determined to make an effort for this alien who has done so much for me. She's all I have now. My need to let her know I cherish her glows within me.

"Can I do anything for you?" I ask her, and Nestra gurgles, as though sighing through liquid.

"Your friendship heals fear," Nestra answers.

"Fear? Are you in danger?" I ask. As soon as the words are out I realize how stupid the question is. She is always in the presence of the queen, which is danger enough.

"The queen. She grows worse." After a moment, she adds: "I am to blame with my thievery."

I close my eyes and concentrate on feelings of love and comfort.

"Our friendship must come to an end," Nestra says.

"What? Why?" I push down the quick stab that burns through me – a child's entreaty inside me crying, *Don't abandon me!*

"I do not believe Queen Tal will allow me to live much longer." Again Nestra sighs. "I have prolonged myself wrongly."

"No!" I cry, and clutch harder at the inflexible limbs in my hands. It is again a child's cry of desperation, less a denial of Nestra's statement than a rejection of the unfairness of the world.

"Also, the brothers are almost ready. I do not believe humans will live when they are hatched," Nestra answers. "I fear for you, my sister." Sadness, comfort, love. "Already there are fewer humans each day."

I can't deny our dwindling numbers. But I've been so focused on Samuel that my passage through streets and the quietness of the dorms has seemed irrelevant background.

Samuel!

Through the fresh stab of pain, my mind whispers to Samuel, *At least you didn't have to see us all die, the battle lost, the human race gone.*

I close my eyes. I can think of nothing to say. Together Nestra and I despair of our deaths, of the end of our friendship, of everything, and still find it within each other to commiserate, to comfort, to console.

A screechy whistle sounds from the far side of the garden and Nestra says, "I am summoned."

As I rise to leave, I say, "I will try to come every day, my sister."

"As will I," Nestra answers as she turns to go. Her tone holds all her doubts that there will be many more days. Even without the physical contact between the two of us, I'm sure Nestra shares my sense of resignation, of endings.

I'm brooding, watching only my feet, walking through the garden toward the back entrance, when I hear the familiar snick of pruning shears. I glance to my right, and there's Tanner, stopped mid-motion, a look of surprise on his face as he sees me. I hurry to leave the garden as he turns to where Diane must be, hidden by some tree or bush. As I rush away, my alarm fading as I make my way down the street away from the garden, it occurs to me Tanner didn't look angry to see me there. Maybe I could have questioned him, learned more.

I shake my head and my sweat dampened hair lashes at my face. I have the important answer. Samuel is dead.

CARAPACE

CHAPTER 41
SAMUEL

Jan and Eli and I have searched the barrooms and clubs Bell frequents. This has been made difficult by the fact we are now all unprotected, perhaps even wanted. If Bell sees us, our lives are in danger. He's proven our lives mean nothing to him. Certainly not mine. He lined up on the front row to watch me die a bloody and public death. I wonder if he's told his masters it wasn't me who died, or whether fear of their reprisal has silenced him.

I'm hit with another pang as the scene plays out in my mind again, the vision of the proud and confident boy I let go to his death in my stead. My guilt is not assuaged by the fact that I didn't believe it would come to death. Even at the end, even at the last moment, I couldn't make myself believe Bell was party to my planned execution.

I believe now. And we have to find him.

I wait in the muggy alley where Jan and Eli have agreed to meet me after our latest reconnoiter. I am crouched behind a large, green trash dumpster, trying to read my watch by the light of the moon. Sweat trickles into my left eye, and I swipe at it with a damp

296

wrist. I hear a low growl, like that of a large dog, and know Jan has arrived. I wait as she crawls behind the receptacle toward me.

"Found him," she says, in a whisper I can barely hear. "Eli's watching the front entrance." She purses her lips downward and blows a stream of air down the front of her sweat-soaked gray tank top, then runs her fingers up through her short, spiked, sweaty hair. "Let's go." As I prepare to follow Jan, the smooth sensation of my perspiration-soaked arm sliding against my slick thigh adds to my feeling everything is slipping away, out of control.

In minutes we are crouched behind broken and empty crates at the back entrance of a dance club. The music is a low sluggish throb spilling into the alley, pounding in dull time with the beat of the pulse in my ears. The thought that Bell is inside enjoying himself raises a blunted anger in me I refuse to indulge. My mind darts away from my anger and toward Khara, but I can't allow this right now, can't focus on my betrayal of her trust, on the pain in her eyes at our last meeting. I have to focus on Bell, and be ready.

Time passes at a slow march, broken only by the sound of the muted music, my breathing in my ears and the rough scuttling of rodents near the back entrance.

With the loud squeal of metal on metal, the door we've been watching opens. A dark head emerges, twists to search the alley in both directions, and then disappears. The door squeals again as it's pushed farther open, and Bell emerges, holding the hand of a plump, big-breasted girl with purple hair. Her giggle chases up the alley followed by Bell's shushing admonishment. She giggles again, but this time with her hand over her mouth.

Jan and I don't move as Bell, after another searching glance up and down the alley, bends to kiss the girl. Their hands wander over each other, and the girl giggles as her hand finds his crotch. Jan opens her mouth, points down her throat with one finger, and mock-vomits into the space between us. I agree with her sentiment. I've only ever seen the suave side of Bell's interactions with women. This doesn't qualify.

We don't move. The girl shouldn't be involved.

Bell is quick to turn the girl toward the wall, lift her short skirt, and enter her from behind. The gusts of his breathing as he moves in her end, and he places his large hands over her small hands on the wall, and nuzzles her ear, perhaps whispering something. She titters, adjusts her skirt, and kisses him before sliding back through the still open door. The last I see of her is her fingers waggling goodbye through the opening.

Bell secures his pants, leans back against the brick, and fishes a cigarette from his pocket. He raises a knee and rests his foot against the wall behind him, then enjoys several long drags, letting the smoke curl out in slow wisps. With another look up and down the alley, he begins moving away from the door, staying close to the dark wall.

Now.

Jan stands, jogs on her toes until she is near Bell, then slows to a walk to match his. She whistles an appreciative wolf-call. Bell

298

jerks to a stop with his back against the wall, and Jan continues to walk past him, turning toward him. Bell glances down the alley where I still crouch, then turns toward her, his back to me. Jan smiles with a suggestive leer.

"She had nice tits," Jan says.

"You always do like them big," he answers. He doesn't sound as certain of himself as he usually does. Again, he glances over his shoulder down the alley toward me.

"Yep. That's how I tell the women from the men. Like you, I don't much go for men," she answers. "But you know that."

"Yes. I know that." Still uncertain. Still waiting for something. His hand moves to his pants pocket, perhaps to fiddle with his cigarettes.

"You too tired now, or are you still up for some fun?" Jan asks. "Got any energy left for dancing?" Jan still smiles, and as I approach Bell, over his shoulder I see her wink at him. Her eyes stay on Bell.

"I, uh…" Bell starts, clearly nervous, and darts another glance over his shoulder. I'm mere feet from him. His eyes widen, and he backs against the wall, eyes moving back to Jan once before he returns his eyes to mine. He gives a small huff before saying, "Samuel." He's not smiling.

"Michael Bellamy," I answer.

Neither of us speak, and in my peripheral vision I can see Jan's teeth as she continues to smile at Bell, this time with chin lowered, looking at him from under her brows, her grin now feral.

299

"Why," I say. It is a steady word that doesn't sound like a question.

"Listen, Mate, I didn't–" he starts, but Jan interrupts.

"Cut the shit, asshole," she says through clenched teeth. Her fists are tight balls that rise between them. Bell doesn't look at her. Something about him seems to deflate as he watches my face.

"Look, Mate," Bell starts, and this time I interrupt.

"I'm not your mate," I say, biting off the last word. "I'm not your pal, I'm not your chum and most especially, I am not your friend." I clamp down hard on the anger that threatens to rise, to cloud my thinking. I need information, despite an unreasoning desire to lift my own fists, to smash his face into the wall. In my mind, I see the proud young boy dropping to the floor of the queen's audience room, blood spurting from the new opening in his throat.

Jan bends and picks up a broken piece of two-by-two from the ground beside the wall and hands it to me, wide of Bell's reach. He shuffles from foot to foot and puts his hands in his pants pockets, giving neither of us a reason to use the stick. I hold the stick in front of me, right hand closed around the base like a bat, left hand palm up, holding the other end.

"Why," I say again.

I see desperation in his eyes.

"They give me anything I want, Ma—," he corrects himself and finishes, "man." His eyes flick away from me, back. "We don't have shit, we're hungry, and they give me anything I want." He takes two quick breaths, and says, "You don't know what it's like. You and Khara" – he spits her name and I hear the anger, the disgust – "have masters. You eat well. You sleep well. You have all the credit you want. The rest of us are hungry, tired, used, and used up." Now his tone is pleading. "I'm no different from you," he whines.

His eyes move to my neck where my collar used to rest, and then back to my face. My face must betray my anger, because he closes his mouth with a small clack of his teeth, and his Adam's apple bobs.

"Look, I don't have to give them much. Just a tidbit here and there. They don't know much," he says. His eyes dart to Jan as she takes a step toward him and then backwards again, fighting with herself. "Just a tidbit here and there," he repeats.

"Like me?" I ask. "I'm a Tid. Bit?" I bite the word off in two chunks.

"I . . . ." Bell pulls his hands from his pockets, holds them out toward me, palms facing me, warding me off.

"They promised I'd be okay, Samuel," he says. He's quieter now. "They promised I'd be one of the humans they keep."

"You stupid shit," Jan murmurs and shakes her head.

"Humans are going out anyway, you know it, they know it," Bell continues, "I just wanted to be one of the humans they keep."

We've all done things – horrible, stupid things – to stay alive, but this doesn't lessen my anger at him. I haven't betrayed a human for my own life.

This thought is followed by the vision of the shining boy who died in my stead just yesterday, and the breath goes out of me as I realize I have traded a life for my own.

It's not the same, a voice says inside of me. *It wasn't the same.* The voice begs for me to admit this. I can think of nothing to say to Bell. I look down at my hands wrapped around the two-by-two and wonder if Bell and I are any different.

Bell fumbles in his pocket, pulls out a pack of cigarettes. He puts the pack to his mouth, pulls out a cigarette with his teeth. He pushes the pack toward Jan and then me, shaking it until a group of three pops forward. "Cigarette?" he says around the one in his mouth.

Neither Jan nor I move. My eyes are locked on Bell's. I am deflated by the vision of the dead boy and the cigarettes his senseless death bought Bell.

I clear my throat. "What do they know?" I ask.

"Got a lighter here . . . ," Bell mumbles, as his hand moves back to his pocket.

I look up the alley at a slight noise and hear a snick of metal from Bell. Just as I register that the snick is not the sound of a lighter, but of something far more dangerous, Jan screams, "No!" and feel a burst of pain in my ribs.

I strike out with the stick in my hand. A jarring tremor travels up my arm as it hits the wall behind Bell before connecting with Bell's shoulder. The blunted blow doesn't do much, if any, harm to Bell. Jan advances as a blur of flailing arms and legs, heavy

302

boots kicking and crunching, fists raining down on Bell's head as he tries to recover from ducking away from my abortive blow.

I raise the stick again, and Bell, still hunched over, twists toward me and lunges at my stomach with the knife. The moon glitters on my blood on the wet blade as it moves toward my abdomen. I can't bring down the stick fast enough to avert being stabbed again.

There is a confusion of limbs and sounds, bone on bone, wood on bone, hoarse yelling, and then I'm lying on the ground, knife buried to the handle into my upper thigh, my own hands wrapped around the handle. Close behind me Bell yells, "Oh shit, no!" and then silence, followed by the sound of a body hitting the pavement of the alley.

"Samuel!" It's Jan. Her hands turn my head upward toward her face. "Are you okay? Where are you hurt?"

I gesture with my eyes downward. I am afraid of the sound I'll make if I unclench my teeth.

"Jesus!" she says as her eyes find the knife in my thigh, and she scrambles down toward it. "Eli, shirt!" she yells, and I'm confused until I hear a grunting sound behind me, and the sound of cloth ripping.

I know what Jan's going to do, but before I can react in any way, her hands close on the knife handle over mine, and there's a searing pain as she pulls it out. I moan through clenched teeth as Eli and Jan wrap and bandage my leg with his shirt.

"It'd help if you'd stop rolling from side to side," Jan says, tone sharp, but she's smiling. She lifts my shirt where it is sticky with blood, examines my ribs, and then says, "You'll live. Lucky bastard."

With a heave, Eli has me to my feet, and between the two of them, we all move down the alley toward shelter. I don't spare much attention to the human-sized bundle we leave behind in the alley other than to notice the limbs don't lie right, but more like those of a broken doll. It's a dark, fallen figure with wide open, glistening eyes.

***

At one of our hidden shelters, my wounds are cleaned, the hole in my leg and the slice in my ribs are stitched, and I'm bandaged again. Jan and Eli receive my instructions around the grunts I release during these ministrations. They leave before the final bandages are in place. I am dead with exhaustion. I have to sleep.

Rex snores in his sleep. It's loud and resonant. I wouldn't believe such a sound could emanate from so slight a young body if I didn't hear it for myself. The hidden room is dark and our cots are pressed close to each other. There's no escaping the sound. The stifling warmth of the closed room would, in all likelihood, keep me from sleeping even without the pain from my wounds and Rex's snoring. My thoughts scramble between our need for a change in plans, Bell's betrayal, and self-disgust at my own betrayal of Khara. Stupid, stupid. I question my ability to lead this local rebellion, and add to my guilt over the boy and guilt over Khara, the guilt that so many have trusted me without good cause. My stupidity has endangered everyone.

You can't quit now. The thought reproaches me from some part of my mind that is not swirling between Bell and Khara, Khara and Bell.

Bell. He knew more about our organization and plans than any other, although, thankfully, not everything. We don't have the time or the resources to move our weapons and equipment caches, and much may be compromised. How much of what he knew did he tell?

We have no time left. We have to attack now even though we're not ready. Bell knew this, but we will have no other opportunity. Now or never. Now or die.

My thoughts race the minutes until morning, our last day of planning. With our new plan, D-day is little more than twenty-four hours away. It'll be before the planned general attacks in the other cities, but maybe this will help.

Sometime after dawn, Rex rolls onto his stomach and the snoring stops long enough for sleep to find me. I dream of Khara, as usual, but this time when I wake, it's not with anger over the fact.

***

Sunlight enters our hidden kitchen from the single high window and gleams off the coffee-colored skin stretched across Eli's massive bare shoulders. His head is bandaged. He's bent over a steaming cup of tea. Jan holds her plate at chin level, fingering eggs into her mouth like a shovel. She looks up and grins at me around a greasy mouthful. She has a black eye.

"So, what happened last night?" I ask. I limp to the table, trying to ignore the pain.

"Bell's dead," Jan blurts. She still grins. "The slimy bastard is dead."

"I saw. How?" I ask. I grunt my thanks as Jan passes me a plate of eggs and a spoon.

"Eli bashed him as he went for you, or that knife would've been in your stomach instead of your leg."

I bow to Eli in thanks, and say, "Go on."

"Meanwhile, you bashed Eli with that stick" – I grimace as I realize where Eli got the head wound – "and I went after Bell. I wanted to take him apart, piece by piece, taking my time, but Eli just broke his neck." Jan grimaces in mock disappointment at Eli, and then laughs with delight.

I look to Eli, who still examines his tea, and then back to Jan.

Jan bumps Eli's arm with her shoulder, but doesn't budge the mountain of a man. "Don't mind Eli. He's just upset with my bloody-mindedness."

Eli raises his head to meet my eyes. "He's dead. It had to be done," he says. But I can see he says this more to console his own gentle soul than to convince me.

Jan chatters through my breakfast about the benefits of being jobless – I am thankful Tamerak mentioned the upcoming purge so I could get those humans who were willing to heed the warning out of the factory – and jokes with Eli in an obvious attempt to improve his humor.

They're getting ready to leave the kitchen for their various cell meetings when a knock sounds signaling one of our people is coming in.

Diane and Tanner enter both breathing hard.

"We saw Khara!" Diane announces. "She was in the garden with Nestra yesterday!"

I feel myself flush with excitement and guilt.

"Yeah, we, like, tried to go after her, but she was really booking it," Tanner adds. "You know, we couldn't yell and run after her or anything." He tosses me an apologetic smile.

Diane continues where Tanner leaves off. "We thought we'd go back today, try to talk to her. If we can catch up with her, she can make the final planning meeting tonight."

"If she's interested in coming," I murmur.

"Khara's okay, man. I mean, she's cool. She'll get it. She's all for humans. She's always tried to help, right?" Tanner's sincerity is charming, but I imagine Khara's feelings of betrayal will keep her from being very excited about facing me again.

Tanner glances from Eli to Jan to me as if just noticing all the bandages, and then says, "Dudes, you guys alright?"

Jan chuckles and I nod.

Diane raises herself to tiptoes to kiss Tanner's cheek, then nods at me with a wide smile. "Khara? Okay?" she asks. I nod in return, and Diane pulls Tanner from the room by his hand. My excitement at the thought of seeing Khara again is mirrored in Diane's ecstatic rush to be on her way.

"Going to be a good day," Jan says, as she claps both Eli and I on the back. One small tough woman between two large men, just one of the guys for a moment of quiet. Then they're off to their meetings, sneaking away in different directions.

CHAPTER 42
QUEEN TAL

"Come," I say, with irritation. I stand erect before the computer that monitors the various aspects of my monarchy: my decrees, my communication with the various seats on the planet, my less than honest communication with the home planet.

This solitary command is directed toward a high-ranking brother from the crèche who cowers, body thrown open in the doorway, outstretched limbs trembling.

"I bring a report, Majesty," he says, voice too loud – probably in an effort to avoid sounding timorous through quivering mandibles. His obvious discomfiture brings a brief pulse of pleasure to me.

"So I might assume, dolt," I answer in gentler tones, pinching my mandibles into a fierce smile. The effectiveness of my smile is confirmed by the brother's increased trembling. I focus all my lenses on the brother, not to see him better, but to intimidate him further – if such a thing were possible. The waft of his colorful fear glazes over me and I draw my mandibles into a bloodthirsty leer as my antennae dance through the scent.

"The final brothers for this city will be ready in mere d… days," he stammers, and again throws his head back, limbs outward.

"How many d… d… days?" I mock. I must take small pleasures where I can, since I do not permit humans into my office, and thus have no one to toy with.

"No more than five," answers the brother, and while he does not stammer this time, his words warble through shaking mandibles.

"And the final shipment for the few remaining cities . . . ," I ask, excitement raising the volume of my voice.

"Gone already, Majesty," the brother answers with haste. He attempts a small smile which makes him look as though he is going to regurgitate his last meal.

"Yessss," I hiss with satisfaction. The humans will be exterminated long before any visitors from the home planet will check the status of this colony. By then, the human relics left on planet will be transformed by our people, and the visitors will join with me in expressing regret at the ages-old mysterious disappearance of what was a once-intelligent race from the planet. Meanwhile, I have had my fun.

I sweep my left arms toward the brother, snapping my pincers in dismissal. My enjoyment at the thought of the end of the soft, repulsive humans is so complete that I do not even take the pleasure of watching the brother cringe and grovel out of my presence.

310

"Majesty?" The word is a shaking whisper.

Anger flares as I realize the toady remains despite my dismissal. I roar as I fling the monitor aside on its tracks and storm toward him, pincers reaching to tear at him.

"Dev'ro!" shrieks the brother, as he falls to his knees and bends his head backward.

I manage to check my anger and bloodlust as I thrust a pincer to the brother's throat and roar again.

"Dev'ro . . . ," whispers the brother, with the screechy, grating sound that comes of speaking with head thrust backward.

"Dev'ro . . . ?" I answer. My own pincers shake with my need to relieve my fury and annihilate this creature.

The brother raises his head, lenses glittering as he close-focuses on my face. "Dev'ro tells me the new Shame Receptor is ready."

Considering how close this brother knows he is to death, his voice is remarkably steady.

"Ah," I say, again smiling. My pincer stays a moment at the brother's throat as I contemplate the pleasure of disposing of Nestra. Then I lower my arms, spin, and move back to my monitor to order the summoning of Nestra. I do not notice when the brother slips away.

***

"I did as you commanded." The escort stands at attention in the entrance to my bedchamber. I lie among the cushions, eating slowly, luxuriously, from a tray held by a brother, my palpus undulating over the food. The anticipation of scattering pieces of Nestra from one side of the room to the other brings me a level of pleasure I have not been able to attain of late.

"Then why is Nestra not with you?" I ask, quite reasonably, I think. I will save my lashing anger for Nestra, not waste it on this brother.

"Nestra was in the garden," the escort answers.

Despite my determination, my anger toward the brother rises. "I gave you specific instructions and permission to enter the garden for this task," I answer. I force myself to remain lying among the cushions, rather than rising to squall at the escort.

"She was with humans," the escort answers. "She was . . . sharing, Majesty, with humans."

I leap from the bed-pit almost before the escort can finish speaking. He does not flinch away when I roar into his face, which startles me. He does not reek of fear. He is either completely loyal or extremely dull-witted.

After a moment of towering over the small escort, I turn away, and walk back toward the tray of food, still being held as I left it. I extrude my palpus and slurp at the tray. I turn back to the escort.

"Were you seen?" I ask.

"No, Majesty," the escort answers.

"Hmmm. Take me to Nestra. Bring several guards," I say as I stride toward the stalwart escort. He bows backward as I pass him, and then follows, scenting the air almost not at all.

Perhaps he knows the pleasure soon to be etched across my features will not likely be from any pain I have directed at him. I chuckle to myself as the escort gathers several guards into my wake.

CHAPTER 43
KHARA

Ilnok shared me freely today, and with more of his brothers than ever before. There was a frenetic energy about their play, and I take this as another sign of the growing scarcity of we human playthings. I'm sore, sticky and beyond tired.

I wonder how much longer I can last. My patch wore off before the end of the session, but the lassitude brought on by the loss of Samuel – soon to be the loss of us all – numbed me sufficiently to endure to the end. My hatred of Ilnok has dulled in the face of my hopelessness.

I stop at a juice vendor to wash the cotton from my mouth, easing the raspy raw feeling from my throat. I need to shower and rest, but more than these, I need Nestra. I crave the comfort she can give me and, beyond that, the warmth of her friendship. Her misery matches mine, yet our friendship still wrenches from us the strength to console the other.

I plod and trudge toward the garden, mind slackening toward oblivion. As I approach the guarded back entrance, I shake myself into heightened awareness. As usual, I pass through unmolested.

Keeping under the cover of the foliage, I wander the garden, searching for Diane and Tanner. I'm still unsure of their reaction, although, again, I see Tanner's surprised – not angry – face in my mind's eye. I recognize my neediness as I entertain thoughts that they, too, could be friends.

Diane and Tanner aren't in the garden.

I look to Nestra's oak, and feel my spirit slump with my shoulders when she's not there. I chide myself for selfish thoughts that all start with *I need* . . . .

I sit in the grass, determined to wait all day if I have to.

As soon as I'm sitting, the smell of my own unwashed body billows up to me.

I should've bathed before coming.

My own odor becomes unbearable, and I swat at the air around me as though swishing away an annoying insect. This does nothing to clear the thick air surrounding me. I walk again, focusing my eyes and ears toward the back entrance, alert to the possibility of Diane and Tanner arriving. I also make sure to stay far from the building entrance Nestra might use, but otherwise, I wander, not paying particular attention to the peaceful beauty surrounding me.

My path takes me toward the secret meeting place Nestra and I use when she comes. I won't sit. I'll just wander through that cherished place, then go back to see if Nestra has arrived at her oak.

I'm through the bushes and several steps into the quiet bower before I think to look up from my feet. Nestra is there! With Diane and Tanner!

I freeze, but before I can move back into the bushes, Diane looks up and sees me. Her face lights with a smile, and she gestures with large come-hither motions of her hand and arm. Her other hand rests on one of Nestra's arms. Tanner jumps to his feet and stage whispers my name as he repeats Diane's gestures. I'm surprised they both look happy to see me.

I stay still, uncertain, until Nestra, too, beckons me with one of her top arms. The gesture doesn't seem natural to her, but seems the repetition of the human gesture, which she has clearly understood. I walk toward the trio.

Tanner smiles and waves at me, but Diane rises to her feet with grace and comes toward me, arms out to hug me, tears in her smiling eyes. When we meet, I surprise myself by returning her embrace.

"Khara," she says, face pressed to my shirt near my armpit.

"God, I smell. I'm so sorry," I say as I let her go. My eyes prickle with tears as well.

"We're so glad you're here!" she says as she takes my hand and leads me to where Nestra and Tanner sit. "Samuel's been just sick looking for you."

"Samuel's dead," I answer, and feel again the wash of pain that leadens my insides.

"No! He's not!" Diane turns to me and takes my other hand, holding both my hands in a firm grip, as her eyes roam my face. A burst of fragile hope puffs through my lungs. "Nestra told us what she saw and what she told you, but it wasn't Samuel. He's fine!" Diane is gushing with happiness and sincerity, but I can't see her through the tears that now threaten to overflow in my eyes.

I blink to clear my vision and look to Tanner for confirmation. He smiles at me, flicks his hair out of his eyes with a toss of his head, and says, "Cool, huh?"

"He'll be *so* glad to see you," Diane says. Then her face is clouded by a rare show of anger, and she says, "Bell's dead."

"Good!" The word bursts from me, along with a flare of righteous anger. Then the flood of relief that Samuel is alive, spurred higher by the statement that he wants to see me, overwhelms me, and I laugh through more tears.

I wipe my eyes and nose on my shirt, then lower myself to sit before Nestra, Tanner to one side of me and Diane settling to the other.

"Sister," I say, as I reach for Nestra's arm. I put my other hand on Tanner's knee.

"Sister-friend," answers Nestra, and our warmth and happiness flows between us.

"Wow. How do you do that?" Tanner asks, sensing somehow that Nestra and I are sharing to a far greater depth than they have.

"Good as a hug," I answer, smiling, realizing the irony of a positive statement from me regarding touching. Diane puts a hand on my arm and another on Nestra's and, for a long time, the four of us don't speak. I want to hear about Samuel, but we have the time now to talk when we leave. For the moment I'm happy just to be sharing with friends.

The sensations and feelings from Nestra change in an instant from happiness and comfort – with fluttery suggestions of resignation and sadness – to deepest fear.

"Friends," she croaks as my eyes fly open, and then my own fear joins hers. Six ants surround us, one much larger than the others. In the susurration of leaves in the breeze, we did not hear them approach. My skin sprouts a fresh layer of sweat.

I pull my hands from Nestra and press them to the grass beside me to push myself up. Diane and Tanner each grab my arms above my elbows, and Diane whispers, "Don't!"

At the same time, the largest of the ants bellows, "Do not!" It's spoken in the ant language, but even if we didn't understand the words, the meaning of the demand is unmistakable.

As I lower my buttocks back to the ground, Nestra unfolds herself and walks to the large ant. She lowers herself to her knees and throws her head back, arms wide.

"My queen," Nestra says, voice raspy.

Queen! Of course! She is as large as Nestra.

The queen looks down at Nestra, pincers snapping for a moment during which I can't breathe, then turns and strides toward the palace entrance to the garden.

"Bring them!" she commands.

The five remaining ants move toward us. As I stand, it flashes through my mind that we'll fight, resist, but Diane reads the desperation in my face.

"Don't," she whispers again.

"We're going to die," I whisper back at her, but she shakes her head.

"Let's not die right here," she whispers.

"Let's trust Nestra," Tanner adds. He slips his hand into mine and squeezes my fingers, then snakes his arm around Diane's waist, pulling her close.

The ants move closer and surround us. Nestra, with a long low sigh, leads the way after the queen.

None of us talk as we follow Nestra, but Tanner's painful grip on my hand shows his fear, or maybe that he knows how tempted I am to run.

Just as we leave the garden for the cool darkness of the entry hall, I whisper again, "We're all going to die." This time there's no vehemence to my whisper. This time I feel they're my last words. Shaking, I step into the maw of the beast.

CHAPTER 44
SAMUEL

Rex helps me as I change the bandages on my thigh. This wound is seeping – although thankfully, the pain has abated to a large degree. As if in response to my thought, a strong stabbing sensation makes me wince.

Rex ducks out to the kitchen as I finish the job, then appears again with a cup containing a bit of a clear liquid.

He smiles as he holds the cup out for me to take. "For the pain," he says. I sniff at the cup. It's gin.

My first thought is I don't need the muzzy distraction of a drink – I've never liked the feeling of impairment – but it's no more than a finger of liquid, and the pain, too, is a distraction. I toss the gin back and smile at Rex as the warmth spreads through my abdomen. I smack my lips, appreciating the piney aftertaste.

"Drinking by noon, huh?" Jan stands in the doorway, smiling. She winks the eye that isn't blackened.

"Everything set?" I ask.

"Everything on standby. Just say the word. We can go now." She shows none of the uncertainty – gloom – that I feel about the odds we face. If our intelligence is correct, the average ant won't resist much once the head of the organization – the queen – is crushed, but this difficult if not impossible to believe.

"Heard anything from Diane or Tanner?" I ask. "Khara?" I add, and hope the emotion that comes with saying her name isn't obvious.

"Nope," she answers.

I heft myself from my stool, bend and straighten the knee of my injured leg to check the bandage, stoop to pull my pants from my ankles, and then limp past Jan to the kitchen.

"How're you doing?" she asks, as she sits next to me at the table.

"Mm," I grunt at her, not in an effort to avoid answering, but because my mind isn't on her question. We are ready in spirit, and yet not ready. But the time is now.

"Really?" she says, and her grin is mischievous beneath one arched eyebrow.

"What?" I ask, puzzled by her expression.

"We could waddle you over toward the garden to get a look," she says, and places the tip of her tongue to her top two front teeth, both eyebrows now raised. "At Khara," she finishes.

I feel myself flush, but there's no point in behaving like a ten-year-old who doesn't want to admit he likes a girl.

"Mm," I grunt again. It'd be better for me to stay here where my people know how to reach me for last minute coordination, but her suggestion is tempting.

321

"So? Let's go now. Need a hand to lean on?" she asks, standing and holding her hand out before me, palm up.

Her idea is terrible, but I grunt my way to my feet, smile on my face. "You are one pushy broad," I tell her.

"Yep," she answers. "There's an apology in order here. I'm always interested in helping my fellow female get an apology she's got coming from some dipshit male." Limping, grinning, I follow her from the room.

***

Because of the buildings surrounding the capitol building, it is easy to find a good rooftop vantage. The only difficulty is climbing the stairs. My thigh aches from the walk despite the heavy walking stick I'm using; supporting my full weight on my injured left leg is not possible. I take the stairs one at a time, right leg up, lift my left to the same stair, then right leg up to the next. And again. And again. Jan is waiting on the roof when I huff up the final step.

"Over here," she says, gesturing.

It takes me longer to settle down behind the low wall at the edge of the roof than I'd like. I am not going to be much use when the time comes to fight. I'm just supposed to coordinate things, but I have – had – every intention of joining the battle. The slash in the skin at my ribs burns as sweat seeps into the bandage there and my leg is throbbing.

"Can't see anything," Jan says. "Shitload of trees."

I pull my binoculars from my pouch and hunker down to scan the garden. I don't need the binoculars to spot a person from here, but part of me hopes they'll assist in seeing through the thick leaves at the tops of the tall oaks and magnolias.

"Think they're still in there?" Jan asks after a moment more of looking.

"Diane and Tanner would've reported back as soon as they left the garden," I answer, hoping this is the case. "They're still in there."

After fifteen minutes pass with nothing moving but leaves in a light breeze – a breeze I wish we could feel on this hot roof – I start to feel foolish. Like a high school boy trying to catch a glimpse of a cheerleader he likes. A stalker.

"We shouldn't have come," I say.

"Not much to see," Jan admits.

After another minute, I grunt and start pushing myself to my feet.

Jan sighs, stands, and puts out a hand to support me. Her eyes scan once more over the garden and she squats again, saying, "Hold on a minute."

I look back toward the garden. I lower myself with such haste that a painful burning shoots through my thigh. I hope I haven't torn the stitches out.

Panting, I hold the binoculars to my eyes and count six ants moving toward us, toward the back wall of the garden. Toward something – or someone – out of sight from our vantage point. I

323

want to shout a warning, but this would be foolish. Instead I focus the binoculars on the point where the ants disappear from our view, our vision blocked by the high wall.

Not a minute later, the ants reappear, walking back toward the building. In their midst, I can make out an additional ant as well as three human figures clinging to each other, ants marching in lock step before and after them.

"Shit," says Jan. I can think of no more appropriate epithet.

"Go," I say. "It starts now. Pass the word. Right now."

Jan looks at me with surprise, but then her face hardens with determination and she says, "Right."

She straightens and takes a step before she realizes I'm not following her.

"Whoa. What the hell are you doing?" she asks.

"I'm staying right here. Have somebody pick me up when you get back over this way. I'll just slow you down," I answer. "Besides, there might be something more to see," I continue when she does not move or speak. Then, "Go! Now!"

"You're not going to do anything stupid, right?" she asks. I look down at my thigh, then back up to her with a look that says her question is ridiculous. There is nothing I *can* do.

"Right. Okay." Then she is gone, running across the short expanse of roof to the stairwell.

I wait until I can no longer hear her tread on the stairs before I put the binoculars back in my pouch, push myself to my feet, and as fast as I can – which is infuriatingly slow – make my way down the stairs, the thump of my walking stick echoing in the confined space.

CHAPTER 45
NESTRA

The chemical flush of emotion racing through me makes my limbs quiver, my knees weaken. I fear for myself, yes, because the queen will kill me this day, but I feel greater terror for my human friends. The fear for them that flows through me is the bright color-scent of the fresh human blood I know I will be seeing soon. I am nauseous as this mingles with sadness, resignation, and – unexpectedly – with a stir of rebellion and disobedience.

The humans who walk behind me seem smaller even than they appear in the garden where trees and hedges tower over them. Here, inside the building, the only height comparison is between the humans and the escorts – escorts who tower over the humans as much as the queen and I tower over these smaller brothers.

I can taste the bright fear of the humans wafting through the air, even above my own. I want to comfort my friends, but I can do nothing. Even knowing I can do nothing, my mind works trying to think of anything I can do or say to convince the queen to let my friends leave unhurt. I am resigned to my own death, but cannot stand the thought of my only friends – the only beings who have ever shared with me – ending their lives right in front of me.

The queen stands in the bedchamber, grand, erect, as brothers rush out the small door at the back of the room. I enter the room and step to the side, not able to bring myself to move closer to the queen. As my friends enter the room, I hear a gasped exhalation from the three. Through my side vision, I see each of them staring upward at the rapier-hung ceiling. Four guards stand as a chain behind the humans, barring the doorway, lower arms linked.

"Leave us!" the queen bellows to the guards, startling the humans who as one bring their eyes down from the ceiling to the queen's wicked face. "Close the door. I will be . . . entertaining myself for the next while."

I cringe as images of disembodied humans and brothers strewn about the room flood my memory. The guards bow backward, then turn and leave the room. The door booms shut behind my friends. No one moves or speaks as the room fills with the swirling reek of crimson fear. The queen's palpus appears for a moment and her antennae flutter as she tastes the air.

The queen moves toward the humans. Tanner, despite his obvious fear, steps forward and pulls Diane behind him. I am filled with admiration and love as Khara places a hand on Tanner's shoulder, and Tanner raises an arm out to his side in front of Khara, including her in his protection.

"Majesty," I say, and lowering myself to my knees, bow backward and open myself. I do not leave my head bent backward, because I want very much to be able to see the queen and my friends. "These humans . . . ."

In one long stride, the queen closes the distance to my friends, and in the same moment, slashes out with one open pincer and tears through Tanner's throat, almost to the bone at the back of the neck. My screeched objection and Khara's cry of anguish mingle and hang in the air as Tanner sways, then topples backward, almost knocking a shocked and silent Diane to the ground as she tries to catch him.

"Majesty!" I leap to my feet and step toward the queen, my pain at this loss of a friend mixing with the pain I know Diane is now suffering, for I have often marveled at the strong link between Diane and her bond-mate. Unable to think what to say to the queen, I shriek and screech my pain.

When I regain control of myself and stop my long wailing scream, I am relieved to find my outburst has at least had the effect of staying the queen from further killing. She stands looking at me as Diane and Khara crouch over Tanner's body, Diane kneeling in the growing pool of blood flowing from the ragged gaping hole between Tanner's chest and chin.

"Well, well . . . ," says the queen. "It appears you care for these creatures, Nestra." The queen's mandibles open and close, making several small clicking sounds in the otherwise quiet room. "It will actually hurt you if I kill another, won't it?"

"Majesty," I croak, begging. "They are bond-friends to me." I am unsure whether this admission will help or put the humans in greater danger, but I can think of no other way to plead for their lives. "They are no danger to you or . . . ."

Diane bends and whispers something to Tanner, kisses his blood-spattered cheek, and pushes herself to her feet. Khara whispers something at Diane in the human language as Diane steps over Tanner's outstretched arm toward the queen. I am amazed to notice I can no longer taste fear from Diane as she raises her arms toward the queen, palms held before her dripping with Tanner's blood.

"You do not fear me?" the queen roars and raises an open pincer to Diane's throat. Again I scream – "No!" – but Diane does not flinch or move other than to close her eyelids. The only scent of fear is that emanating from Khara and from me. The queen tilts her head at the small human standing before her, then closes the pincer and rips out the soft throat.

I wail, and fall to my knees as Diane's small body crumples forward into the queen. The queen catches the slack body before it can reach the floor and flings it at me. I dodge the flying body. It sails through the air like a limp rag with odd flailing limbs, and lands with a dull crunch against the wall at the far edge of the room.

I can still taste the warm purple-blue passion with which Diane has gone to her death. Again I wail, head thrown back, which adds a grating rasp to the end of my keening lament.

When I lower my head, the queen is standing over me, hungrily tasting my pain, lower arms questing closer for the intimacy of sharing.

"Majesty, I beg you," I say, in a voice almost a whisper, rich with pleading. The queen presses her slim fingers to my shoulders and I hear a sharp intake of breath from her as she throws her own head back and revels in the taste of my anguish.

Khara has not moved from her position crouched near Tanner's splayed knees. She is watching the queen and me, while tears roll down her splotched face. As I share my pain with the queen and try to avoid feeling her sick pleasure, I long for my friend and try not to long for her, knowing the queen will taste this as well.

The queen sighs and lowers her head, wicked smile directed at me. With fingers still resting on my shoulders, the queen looks toward Khara and asks in warm, almost loving tones, "Shall I kill this one too?" She opens the pincer of her upper arm, and then snaps it shut over my head.

I can feel my terror for Khara rising in me, but before I can answer or even think what to answer, she continues, "Or shall I toy with it first?" My shock mingles with the flavor of my surprise as I realize that having the queen merely kill my friend will be a far kinder fate.

"Yesss. Just as I thought," says the queen, and releases her grasp of me. Turning toward Khara, the queen says, "You will be my toy for a while."

Believing Khara cannot understand our language, the queen follows this statement with a short statement in the human language. "You. Come. Here." Her mandibles click with the effort of the human words.

Khara stands up. "I understand your language," she says. "I will be your toy, Majesty."

The queen's startled laughter chirrups through the room. "How splendid, Nestra! It is no wonder you enjoyed this creature." Again, delighted laughter fills the room.

"What is it you wish of me, Majesty?" Khara asks.

While I admire the strength and audacity of my sister-friend Khara, I shake with horror as I realize Khara thinks to buy time by allowing the queen to use her as her master does.

No! You don't understand!

I want to shriek a warning, shriek my pain, but clamp down on my self-control, determined to be as strong as Khara is proving herself to be. I console myself with the knowledge the queen will not let me outlive Khara by long and this agony will soon come to an end.

"Join me here," the queen says to Khara as she leaps to the bed cushions, her excitement broadcasting to me through her gestures and her scent.

Khara moves toward the bed-pit, then reaches into her pants pocket and extracts something small, which she holds in her fist. "May I use this, Majesty?" Khara asks.

"What is it, creature?" asks the queen, purring in her pleasure.

"It is a drug, Majesty. It will comfort me and allow me to last much longer as your toy. My comfort will be your pleasure."

Again the room fills with the queen's laughter.

"Please!" answers the queen, then turning to me, she says again, "Delightful!"

I still kneel, frozen, not knowing how to help my friend, not able to stand what I know I am about to see. I watch as Khara slaps a hand to her throat.

Khara stands for a long moment, perhaps allowing the drug to begin its effect on her, perhaps buying more precious minutes of life. The scent of her fear is still strong. The queen allows several minutes to pass before her patience lapses and she bellows, "Come!"

Khara removes her clothing and moves with languid motions toward the bed cushions. She crawls toward Queen Tal, rolls over, and lies on her back, eyes closed, very near the queen.

The queen opens a pincer and places the open pincer over Khara's neck, pinning her head to the bed cushions, but does not close the pincer. With a cruel smile directed toward me she says, "Come here, Nestra. I wish to enjoy your reactions close at hand." When I do not move, the queen bellows, "Come!"

I jerk myself to my feet and approach the queen. I expect a pungent odor of fear as I approach Khara; instead her terror is now muted by her drug. I should kill Khara now and save my friend the pain that is to come, but I do not have the strength to take my friend's life.

I am weak.

I lower myself to the bed cushions on the other side of the queen from Khara.

As soon as I settle myself, the queen reaches with a small lower pincer toward Khara's foot, and after placing the pincer to ensure taking only the smallest appendage, clips the appendage from Khara's foot. Khara gasps and jerks her leg up, knee bending up to her chest, arms flailing. A bright spray of blood splashes over Khara's stomach and other leg, as well as onto the queen's torso. Several small drops fall on me and I can taste Khara's fear swell and blossom despite her drug. I moan and thrash as though the queen had cut a portion of my foot as well.

The queen does not hesitate, but with a lower arm, holds Khara's bent leg in place, knee pushed to chest, and clips the next appendage from Khara's foot. This time Khara does not gasp, but screams, long and loud. I scream with her.

"I never thought of making you a part of my little play sessions," says the queen, when I have stopped screaming and Khara's scream has reduced itself to small moans escaping between weak gasps. "This is wonderful!" The queen raises her head to look at the barbed ceiling and seems to swoon.

Then she grasps Khara's other leg, and again starting with the smallest appendage, clips it off. Khara's scream lasts longer this time, and her fear billows off her in gross, nauseating waves. The

queen reaches to retrieve one of the small pieces of bloody bone
and flesh, wipes it across one mandible, and then flings it across the
room. Khara thrashes and rocks until blood blooms on the side of
her neck where the queen's pincer holds her pinned. Blood from
her feet soaks the bed cushions and decorates much of Khara's
body in a grotesque pattern of large and small blotches of red.

"Majesty!" I roar, hoping even as I pull at the queen's arm
which holds Khara's head to the bed cushions that the queen will
just hurry and finish the job, close the pincer at Khara's throat and
kill her.

I am confused when the queen releases Khara. Khara rolls
away from the queen, and with two small groans grabs fistfuls of
linens and jams them against her bleeding feet to stanch the flow of
the bright red blood.

The queen turns to me and says, "Yes, Nestra, dear?"
Gloating pleasure rasps her voice, even through the warmth of her
words.

You are sicker than I knew. This is wrong! Can you not feel that?!
But I do not speak aloud.

"You wanted my attention, Nestra, dear?" The queen
speaks in a soft, warm voice, as if to a dear friend. Still I can think
of nothing to say.

"Ah, perhaps you fear for your queen. Perhaps a
downloading session is in order?" The queen purrs the words at
me.

Teal-violet shock.

I cannot do this right now!

As she moves into position above me, the queen jerks her head toward Khara, who still sits hunched, clutching linens to her bloody feet.

"You can't escape," she snarls, all the warmth gone from her tone.

Khara continues rocking and moaning to herself, giving no sign she has heard the queen or even recognizes her surroundings.

Just as the queen begins extruding her palpus toward me, she whispers, all softness and warmth again, "Don't worry, Nestra, dear. This will be your last time."

The brief spurt of shock that flows through me is overtaken by resignation, and even thankfulness, and then the queen's palpus is on my own and the black flood begins. I float toward the half-trance state that will allow me to retain sanity in the midst of the poisonous flow. That part of my mind that remains my own wonders at my effort. Wonders at my desire to continue living or to maintain my sanity. But the desire is there. A sudden anger grows in me as the selfish, normally suppressed part of me comes to the fore – anger that I risk my sanity and my life for this queen, who should, by all rights, perish by her own black bile.

Without any conscious decision, I find myself facing the golden dewdrop of the queen's strength. Without guilt, I taste of the dewdrop – not a small nipping lap at the beautiful golden liquid, but a strong draft, plunging myself into the dewdrop, soaking up and sucking at it with a ravening ferocity. Feeling radiant and renewed, I act on my anger and do the unthinkable: I deflect the Shame into the queen, sending the Shame back up the same channel from which it floods into me. The sharpness of my anger punches through, and I feel the exhilaration of being emptied of the poison, instead of filled. Gathering even more strength from the queen, I push and push until the last of the poison leaves my body, and with it, the last of my sharp black anger.

With the shock of my sudden cleanliness, I break the half-trance. The queen thrashes above me, wild, striking me over and over, pincers opening and closing with a violence I have never seen. I roll from the bed cushions and realize the only reason I am not now dead is because the queen is not in control of her body, and she cannot direct her blows. The queen's own mandibles slice closed over her retracting palpus, drawing blood.

Fear/regret/excitement/shock thrill through me. I am at a loss what to do.

"Guards!" I yell.

"GUAAAARDS!" roars the queen in a terrifying parody of my shout. I cannot determine if the queen even knows what she yelled. Still her arms and legs thrash and kick, still her pincers and mandibles open and snap closed.

Two guards rush into the room, pause, scenting shock and fear into the already thick atmosphere of the room, and then rush to the queen. Both guards bend to restrain the flailing limbs as I back away and move around the bed cushions to where a wide-eyed Khara sits. She flinches when one of the queen's limbs dashes

336

in her direction. I lift Khara in my arms and move her over to the lounge, careful that the linens she clasps to her feet travel with us. I pour love and comfort into Khara, wishing I could also transfer the strength I now hold within me into my dear human sister.

I turn at a rasping strangled sound from one of the guards to discover that the queen, in her thrashing and pinching, has managed to land a deathblow to one of them. The other guard redoubles his efforts to restrain the queen, but after another moment of dodging kicks and pincers, stands back, releasing the one limb he has pinioned. With a scream the queen lurches and closes a pincer on his neck, removing his head with the violence of her motion. His body clatters to the floor, legs bent and embracing his own head. And still the queen thrashes as Khara and I watch, horrified.

"NESSSS . . . ," the queen roars, but cannot finish my name as her mandibles clack together in jerking spasms. I turn my attention back to Khara and while keeping watch on the queen, again try to fill Khara with the flow of my comfort and friendship. Soon the queen thrashes with less violence, her body perhaps tiring from its violent spasms.

I embrace Khara, all the while transferring as much comfort and love as I can into her and try to think of what to do next. I wonder why no other guards have come to the room to investigate the commotion.

Perhaps I can take Khara to safety?

I disentangle myself from Khara, and leave her to peer out the door and down the corridor. Before I can reach the open doorway, Khara screams again, and I spin to see the queen lurching, jerking, twisting across the floor, almost to Khara, pincers reaching, snapping, as Khara scrambles to move off the other side of the lounge.

I leap for the queen.

CHAPTER 46
SAMUEL

My leg throbs as I lurch across the street, and then down a wide, short alley toward the back entrance to the enclosed garden. The sharp *tack-tack* of my walking stick striking the cement batters against my ears as I try to force myself to move faster. My pants below my wound are stuck to my leg by a warm fluid. I refuse to look down. I don't want to acknowledge the fluid is my own blood.

I have no plan, other than to do what I can to save my friends, to save Khara.

I have an apology to deliver, teasing myself in Jan's stead. I try to smile, but it can't break through the pain-generated grimace stretching my mouth.

I can see the small guard booth across the street from where I stand. I pause, take a deep breath, try to ignore the throbbing in my thigh which pounds in time with my heart. My left foot feels swollen and warm and wet in my boot. As usual, there's only one ant-guard in the booth. I glance up and down the short stretch of street. There are no other people or ants in sight. This bit of road behind the capitol complex never gets much traffic.

"Help me," I yell, as I start hobbling toward the guard, I imagine the sight of me will convince the guard my plea is genuine, although he won't care or attempt to assist me. "Help me," I yell again, and feign stumbling. My pretence almost causes me to fall and I have trouble recovering. The guard doesn't move, although I am certain he's watching me.

As I step up the curb near the guard booth, I reach down and touch my leg below my wound. I bring my hand up and hold my palm toward the ant as I say, "Master, help me." My palm is red with blood.

"You go," says the ant. "You go." He steps out of the booth to meet me on the wide sidewalk. He gestures toward the alley mouth from which I emerged. When I remain where I am, panting at him, he motions up and down the empty street, saying again, "You go."

I sigh and take a small turning hop so I'm no longer facing the ant. I wait a moment before looking back. Satisfied I have understood him and am leaving, he turns back to re-enter the small booth. Gripping the walking stick in both hands, like a long bat, I take several quick, painful strides and swing at the ant's head. His head snaps toward his shoulder and his rigid body tilts to one side, off balance, one leg off the ground. Before he can recover, I plunge my knife into the base of his skull, and up into his brain. The ant falls forward half into the booth. Keeping my grip on the knife, I'm pulled with him to the ground. My elbow smashes against the wooden doorway of the booth and the fingers of my hand tingle with the transmitted pain.

Pausing only to recover my breath and flex my hand and elbow, I retrieve my knife, now covered with the thick viscous yellow-white fluid of the ant's blood. The pincer closest to me opens, and I jerk away from it, unsure whether this is a post-death reaction, or whether the ant is reviving despite my wound to its head.

I scramble backward to retrieve my walking stick. The ant doesn't move again. I consider poking at it, but I've done what I set out to do. I've gained entrance to the garden.

As I limp and stumble through the garden, I marvel at the small world Diane and Tanner have helped to create here, away from the heat and filth of the city. The surreal character of the sunlight dappling the paths and the slow-motion bobbing of flowers and branches makes me wonder if I'm becoming delirious.

How much blood have I lost?

I slow as I approach the open entrance to the building, lifting and placing my walking stick with care to avoid making any more noise than that of my limping shuffle against the stone. Hands cramping as I grip the handle of my knife with one and the walking stick with the other, I push my head around the edge of the entrance. I blink as my eyes adjust to the darker interior, hoping no one is approaching during my blindness. I can't hear anything moving nearby.

As my vision adjusts, I am happy to see that no ants are in sight down the long corridor. Maybe this is because the garden is forbidden, or because no one wants to be near the queen.

I move inside. I forget for a second and my walking stick cracks loudly against the hard floor. I hold my breath then move back out to the garden, sit on a bench, and cut off the bottom of my right pant leg. I wrap the cloth around the bottom of my walking stick to muffle it. My left pant leg has a wide stripe of red from my upper thigh to the cuff. Not good. I remove my shirt and cut it into strips that I wrap around the outside of my pants over my wound, pursing my lips and chuffing at the pain. I don't have time to do more.

Leaving my pack in the garden by the bench, I move to the entrance, and again wait for my eyes to adjust.

The noise hasn't brought anyone to investigate.

I have no idea where the ants have taken Khara and Diane and Tanner. I can only search, hoping to find them without being seen. With the current passage clear before me, this seems possible. I can't think beyond finding them. I hope they're not in the main audience chamber, which I imagine packed full of ants and humans, as last I saw it.

I move down the corridor. It is lined with the occasional almost human-sized vase full of flowers and ornamental branches, interspersed with small potted trees I don't recognize. The delicate blossoms on the trees tinkle as I pass.

At the first intersection of corridors, I pause, looking both ways. On my right, about half a dozen ants move away from me in a group. The left corridor is empty. I move on, grunting with small breaths as I put too much weight on my injured leg.

It's quiet. This should comfort me, but doesn't.

I've passed two more corridors when I enter a portion of the hallway that has doors opening into the passage on both sides. I creep past the first two. The thought that any of these doors could open at any moment causes my flesh to crawl and prickle with sweat. My heart speeds up and my breathing is irregular. The corridor lengthens in my vision as I count six more sets of doors before the cross-corridor at the end of this one. And I still have no idea where I'm going.

I lurch forward slowly, too slowly. I blink my eyes to relieve a bout of dizziness, and press forward.

Stiffening at the sound of a door opening behind me, I stifle the urge to turn swinging my walking stick. Instead, I cram my knife into my pants pocket and turn to face my enemy. An ant walks toward me, looking at papers held in one lower arm. It raises its head, probably smelling me, and stops.

"Human," it says.

Painful as it is, I do what seems safest. I lower my walking stick to the corridor floor, bend to my knees – excruciating! – throw my arms wide and my head back, and say, "Master."

"Why are you here?" the ant clicks, moving toward me, head turning from side to side to scan the corridor.

343

"The queen," I answer, both because it's the truth and because I can't think of any other answer.

The ant pauses, waving the papers back and forth through the air. Then it moves toward me.

"You are lost," the ant says.

"I am lost," I answer.

"Follow," it says, as it turns back in the direction I have already come. Apparently, he's decided the queen can deal with me whether I belong here or not. He doesn't see me as a threat. I can only hope to be.

The ant pauses before turning left down the last corridor I passed. He waits until I've almost reached him before he turns and heads down the corridor. Twice we pass other ants; a group of two which passes without greeting, and one with whom my escort locks lower wrists.

A faint human scream comes from the direction we are walking. *Please, not Khara!* My heart races and I stumble as I try to increase my own speed. My escort doesn't turn to look at me and doesn't change pace.

I can't arrive with my escort into the queen's presence. I don't need any more ants to fight than the queen and however many of her entourage she has with her. I look down the corridor behind me. My escort and I are the only ones present. I increase my pace yet again to close the distance between us.

I raise my walking stick, grunting as I have to put my full weight on my leg to keep walking. As I did with the guard at the entrance to the garden, I swing at the head of my escort. He topples to the floor. The rattle of his armored body hitting the floor joins the clatter of my walking stick as I throw it aside. As he struggles to raise himself, I leap onto his back and jab the point of my knife toward his head, aiming for the jointed area at the base of his skull. I miss, and my knife glances off the thick skull. As his pincers rise toward his shoulders and me on his back, he emits a short shriek, but before he can reach me, I plunge the knife into his head through the base of his skull.

As much as I need rest and a moment to breathe, as much as the pain in my leg screams I can't go any further, another muffled human scream sounds from around the corner, and I know I have to move and move quickly. I drag the body of my escort toward the far wall, retrieve my walking stick and limp toward the end of the corridor.

I push my head around the corner and then jerk it back. With my brief glimpse, I notice that unlike the other corridors, this one has a carpet running down the center, and far more potted trees to each side. Again, I peek around the corner, this time noticing the two guards at the mid-point of the hallway, one moving toward me, probably in response to the shriek of my escort.

My accent is terrible, but I put my hand to my mouth and with my voice muffled with my fingers, call out some of the few words I remember from Diane's lessons in the ant language. "Assistance please." I hope only the one guard that was already moving toward me comes. I can't take two. I'll be lucky to take the one, since this one will be coming toward me, not moving away. Should I try stabbing the ant from under the jaw up into his brain, or try stunning it first with the walking stick? The thought of mandibles and pincers reaching for me decides me. I grip the walking stick in both hands and lift it up and over my shoulder, waiting, pressed to the near wall.

The guard comes around the corner so quickly he's past me before he realizes I am here. He moves toward the body of the ant sprawled on the floor at the base of the far wall. He turns — perhaps at some small noise I have made, perhaps because he's caught my scent — and he faces me as I slam a home-run blow to the side of his head, and then another on the back swing. I manage to hit his head with a third blow before he hits the floor, and he isn't moving as I plunge the knife into his skull.

I dispatch the second guard with the same tricks, luck, and speed. I don't bother to move the last body to the side of the corridor.

I peek around the corner. Much farther down, I can now see two more guards, standing with backs to a large closed doorway. My mind races, trying to think how I can lure these two guards — one at a time — away from the door behind which I am certain lies my goal. As I watch, there is a roaring bellow, this time from an ant, although I can't understand the word or words. I hope it's a roar of pain or despair and not a roar of triumph. The guards throw open the door and rush out of sight. A brief flare of hope rises in me.

Atta girl, Khara. Give them hell. The thought is irrational.

I wait a moment more, but the guards don't return.

Now or never, Samuel.

I turn the corner and head down the corridor toward my woman. I move with a terrible limp, but I won't lower my walking stick. I may not have the time or the strength to raise it again, if needed. Every couple of steps, I glance behind me to assure myself I'm still alone in the long expanse. I am not certain I'd hear anyone approaching me on the softness of the carpet and over the strange noises coming from the open doors before me.

I'm near the door, moving with more caution, walking stick still in both hands and over my shoulder when I hear another very human scream – pain and terror given voice. I don't hesitate. I bound around the corner of the doorway.

Blood. Everywhere blood. On the floor, on the bed cushions, everywhere. Human bodies crumpled to the floor in front of me – *No!* – ant bodies strewn on the floor near them. Steel sword-like projections stretching down from the ceiling. I take in this vision of hell in an instant.

To my right, I see two giant ants and another human body, nude, covered in blood, this human moving, this human the source of the screaming, which comes again and again. *Khara!* I rush toward the ants, my own scream tearing from my throat, trying to make sense of what I see. While the ants attack each other, the one closest to Khara seems to be trying to push the other back.

Protecting Khara!

I twist my advance toward the other and bring down my walking stick on flailing outstretched arms. I've hit the arms of the attacking ant, but I've also probably hit the arms of the protecting ant. I can't focus on this as the attacking ant roars again and turns toward me. Its movements are strange and jerky, but I can't mistake the malice in the snapping mandibles and grasping, snapping pincers. Only one higher arm moves toward me. The other seems disabled. I hope this is because of my blow.

I stumble as I try to back from the attacking ant and prepare to swing again. The swing of my stick glances off the upper torso of the tall, raving creature coming toward me, but doesn't appear to do any harm. As I try to pull the stick back around for another swing, the ant's pincer closes on the stick and snaps it in two. I back another step and trip over something behind me. In slow motion, the ant's pincer swings toward my head as I fall.

The pincer swats my head with the force of a moving truck. My head cracks against something hard as I hit the floor, and lights pop before my eyes. My ears fill with a dull roar like rushing ocean waves.

I try to blink the redness from my eyes. As blackness closes in around the red, I stare up at the glinting silver swords, sure I am rising toward them. Nothingness takes me.

CHAPTER 47
KHARA

My world swirls violently around me: The swirling of the drug through my veins making my vision twist through fun-house mirror distortions; the swirling of the pain throbbing in taut burning lines from my feet to my brain; the swirling of the two ants, eight upper limbs dancing in macabre flashes of blue-black shell.

I scream again in fear of the mad queen, in fear for my gentle friend Nestra, in pain as I slip from the back of the chaise lounge to the floor, wounded feet pinned under me. My agonized cry is echoed by another shout, this one harsher and pitched lower and glazed with anger.

I turn my head in the direction of the hoarse shout, and the room spins and rocks, slowly following my eyes. I can't focus on the blur of motion rushing toward the towering, battling ants. I turn my head back to the ants and the figure that has now joined them and again wait for the room to catch up with the turn of my head.

Focus, damn you!

I feel a trickle of hope as I realize the figure is human and an explosion of ecstatic relief as I recognize Samuel.

My beautiful Samuel! I realize I hadn't really believed he was alive until this second.

The queen is attacking him, and I see the blur of a large stick as he tries to strike up at the towering crazed figure. Before my ecstasy at seeing Samuel – being rescued by Samuel! – can blossom, I hear the crack of the blow as her bowling ball-sized pincer connects with Samuel's head, and he's gone, crashing to the floor to join Diane and Tanner, head bent toward one shoulder, eyes open staring at the ceiling, one arm pinned underneath him.

"Samuel!" I scream, and weep, wailing, eyes locked open, seeing only Samuel, my Samuel, through the renewed torrent of tears. "Samuel . . . Samuel . . . ," I moan between my sobs.

I'm shocked from my agonizing preoccupation with Samuel by the slamming of a pincer into the chaise lounge, which comes so close to my face the breeze brushes my skin. The force of the blow bursts the cushion of the chaise, and the small white foam beads that fill it pour into my lap and onto the floor in a slow lazy cascade as I crab-crawl backward toward the wall behind me.

The queen roars, and Nestra roars, and the sound mixes with my own renewed screams. Nestra charges the queen and batters her back away from the lounge toward the filthy bed cushions. Pincers weave and dodge between the two, mighty blows are traded, and I can only hope Nestra's greater control will win over the maddened strikes from the queen. Both are mottled with the pale yellow blood of their wounds.

Nestra draws back and again rushes the queen, both pincers lancing toward the queen's throat, both lower hands thrust out to her sides. The queen lashes and swipes in wild arcs through the air between them and bats Nestra's pincers away as the two gigantic ants fall to the bed cushions. Nestra's arms tangle with those of the thrashing queen beneath her.

I look again to Samuel. He hasn't moved. He's dead, I'm sure. With small moans, and frequent glances toward the bed-pit where the two ants struggle, I crawl from behind the lounge toward Samuel's body. A small coal of hope burns in me that he's still alive. I have to know the answer, if only to extinguish the hope once and for all.

I'm almost to Samuel when the queen, gaining some leverage among the cushions, rolls to one side pinning Nestra beneath her. Her mandibles click and crunch at Nestra's face and throat. In a moment of random flailing with her pincers, I watch as the queen snips the slim fingers from Nestra's lower arm. Nestra's blood oozes from the stumps and mingles with mine on the bed cushions. I crawl with more speed toward Samuel, realizing this battle will be over soon, and determined to reach him before I, too, die at the queen's hand.

My hands are on Samuel's chest, but I can't tell if he's breathing. I inch my knees closer and closer, sharp pain stabbing my feet. I lower my head to his chest, either to detect breathing there, or to bury my face in his warmth. As I put my right knee down close to his body, I flinch with a new pain. My knee has landed on something hard, maybe metallic. I look down and see a knife handle extending from Samuel's pocket, resting on the floor. At first I think to bat it away so I can move closer to him, but instead, I close my hand around the handle and slide the blade from Samuel's pocket. I look to the bed cushions again as with another great roar, Nestra rolls back, again pinning the queen.

I bend and whisper into Samuel's ear. "This one's for you."

The tickle of Samuel's damp hair against my nose, the smell of his sweat, ignites an anger in me that overcomes the pain in my body. That we should be this close and forever apart after all of this enrages me. I pull the bloody rags from my feet, grip the knife, and kiss Samuel's slack lips before I push myself up to stand. My gait as I move toward the thrashing figures on the bed cushions is halting but sure.

I reach the edge of the bed pit and crawl toward the heads of the flailing ants. Nestra is still on top of the queen but is only barely in control of the fight. The queen's pincers and arms strike at Nestra and strike at the cushions to either side of the battling figures. One pincer slams into the cushions near my knee, but I'm beyond fear. I move in a slow dream-like trance. I crawl forward another foot.

The queen's pincer opens and slashes toward Nestra's throat, and I'm sure Nestra won't be able to defend this blow. My trance evaporates and, in a flash of speed and determination, I raise

352

the knife over my head with both hands and bring it down into the face of the raving queen. Again and again, I lift the knife and plunge it down, into the queen's eyes, into her throat, in between her snapping mandibles and into her palpus underneath. Again and again, my own war cry pierces the room.

After a time, I realize the queen no longer moves, that Nestra is rising, pushing herself away from the queen. As I look into the horror that is the queen's face — more hideous than the horror of her living face — the yellow mucus of her blood all around me, I realize what I've done. What we've done.

We're alive.

Nestra moves around the bed cushions to the side nearest me. She's bleeding from countless wounds. I reach my arms out to her as she approaches in the silence of the aftermath, ready to welcome her embrace, to thank her.

The noise of gunfire in the corridor causes us both to pause, to turn toward the door. I look back to Nestra and she meets my eyes with her own large faceted ones. Although we aren't sharing, I'm sure she's filled with the same resigned knowledge that after all this danger and battle and blood — on the verge of our victory — we're now going to die at the hands of the queen's guards. Nestra takes another step closer to me, three limbs stretched toward me, injured lower arm tucked into her torso.

The commotion, sounds of yelling and banging, reaches the door. I look up to see, not the ant-guards I've been expecting, but humans rounding the doorway and bursting into the room, rifles raised, muzzles swinging in arcs. They pause to take in the devastation, and then one points at Nestra and yells, "Get that one!" As several people bend to inspect the dead, two men leap over the bodies strewn at the door and rush toward Nestra, growling threats.

"NO!" I screech, and manage again to rise to my feet, standing tall amid the bed cushions. I'm pleased that the sight of me – nude, covered in blood – seems to startle the advancing humans, who stumble to a halt, astonished looks on their faces.

"This is my friend," I say, just before my world drains down a tight black tunnel and I fall toward Nestra's outstretched arms.

CHAPTER 48
NESTRA

I taste Khara's relief at the sight of humans entering the room. I wish I could share that relief. While I am not an enemy to humans, they cannot know this.

In my side vision, I see Khara crumple and fall toward me. Without allowing my head to turn away from the sight of the guns trained upon me, I reach for my friend and catch her before she can tumble to the floor and perhaps injure herself further. While I do not believe the humans will shoot at me while I hold Khara, I cannot know this for a certainty, so I bend to the bed cushions and, despite my trembling and my pain, arrange her body with care among them.

I can taste the emotions that so filled Khara at the moment of her collapse: her relief at the sight of the humans – yes – but beyond that, her passionate feelings for her bond-mate, her hatred of the queen, her courage and determination to protect me. Unable to stand the sight of the evil queen so close to my human sister, I push the queen's body as far from Khara's as my reach will allow.

I rise to face the two humans who still stand where they stopped at Khara's command. I bend my head back and open my arms to the humans in a show of submission. Blood from my severed hand drips to the floor beside me.

Never until this moment have I regretted not learning the human language. Before befriending Khara and Diane and Tanner – I quiver anew with a pang of the loss of two of my friends – I had never cared to learn their language. After sharing with my friends, I did not wish to temper their pride and enthusiasm for learning our language by learning to speak theirs. Now, I am faced with humans to whom I cannot speak, even to beg for mercy. I console myself with the thought that even if I could speak to them in their language, they would not believe my professions of friendship. I keep my head bent back and wait for the death I have thus far eluded.

It does not come.

Arms still open, I bring my head back to the upright position, trying to catch the scent of the humans over that of my own fear and the thick cloud of flavors remaining from the terrible battle with Queen Tal. I cannot. The two humans still have not moved from their positions. The other humans have completed their examination of the dead guards and move to the bodies of the humans. I focus upon the remains of Diane and Tanner and am again awash in pain and regret over the loss of my friends.

Worried Khara will perish from the blood lost from the wounds, I gesture to her feet. Will they understand me? My concern? With the flavors of the battle dissipating, I taste the revulsion and anger that flows from the two humans guarding me. Still, they do not approach. Still, they do not fire their weapons.

I cannot let Khara perish through inaction. Without moving my head, I search the room for the linens Khara used to stanch the flow of blood from her feet. I find them near the body of her bond-mate. I do not move to retrieve them, afraid of antagonizing or frightening the humans crouched nearby. Instead, I reach for one of the smaller bed cushions, my movements cautious. With a pincer, I tear the covering open and press Khara's near foot through the opening and into the padding within. The wash of approval from the two humans gives me the courage to move more decisively in reaching for another cushion to apply to the other foot.

I am startled by loud sounds and gestures from the humans crouched near Khara's bond-mate. They are surprised and happy – perhaps that he is not dead? I remind myself they cannot smell the dulling pall of death as I can.

Three of the figures attempt to lift the large human from the floor while another rushes to support the drooping head. I can help them. I want to help, if only for Khara.

"Ssssamuel," I say, remembering the name my friend used when talking of her bond-mate. The two humans guarding me stiffen in their posture and raise their weapons. The other humans pause in their struggle with Samuel's body and their faces all snap toward me. "Ssssamuel," I repeat as I move one cautious step toward them. The humans helping Samuel stop all movement, but the two guards advance toward me. I am failing in my feeble attempt at communication. If I do not find some way of calming the humans, I will die, and Khara and Samuel may also die from their injuries. I decide to repeat the last human word Khara used before her collapse, the word that seemed to stop the humans from advancing toward me.

"Friend," I say. I can taste a small measure of surprised relief from the humans nearest me. Anger dissipating. Flush with my small success, I repeat the word. I move toward Samuel, body posture submissive. "Ssssamuel," I say again as I bend over the body. I lift the body easily from the arms of the humans. One of the humans speaks in anger and tries to reach around Samuel's body to restrain me, but another holds the irate human from me. The scent of fear and concern billows toward me.

I place Samuel next to sister-friend Khara. I arrange their adjacent arms so their hands lie one atop the other. Conscious or not, they can engage in whatever level of sharing is possible to them. Having done all I can, I turn again to face the humans and open myself in submission.

The humans exchange several words. One of them bends to the bloody linens Khara left near Samuel and, using a knife, cuts them into several strips. Another human brings the strips to me and gestures at my still bleeding arm. I wish I could share my gratitude as I take the linens and bind my wound.

***

Much of the day has passed. Samuel and Khara have long since been taken from the room and only one guard remains, sometimes squatting near the door, sometimes pacing, always with gun at the ready. I crouch in the corner farthest from the door. I cannot see the queen where she rests in her bed pit, blocked from my sight by cushions. Determined to remain motionless, to give the guard no reason for action against me, I listen through the hours to the staccato bursts of gunfire that come in muffled bangs through the closed door.

A confused mix of emotions swirls through me as I think through what I have done this day – saved my bond-friend, lost my other friends, betrayed my queen, rejected evil. Guilt, pain, pride…

I escape into trance state in an effort to restore peace to my mind. My path shines and is navigated with ease and without the roiling poison that has so long choked me like a malignancy. Serenity is found and a lightness suffuses me. If not for concern over my bond-sister and her mate, if not for my fear of my fate, I could rise from the trance and fly through the air like the small creatures in the garden.

***

I walk the halls of the palace, human guards before and behind me. My new-won tranquility abandons me by degrees. I am sickened at the evidence of battle as I move past many dead, my kind as well as humans. The ugly mingling of the two colors of blood smears the hallway where the bodies have been dragged to the side. I am filled with sorrow at the unnecessary loss of so many lives – unnecessary, but for the sickness of the queen.

We enter the throne room. One side of this vast room houses a great pile of dead brothers. I turn my eyes from this horrific vision and toward the more hopeful sight of living brothers bunched under loose guard at the far side of the room. As I approach, I taste more relief than terror.

Have these brothers been spared? My own hope rises as an antidote to my sadness and fear. A small brother approaches me as we near this group.

"Fatchk," he says, and opens himself to me.

"Nestra," I answer, opening in my turn. I am certain he can taste the sour yellow-green of my questioning thoughts.

"I am friend to the humans," Fatchk explains, "as, I know, are you." I taste the soft gold of admiration across the small space between us and am surprised and buoyed by this. "I am assisting the humans in separating the infected from the healthy."

A human speaks to Fatchk and he answers in their language. I envy and admire his talent. After a short conversation, I taste Fatchk's consternation as the human takes my arm. Two other humans gesture with guns as I am pulled from Fatchk toward the side of the room where so many of my people lie dead. Fear blossoms anew in me. Fatchk raises his voice to the humans and moves to stand in front of me before he addresses me in our language.

"I have promised to touch each of our people and to give the humans a determination of their illness – some can be helped, some are too poisoned. I have explained you are the queen's Shame Receptor, and for this reason, I cannot touch you. They have decided that if you cannot be declared safe, you must die. I would not have this, but I cannot make them understand!" The flavor of Fatchk's pain and frustration overwhelms me, strengthened and propelled as it is by his near panic.

I am saddened at my fate before I realize there is no need for Fatchk to be repulsed by what he believes he will taste on me. I am clean.

"Fatchk, you may do as the humans ask. You may touch me and make your determination." The teal-violet shock of the brother's reaction is almost palpable. I continue. "I am clean. You will not taste the queen's Shame on me. The queen took all her Shame to her death, I assure you. Furthermore," – this with a renewal of the rebellion which led to my battle against her – "the queen is no longer here to punish you or me for your breach of her decree." When Fatchk does not answer, I say, "We must work together, brother, to help our human friends. We have much to atone."

Fatchk lowers himself to his knees and opens before me, as if facing the queen. Again the soft gold of his admiration washes over me. He rises and comes to me, arms still open. I quiver with each step he takes in anticipation of touching, sharing – for the first time – with one of my own kind. When he is close enough to me, his arms gather around me, and after a slight hesitation, I bend and move mine to enclose him. I lower my head as he bends his head back. Mandibles open and our palpi come together.

Overwhelming, the sensations that wash over me! Visions of his interactions with humans, with other brothers; scents of secrecy, pride, admiration; taste of regret at his role in the deaths of so many brothers, and acknowledgement of the necessity. As I reel under the beautiful assault, I conjure images/scents/flavors of my pain at the hands of the queen, of my loneliness, of my friendship with my own human bond-friends. I am as lost in the midst of this communion as I have ever been floating in trance state. I am unaware of the passage of time, yet fully aware of the flavor of understanding that passes between my brother and me.

I am disoriented when he releases me. My arms remain raised and curved. With my posture, I beg for another embrace. Fatchk backs from me and turns to the humans who stand waiting for his determination.

He speaks in their language and then translates for me. "This one is healthy," he says. With a waft of affection, he continues.

"This one is the best of my people."

CHAPTER 49
SAMUEL

I wake with a sharp intake of breath. I flush with a sense of panic and disaster as I remember... The hideous sight of huge, terrifying ants battling to the death, Diane and Tanner dead, blood smearing the floor and the bed, and Khara screaming, screaming.

"Khara!" I shout, trying to rise from the surface on which I lie. A heavy weight descends on me and I kick and punch against the various forces attempting to restrain me. It takes a moment before my mind registers that the grunts and exclamations that follow my blows are human utterances.

A voice I recognize says, "Cool your jets, damn it!" I stop my flailing to see Jan lying crosswise atop me and Eli at my feet. "That hurt, you big lummox," Jan says. Her head is twisted to look at me and her mouth is bent in a wry grin.

"Jan! Eli!" I say with a huff of relief. Then, "Where's Khara?" My head snaps to either side of me as, in my mind's eye, I picture the nightmarish room in which I last saw her. I'm in a smaller room now, lying on a cot. Khara is not here.

Jan stands and, with tentative fingers, rubs her face where I must have struck her. "She's fine," she says.

"I didn't ask *how* she was. I asked *where* she was." Jan looks surprised at my tone, maybe a little hurt. I close my eyes, release a long breath, open my eyes again. Putting a hand on Jan's, I say, "I'm sorry. I didn't mean to bark. I just really need to see her."

Jan breaks into a smile, bends and gives me a quick peck on the cheek. "Yeah, I know," she says.

Eli steps toward me with a glowing smile and a huge hand extended toward me. I take his hand and he pulls me to a sitting position. In his characteristic soft-voiced rumble he says, "She's just down the hall. She's getting patched up."

"What happened?" I ask. "How long have I been out?"

Jan pulls my pillow into her lap and sits next to me. "You were out for a good thirty minutes after we found you. Queen Bitch knocked you for loop. Nestra and Khara did some whomp-ass on the queen – who is now very dead – and then just as we busted in, Khara passed out. *She's fine!*" Her last statement is in response to the panicked snap of my head in her direction. She pats me on the leg. "In all honesty, we were more worried about you. I *told* you not to do anything stupid!" Jan punches me in the shoulder. By the force of her blow, I know it's not all good-humored – there is some anger there amongst the playfulness. "Then this big damned ant tries to pick you up. Completely freaked me out and I was ready to take it on single-handed . . . ."

"Yeah, she was," interrupts Eli under his breath.

"But, turns out it was Nestra who, according to your buddy, Fatchk, is just as good as Khara said." Jan's face clouds and she drops her chin to her chest. "Diane and Tanner are dead," she finishes.

"I know," I say as my mind flashes to my memories of entering the room. I shake my head and swallow hard. They were good kids. I'll miss them. "At least they're together, which is all they ever wanted," I say. This doesn't help alleviate my sense of loss.

"Yeah, somehow in this rotten world, they found love," Jan says.

Love.

"I want to see Khara," I say. Even if she never forgives me, I have to see her, make sure she's okay.

"She was just as worried about you as you are about her," Jan says, and I don't think I've heard more welcome words in my life. "Eli had to carry her to get her out of here." Then grabbing my hand and pulling me from the cot, she says, "How're you doing? Dizzy?"

I shake my head. "I'm fine."

"Come on. We'll take you there. You could use some patching up anyway."

***

We – humans – have won our planet back, and without much of a war. I can hardly accept this fact as reality, but it seems all Fatchk told me about the "true nature" of the ants is genuine.

With Nestra, Fatchk, and others of their ilk working to rid us of any infected ants left, my greatest challenge is with my own people, with humans. I can't blame humans for their anger and fear of the ants, but at the same time, I can't condone the outright slaughter that's been going on.

Not that I was at all upset to discover Ilnok had been killed. Khara neither, and even though she loves Nestra and the other gentle ants, I can't help wondering if she wishes she could have done the job.

From our best guess, there are only about thirty million humans left on Earth, and all of us are pretty near here. After wiping out the other half of the world at the beginning of the invasion, the queen had been tightening the noose closer and closer around where we are now. Surprisingly, we have discovered caches of humans across this continent that had been protected and hidden by groups of uninfected ants – more proof that Fatchk's characterization of his people was accurate – but no more than a couple of thousand at a time. We are searching for other caches of humans, and hope to find more, but there are still too few of us left. Without Nestra, Fatchk and the other ants who helped us, we'd be gone.

Since the war, our thirty millions have wiped out three times as many ants. Of course, it helps when the ants don't fight back. Fatchk is taking greater and greater numbers of the uninfected to spread the chemical message of surrender. He says that most of the ants on the other continents are uninfected – all but the few highest in the hierarchy who regularly came here to met with the queen.

Nestra set up a sort of rehab center for those ants who weren't poisoned beyond redemption. She and others are flooding those ants with the "good" chemistries that, according to Nestra and Fatchk, are natural to their species. She's hinted that this process would work faster if she took the infection from them, but I don't blame her for not agreeing to go that far.

Now, with the coordinated effort of so many ants working with us and for us, our effort to rebuild and take back our cities is going faster than any of us could have expected.

As an added blessing, Khara has forgiven me. We no longer hide our relationship and our feelings for each other. This has led to Khara being the butt of Jan's jokes about Khara's initial don't-touch-me attitude, but Khara takes them well. She and Jan are good friends now. Khara spends her daytime hours split between me and Nestra, acting as translator for us both, while trying to teach us both the other language.

Now that we can see daylight, the question remains what to do about the ants. Khara tells me they have started a new queen growing or fermenting or whatever it is they do. I haven't told any other humans yet. I have my own fears about a new queen and don't imagine this news will be well met. I can see that with the devastatingly reduced human population, the help the ants provide is essential, but the consensus of my fellow humans seems to be that they must leave our planet – dead or alive. I can't blame them. And yet . . . .

CHAPTER 50
KHARA

The conference room is small – it'll seem smaller still with Nestra in it. The table in the center of the room is tiny, only a four-foot round oak table, with four chairs around it. Three of the chairs match, but the fourth is huge. Samuel is in the chair beside me.

The table reminds me of the Ethan Allen kitchen table in my mother's breakfast nook, but unlike the table of my memory, this one is shiny and smooth instead of care-worn and notched with years of abuse from my brother and me. As I relax in this moment of quiet waiting, my mind conjures images of my family gathered for dinner, of my brother and me playing cards. It's been a long time since I've had any memory of my family other than the day of their deaths.

Afternoon sunlight slants through the two high windows highlighting floating dust motes. I'm canted sideways to the table, with my bandaged feet resting on a small stool to the side of my chair, my head thrown back in luxurious leisure.

My eyes fall to Samuel as he puts his large hand on my shin.
I wiggle my remaining toes at him, the bandage performing a small
wave, and then wince.

"Don't hurt yourself," he says. His voice is warm with
concern and affection, and a small intimate smile curls his lips. I
gaze at him in a dreamlike stupor and consider leaning up to kiss
him, but I'm too comfortable.

We're waiting for Nestra. I've spent a lot of time with
Nestra since the death of the queen and the almost easy success of
the short battle that followed, but for this meeting she sent a
messenger with a rather stilted request for a conference. Samuel
insisted on coming, which didn't bother me in the least.

Outside the door are human guards, which I think
unnecessary, but which Samuel insists are needed for Nestra's
protection. The wholesale slaughter of aliens in this city has trickled
to almost nothing but killings do still happen. Even so, I can't
imagine anyone wanting to kill my gentle friend.

The door opens and Nestra enters, a small brother coming
in behind her.

"Fatchk!" Samuel stands and limps to his comrade and
friend. Fatchk opens his arms and throws his head back, and
Samuel does the same, each showing the other mutual respect.
"Fatchk!" Samuel says again, and I can hear his smile in his
enthusiastic repetition. Samuel throws his arms around Fatchk
between the alien's upper and lower arms and pounds him on the
back. "I'm glad to see you back from your travels, friend."

"And I you, friend," Fatchk responds, lower arms encircling Samuel, while his upper arms remain thrown back, a new mix of human affection and alien respect. "I hope your injuries are healing."

"Yes," Samuel answers and, with a final pound on Fatchk's back, leads the alien to the empty chair next to his.

I lower my feet to the floor in preparation of standing to greet Nestra, but she rushes around the side of the table toward me. "Please, sister Khara, do not rise." She places her remaining lower hand and her healed stump on my forearms, and my pleasure that she doesn't hesitate to share with me overrides my sorrow at the reminder of her injury. Neither of us escaped our battle whole and yet we're both more whole for what we've come through together.

Nestra lowers herself to the large chair at my side, fingers resting on my arm for another long moment. The warmth of her friendship flows into me, but there's also an undercurrent of tension.

"We're here. Tell me the purpose of this meeting," I say. My own tension rises in response to Nestra's. She removes her slim fingers from my arm.

"The new queen we have begun is sick, like Queen Tal."

My apprehension skyrockets with my pulse.

"She cannot be permitted to survive," Fatchk adds and I'm embarrassed by the huffing sigh that escapes me with the instant release of anxiety.

"We have contacted the home planet," Nestra says. I feel like a rollercoaster car as my tension rises again. I imagine more aliens coming to subjugate our newly re-won planet, although Nestra has assured me this won't be the case. *But why the tension in Nestra, then?*

As the silence stretches, I look to my three companions at the table. All their eyes are on me.

"Yes?" I swallow in a dry throat and try to sit up straighter, which is difficult in my semi-reclined position.

"We have a favor to ask of you, sister Khara," Nestra says.

We? I wait for Nestra to continue.

"As we have said," she says, "the new queen developing in the crèche cannot be allowed to mature to adulthood."

"Yeah." Why repeat this?

"Our people need a queen," she continues.

I'm going to go crazy if Nestra doesn't get to the point. She is stepping her way toward something but I wish she'd just get there. I take a deep breath and center myself, remembering how much I love my friend.

"As you also know, only a sister can be queen." My maddening impatience keeps me from asking her again why she can't be the new queen, since she was grown from a queen egg. I doubt I'd understand her explanation any better this time than in past conversations – something about her body having been altered by Queen Tal, something about being infertile, and politics. All I know or care about is that my kind friend would be an excellent ruler of her people.

"Our people – home planet – has requested that in the interim, while a new queen is in transit here… you will be queen of our people on this planet. That you act as ruler of my people and our ambassador to the human leaders."

After a moment trying to rearrange her words into something that makes sense, I say, "What?"

"You are female and to my people I have declared you sister," Nestra explains. "Queen Tal was an aberration among my people. Sick, as I have explained to you. My people wish to make this gesture of peace in the hopes our combined peoples can live and work together on this planet, and on others. However, when the new queen arrives, if humans determine we must, she will lead us in leaving your planet – after helping you repair the damage we have caused." Nestra says this last bit in a rush of words, as if still feeling the need to reassure me of their desire to help us rebuild. This reassurance is unnecessary considering how much they've already done.

I'm exhilarated with the idea of humans having our planet to ourselves again, but I glance at Fatchk and Samuel and back to Nestra, and I can't imagine not having my friends – my alien friends – in my life. Then another thought thrills through me as my mind runs over her words again.

"Other planets?" I ask. It never occurred to me the aliens could give us star flight. I've been too focused for too long on surviving, and then on the glory of having control of our own planet back in our hands.

"If your people wish it," Nestra answers.

After a moment of swirling thoughts, I say, "But I couldn't possibly . . . I don't know anything about . . . ." I turn to Samuel for help. He's smiling at me. I'm tempted to punch him in the shoulder, and determined to ask him later if he knew about this in advance. He doesn't seem as dumbfounded as I am at this request.

"You speak their language as well as anybody," Samuel says.

"You share more than all but a very few humans," Nestra says.

I look to Fatchk, who until now has said nothing.

"Our people ask you to assist in healing this terrible, terrible breach," Fatchk says.

My mind comes back to the same objections. I know nothing about governing – I've barely managed to handle my own day-to-day life – and almost nothing about the aliens they're asking me to govern. I stare at the table, not seeing it, but terrified at what they're asking of me. I can't do it.

Nestra again rests her fingers on my wrist. Her warmth and friendship and trust flow into me.

"If you wish it, you may choose advisors," Nestra says, and again I'm flooded with warm, comforting feelings.

I take a deep breath, thinking of all the positive ramifications of cooperation between our species. And with this friend by my side, I can do anything. I let my breath out in slow stream, and then smile, and say, "I choose you, Sister Nestra."

Nestra moves her fingerless limb toward Fatchk, who locks his wrist with her arm. I can feel through my connection with Nestra her affection for her bond-friend. Fatchk reaches his free lower arm toward Samuel. Samuel places one hand on Fatchk's arm and the other on my leg, and together we make a circle of comfort and friendship that overrides my trepidation and insecurity.

"Come," Nestra says. "Meet your people."

"What! Now?" I almost yell the questions, and sit forward in my chair with a jerk. My feet fall from the low stool, and I emit a small squeak at the jarring pain. Now I understand why this conference was held in the capitol building. I am filled with nauseous tension.

Nestra and Fatchk's chittering laughter mixes with Samuel's booming guffaw. Nestra floods me with her love, and the laughter continues until I'm laughing with them, helpless.

"Tomorrow – or the next day – will be soon enough, I think," says Nestra, still chirruping with laughter.

"Good!" I say. And then in a moment of girlish nervousness, "I need to do something with my hair!"

***

The new queen will soon be on Earth, and I'm more than ready to be done with the incredible work of governing a species I don't understand – it's only been possible because of Nestra. To the rulers of the still disorganized and largely depopulated North

375

America, I'm ambassador to the aliens. I've had to work to overcome the natural human dislike and distrust of the aliens, but their gentle nature and Herculean efforts at helping humans rebuild have accomplished at least as much as my efforts.

"Come to bed," Samuel says to me from across the room, his voice rumbling with a burr that tells me he's already been dozing.

I look once more at the screen in front of me and decide I can't do anything more this evening. I curl into his arms, happy, and feel him hunch closer to press against my back and buttocks. His hand rubs my distended abdomen, and I feel a kick and then a crazy roll from our growing child.

I recall the time, not so long ago, I thought it the worst possible crime to bring a child into this world. Now it's our duty as well as my pleasure. I put my hands on top of Samuel's and stroke with him.

"Things have certainly changed," I say.

"What?" Samuel nuzzles into my hair.

"Let's have lots of babies," I answer, happy in the knowledge they will be coming into a better, gentler world. The world Samuel and I – and Nestra – have given them.

I wait for Samuel's answer. He snores gently into my ear.

Davyne DeSye

Thank you for taking the time to read

Carapace!

If you enjoyed it, please leave a review on Amazon!

If you want more…

Check out *Soap Bubble Dreams and Other Distortions*,

an anthology of my science fiction and fantasy.

CARAPACE

ABOUT THE AUTHOR

Davyne DeSye grew up traveling the world with her diplomat parents, and has lived in Germany, Bolivia, Somalia, Afghanistan, Japan, Korea, and Mexico (and has visited plenty of others).

After several career choices (including computer programming and fine art photography!), she finally settled into the law and was an attorney for over twenty years, although writing has always been her first true love.

Davyne lives with her husband and cats and together they always look forward to the visits of their five children.

Interests: Learning new things, reading, writing, cooking, laughing...

Loves: Intriguing mouths, good food, books that make her wish she didn't have to stop, Christmas, beautiful shoes, and my family.

For more information, please visit Davyne at www.davyne.com.